SAXONHURST SECRETS

JUSTINE ELYOT

Published by Xcite Books Ltd – 2012
ISBN 9781908262684

Printed and bound in the UK

Cover design by Sarah Ann Davies

Chapter One

What exactly it was that drew him out of the vicarage study and into the unseasonably warm April air was never clear to Adam Flint. One minute he was unpacking a crate of theological texts, lining them up in neat subsections along the dark wood shelving. The next, he was sweating and giddy, inhabited by the most powerful urge to get outside and be part of the village springtime.

'What's this? Some kind of spring fever?' He spoke to himself, a habit he had got into over the years of rehearsing rhetorical questions for his sermons. Nobody else ever gave him properly satisfactory answers besides. 'Well, a bit of fresh air, what's the harm?'

But if somebody had been there to answer that question, before he grabbed the old-fashioned hat and walking cane he liked to affect, despite his being only 31, perhaps he would have stayed indoors. What was the harm? He would know soon enough.

Saxonhurst certainly didn't look like the outpost of godlessness he'd been led to expect. The circle of honey-coloured cottages nestled around the church had all the correct bucolic fixtures and fittings – flowery trellises up the walls, diamond-paned windows, thatched roofs. He breathed in the aroma of hyacinths, the sweetness steadying him somewhat, bringing him back to his senses. There was nothing odd or sinister about this place. It was simply a village that had fallen prey to the common 21st century syndrome of entitled materialism and the consequent atrophy of faith. They were good people who looked after their homes, capable of redemption.

From the corner of his eye, he caught the twitch of a lace curtain. A black cat ran across his path by the National Trust pub. The strong feeling that he should be walking out toward the arable farms on the northern outskirts of the village overwhelmed him, turning his footsteps away from the recreation ground and the infants' school, along a narrower lane.

The cottages soon gave way to acres of polytunnels housing tomato plants and courgettes. On his left loomed the ruins of Palmer's Barn, where local legend had it that a man had killed a girl then hanged himself. He almost fell over the wishing well, hidden by weeds, as his curious eye outlined instead the brutal skeleton of the mythic building. It looked evil and brooding. Perhaps he should perform a consecration there, bring the grace of the redeemer to that burnt-out wreck. Or perhaps he should just write to the council and suggest its demolition. What was the good of keeping it there, a reminder of wickedness past? It couldn't be good for village spirits.

When he tried to tear away his gaze and move forward, toward the endless fields of bright yellow rape and the hills beyond, he found that he couldn't. The blackened timbers held him in thrall, calling to him. *This way. It's this way.*

He hacked a path through brambles and weeds with his walking cane, struggling slowly towards the barn. And then he heard voices, a male shout, some laughter, a high-pitched female shriek that reminded him of a siren's song.

There were people behind the barn. Parishioners, he supposed, on a picnic, or maybe some truanting schoolchildren. Whatever they were up to, it sounded rowdy, bacchanalian even. Adam's eyebrow twitched, a sign that the devil was present and close. He moved forward into the shadow of the barn.

He stopped.

Six men, burly young fellows who shone with physical health and strength, chased a woman through the bushy green wheat. It was clear that she was enjoying herself, whooping and laughing as she dodged their great lunging hands. It could be a simple game of chase under the spring sunshine. Except that the men were all painted green and she was completely naked.

Each of the six male players wore goat horns on his head, and each sported a loincloth, beneath which obvious signs of erection were visible. But they were of mere peripheral interest to Adam, who watched with unflinching fascination the figure of the young woman as she twisted and wove through the wheat, eluding her swains at each turn. She was the most beautiful thing he had ever seen. Her hair cascaded down to the dimple at the top of her buttocks, which were full and round, like her swaying breasts. Wanton lips curved in a smile that revealed a wide gap between her front teeth, seeming to invite kissing. Her eyes glittered with sensuality and joy. She was a devil. She had to be.

One man roared in triumph, his fingers closing around her upper arm. She tumbled down with him into the greenery, rolling over and over while the remaining players crowded around, punching the air or beating their chests.

Between the tunnels of their legs, Adam caught sight of the couple kissing fiercely as they struggled. Despite the girl's resistance, it seemed clear that she was a willing participant in whatever this was. It wasn't until the man lifted his loincloth and roughly spread his partner's legs that Adam thought about intervening.

'Fornication,' he whispered. 'Sin. The devil.'

The man's cock – which was still pink, unlike the rest of him – slid easily into the girl's shining sex. There was a cheer, then some kind of odd chant, the words of which Adam couldn't make out.

If he could have made them out, perhaps he wouldn't have heard them anyway, for the rush and drum of blood in

3

his ears.

'Sin.' He fumbled with the fly of his trousers. 'Fornication.' He put a hand on his cock, feeling its heat and rigid tension. 'The devil.' He began to stroke it in rhythm with the man's thrusts into that beautiful witch's tight cunt.

'Depravity.'

She arched her back, mewling and spluttering, then her fingers slipped between those plump lower lips of hers and set to work. Her flesh was white as pearls amid the green; she looked as if the merest hint of pressure would bruise her.

'Bruise her.' He threw back his head, panting, his blood filled with wild red heat.

There was a grunt from the male sinner, and then he rose, his cock departing that obscenely gorgeous body.

She sat up, propped on one elbow, pouting.

'Oi, Jake Summers, I ain't done yet.'

Adam's hand stilled on his cock. He felt shooting pains in his wrist from the speed at which he'd been masturbating. His fingers were numb. What would happen now?

'Just as well we're here, then.'

A second man dropped on to his knees in front of her, exposing his willing cock for her approval.

She smiled and pushed him back by his shoulders until he sprawled on the ground. Straddling him with pale thighs, she crept up his body until her pussy hovered over his shaft. Her hair drifted along the green-painted chest.

'Must tickle,' whispered Adam, imagining it.

Life returned to his hand and he stroked himself all the harder, watching the girl lower herself over her second lover and rotate her sinuous hips.

The chant started up again. The first man, now flaccid and regaining his breath on the ground, tried to join in but his efforts were half-hearted at best.

The girl fucked her man hard, tossing her hair, tightening her arse muscles, giving him the ride of his life. Her orgasm came first, a shrill sound like sorrowing birdsong. It hastened Adam's own finish, his seed landing on the burnt ground in the barn's long shadow.

He fell to his knees and put his forehead to the blackened tufts of grass. His hat rolled off his head and lay to one side while Adam poured forth silent, self-loathing lamentation.

Punish my sin, Lord. I am weak.

Lusty cries from beyond his crouching figure suggested that the girl was now on to her third lover. He shut his eyes, listening to the growls, the savagely spoken obscenities, the chanting and the thud thud thud.

'Fuck me raw,' she said, her voice now harsh and ragged. 'Fuck me, you pussy. Proper, like a man, not like a bloody boy.'

When Adam looked up, she was on to her fourth, on her hands and knees, getting fucked from behind. He wanted to find his feet and get out of there before his soul turned to ashes, but he couldn't get up, couldn't look away.

Lord, no Lord, please ...

He groaned out loud, feeling his cock twitch again. For a second, he feared that the revellers might hear him, but they were far too involved with their ritual, cheering on their mate as he slammed hard into the girl's cunt, driving her face and her arms deeper into the dirt with each thrust, finally smacking her bum as he filled her with her fourth helping of spunk.

Surely she couldn't take two more?

Adam lay on his belly on the ground, trying to ignore his cock's insistent cries for attention as it hardened painfully against the earth.

Don't touch it. Don't let the devil win.

But the fifth man sat down amidst the wheat, pulling her on to his lap, kissing her and fondling her breasts for a long time, apparently knowing that she needed a break. Her nipples were ripe and dark red as cherries. When the fifth man put them in his mouth and sucked, Adam half expected juice to ooze from them. While he attended to her tits, the sixth man nuzzled up behind her and began to kiss and lick the back of her neck. Her face melted into pleasure, her body stretching and arching like a cat's. Adam could barely breathe, watching her heavy eyelids fall, the thick, black lashes fluttering against her cheeks. Her lips were beestung, kissed into swollenness. She ran the tip of her tongue along them, leaning back to offer her breasts even more blatantly than before. She stroked the fifth man's cock while he teased her nipples, pushed her bottom back against the sixth and ground it into his pelvis.

'Whore.'

Adam's eyes filled with tears. He couldn't fight arousal as powerful as this. The devil was going to win again. Her skin was damp and shining with sap. Brown streaks from the earth adorned her like primitive tattoos. She was a creature made of sex, a nymph of some kind. She had to be. No human woman could take six lovers, one by one, the way she did.

While she eased herself onto the fifth man's cock, Adam began to hump the ground. It didn't count if he didn't touch it himself. It wasn't the same.

When the sixth man parted her buttocks and pushed his fingers, lubricated with her own juices, into the tight pucker between them, Adam uttered a strangled cry.

'Wanton bitch on heat. Strumpet. Harlot.'

His legs kicked behind him with each rough motion on the ground. His fingers curled in his hair, yanking at it. He was almost blind with sweat, the bodies of the lovers blurring before him.

But they weren't so blurred that he couldn't make out the long, thick cock of the sixth man gliding inside the girl's bottom even as she bounced up and down on the fifth. A sight he should never have seen, wickedness, depravity ...

'Filth.' His pants filled with warm liquid, the evidence of his guilt.

When the lovers came, one, then two, then three all

within a minute of each other, he was sobbing with his face in a patch of scrubby grass.

'Fuck me, Evie,' someone said. 'You get dirtier by the day. We'll have to find a number seven for next year.'

Her laughter was raucous and free.

'Maybe make it Charlie Stack. He's filling out nicely.'

'Well, I can't see as Robin Goodfellow has anything to complain about there. We should have an even better harvest this year.'

'Lush.' Evie. That was her name. 'Come on then, what we waiting for? I'm gasping for a drink. Is the pub open yet?'

Adam held his breath, maintaining his prone position under what remained of the barn's eaves. Surely they would see him as they passed? His career in this place was over before it had begun.

But the heavy footsteps of the men paraded by him at a distance of mere feet without the passing of any remark. Her lighter tread came last. He smelled her, her scent stronger than that of the parched grass that tickled his nose. Such an aroma, of vegetation and sex, each element as strong as the other. Adam felt a kind of dissolving in his stomach. That fragrance would stay with him for ever.

Their careless voices faded, shouts and giggles flying up into the sunshine.

They hadn't even dressed before they left.

Adam waited a long time, maybe ten minutes after the final distant yell, before lifting his face and squinting out at the scene of the dissipation. His head ached and the bright green wheat giving way to the brilliant yellow of the rape beyond and the overarching gleam of the sun was too much. He returned to the comfortless dark of the ground.

Had it, in fact, really happened?

The hammering at his temples led him to hope that perhaps this was some kind of vision, a hallucination brought on by many sleepless nights praying that his ministry in Saxonhurst might soften the hearts of the villagers and bring them back to the church.

'And I had no breakfast,' he murmured into the scrappy tufts, before braving another look up. 'Lord, are you showing me something? Are you showing me the challenge I have to face? People steeped in sin, needing your humble proxy to help them on to the true path? Is that it, Lord?'

He pushed himself back onto unsteady knees. The shameful chill of the slime in his pants almost made him fall face-first in prostration once more.

'Forgive me, Father,' he whispered. It was a dream, one of those that the devil puffed into his brain with his demonic bellows. He couldn't be held accountable for what happened in his sleep.

He rose to his feet and dusted himself off. After shaking some life into his cramped limbs, he took a few steps down to where "it" had happened. The vision. The hallucination.

The wheat lay flat in patches.

'No,' muttered Adam. 'No, this is for some other reason. It was already flat when I arrived here. Village kids playing at making crop circles. That's all.'

Retrieving his hat and putting it back on his dusty head, he looked up at the ragged outline of the ruined barn. It seemed to him to have a human quality of malevolence, as if the spirit of the long-ago killer inhabited its dead wood.

He would stay away from this place in future. And he would write that letter to the council.

His walk back to the vicarage was accompanied by bitter thoughts. He knew why the diocese had appointed him to this backwoods parish – they were embarrassed by his old-school evangelism and this was effective banishment. True, Saxonhurst, with its infamously empty pews, was only one of three villages under his pastoral care and the other two had stronger congregations, but there it remained. He was exiled, in what the clerical grapevine called "the most godless village in England".

In an attempt to put a positive spin on the appointment, he had told himself that it was his unique blend of moral strengths that had led to him being chosen for the role. God moved in mysterious ways, and His purpose would soon become clear. And what a coup it would be for him, if he could transform the moribund church attendance and have the pews full by Christmas.

His step grew sprightlier as he began to plot his campaign. He would need a big opening event, something that would lure the villagers by appealing to their baser natures. Something with prizes, perhaps, or some kind of silly talent contest, since they were so popular these days. A youth club, of course, and perhaps a parent and toddler group.

By the time he reached the heart of the village, he was too preoccupied to even think of peering into the pub windows to check for green men and naked women. He turned the corner into the vicarage grounds, enjoying the crunch of gravel beneath his feet and the sweet smells of the flowers in the borders. Birdsong and the swish of leaves in the light breeze conferred a glow of well-being that lasted through the door and into the living room.

Which was not empty.

'Visitor for you, Reverend,' called his housekeeper, Mrs Witts, from the kitchen.

'So I gather. Good morning.'

The visitor sat on a chair, in that kind of folded-up stance that suggested she was trying to take up as little space as possible.

On seeing Adam, she rose and held out a hand.

'Good morning, Reverend. I'm Julia Shields.'

Her hand was cold and thin, like the rest of her. She was pale to the point of translucence, from her colourless hair downward.

'I'm pleased to meet you, Ms Shields.' Shaking the hand was like shaking frigid air. 'What can I do for you?'

'Oh, I just wanted to welcome you to Saxonhurst,' she said, smiling tightly. Withdrawing her hand from Adam's, she began a slow excursion around the room, picking up ornaments and putting them down as she went. 'It's a long time since I visited this house. I used to come here, as a child.'

'Did you? You're born and bred in the village?'

'Yes. Actually, I'm the lady of the manor.'

'The lady of the manor? Well, I'm honoured.'

Adam felt foolish, wrong-footed somehow. This woman's motives were veiled in mystery and something about her filled him with profound unease. Talking to her reminded him of trying to talk to girls he fancied back at school – all the conversation flew from his head, leaving him with awkward remnants of words.

'You should be. Nobody ever visited the last vicar. You're much younger than him.'

She turned from examination of a watercolour of the church over the fireplace and gave Adam a piercing glare.

'I'm 31,' he said, wanting to kick himself for sounding so gauche.

'Thirty-one. That's young.'

'You can't be much more.'

'No. I'm 29. But I don't have a job to do, as such. I don't have such a very, very difficult job to do. What made you want to come here?'

'I like to look upon it as God's decision.'

'Oh, so you didn't want to come here?'

Her smile was like the glimmer of light on a blade.

'I ...'

'Well, anyway, this is all small talk. I do actually have a purpose in visiting you. I have a problem and I want your help.'

'Oh. A crisis of faith?'

'No.' She looked at him pityingly. 'Sit down, for heaven's sake. You're so tall, and in all that black, you loom like a huge crow.'

'I'll have Mrs Witts bring us tea.'

'No, no tea. Do you have any sherry?'

'I don't drink.'

'Ugh. Well. I'll begin. I told you I was the lady of the manor.'

'Yes.'

'My title is in jeopardy. I am still the lady, but I have no manor.'

No manners either, thought Adam, smirking at his unspoken witticism.

'Oh dear, how come?' he asked politely.

'Money. That's what it all comes down to, isn't it? I ran out of money. I tried all sorts. I took in paying guests, hosted those awful murder mystery parties. But I couldn't afford to maintain a place that size. I had to put it on the market – or rather, my bank did. It was bought at auction a few months ago.'

'I see. I'm sorry to hear of your troubles. I can, of course, pray for their easement, but ... I don't think that's what you want from me, is it?'

'Of course not. I'm an atheist, for one thing.'

Adam winced. He should have ordered that tea anyway. He felt the need for something hot and sweet to anchor him, a handle to hold on to. If only he could go upstairs and change his trousers, then he wouldn't have that creeping feeling that Julia Shields knew what he'd been up to that afternoon.

'Then, may I ask ...?'

'I think you'll agree with me that the new owners need to be drummed out of the village when I tell you what they're doing in my ancestral home.'

He leant forward, finally interested in what this apparently batty woman had to say.

'What's that?' Images of Evie frolicking in the corn wound through his head as if on a film reel. Before Julia's words were out, he knew sex would be in the equation.

'They've turned it into a porn set.'

'What? A what?'

'Exactly! It's horrifying! My childhood home, the seat of the Shields since 1609, is being used to make blue movies.'

'Are you sure?'

'Am I sure? Yes. Come with me. I'll show you.'

'Show me? They surely won't ...'

'Just come.'

'I don't know about this.'

Adam was far from prepared for a second round of voyeurism that warm April afternoon, but Julia had already left the room and waited impatiently for him by the front door.

He knew where the manor house was – it was almost directly opposite the vicarage, but its handsome grey stone façade didn't give any inkling of the corruption within.

'I don't know about this. What makes you think this is going on? Have you seen them filming?'

But Julia wouldn't answer any of his questions, guiding him silently along the garden wall until they left the road and followed it through thick foliage, eventually arriving at a small, broken-down section that could be climbed over, with some effort.

'You want me to break in to the garden with you?'

'It's not breaking in. This place belongs to me.'

'I don't think the law would recognise that.'

'I thought there was a higher law, Reverend. Or have I misread that?'

'No, no, Jesus never advocated law-breaking. I can't follow you.'

'Shh. They're close by.'

Julia, who had managed to climb the wall and drop down into the trees on the other side, crept noiselessly towards the lawns.

'You'll be able to hear them anyway,' she whispered.

He heard a sharp click and a cry of, 'Action!' Almost immediately a loud chorus of moans floated through the thicket, the effect eerie to Adam's already nervous ears. Julia moved back and forth, peering through the branches then reporting her findings to her companion.

'They're fucking up against a tree,' she said matter-of-factly, then, 'she's tied him to the tree and she's sucking him off. He really is enormously well hung.'

It occurred to Adam that she could be making all this up, but the sound effects were so lewdly realistic he thought he should believe her.

'She didn't swallow. I suppose they prefer a money shot, don't they? Anyway, he jizzed on her tits in the end. You must come and look. I think they're setting up a threesome scene now.'

'Are you absolutely sure?'

'For heaven's sake. Get over the wall and see for yourself. It's all terribly immoral, but you mustn't take my word for it.'

Commending his soul to God, Adam scrambled over the wall. He stood beside Julia, suddenly hideously aware of the dried semen stain inside his pants, and followed her line of sight.

A naked man lay on the lawn, being closely attended to by two beautiful women. They were a far cry from the pneumatic bottle-blondes his vague knowledge of such productions might have led him to expect. These looked like art students, adorned with exotic tattoos. The girl on the right had purple-streaked hair and interesting piercings while her counterpart's dark skin glittered with pasted-on jewels, contrasting exquisitely with the helpless man's golden tone. They feasted on the man's cock and balls, occasionally rising to kiss and fondle each other with tender enthusiasm. The man's hands busied themselves inside the widespread slits of his partners while they pushed their tongues into each other's mouths and twisted each other's

13

nipples. Around them, people ran back and forth with cameras and sound equipment.

Adam shut his eyes, suddenly faint. His cock was hard again.

'So there you have it,' whispered Julia, triumphant. 'My beautiful lawn being used as a porn set.'

'Yes. Yes, I see.' Adam tried to clear his throat discreetly, looking away from the action.

'The question is what are you, as the moral compass of the village, going to do about it?'

It seemed to Adam that Julia's objections were less morally than materially based, but he kept the observation to himself.

'I … I think a pastoral visit may be in order. Can we go now?'

His peripheral vision caught the sight of one girl sitting on the man's face, bending over to lick the other girl's offered pussy. He turned his back and strode swiftly away.

Julia scurried after him.

'Pastoral visit?' Her whisper was harsh and urgent. 'Is that all? Make them see the error of their ways? That'll be the day. We need action, vicar. Direct action.'

Scissoring both of his long legs over the wall, Adam shook his head.

'I disapprove just as strongly as you do, Ms Shields. But we must observe the law, which they don't appear to be breaking.'

'Well, they might be. And call me Julia. We've only seen a snapshot of what they do. Could you give me a hand, please …? Thanks.'

She landed on the other side of the wall and held on to his steadying arm a little longer than was necessary. She was so cold. Why was she so cold?

'But they could be up to even worse things,' she continued. 'Teenagers or – you know – illegal stuff. I want to organise a surveillance rota. I want to catch them out.'

'A surveillance rota?' Adam removed her bony fingers from his forearm and stared at her. 'You mean – trespass the premises and spy on them?'

'I can't trespass on my own land,' she insisted. 'And yes. That's what I plan to do. I have friends who are in. They'll help out. We were rather counting on your support, vicar.'

'A pastoral visit,' he said firmly. 'That's what I can offer in the first instance. After that, we can reconsider our strategy. We can stage protests, marches, involve the local press. But first I want to talk to them.'

'I don't see what talking will do. They'll fob you off.'

'Have you tried talking to them?'

'Of course not. I don't talk to thieving pornographers.'

'Jesus would have done.'

'Well, you're not a very good clergyman if you haven't worked out that I'm not Jesus. Look, I'll leave you to it. Talk to them if you must. But do it today, and report back to me.' She took a business card from her handbag and shoved it in his hand. 'Here's my number. I'm renting a ground-floor flat at the Malt House. It's a short-term let, because, believe me, I'll be back in the Manor by Christmas.'

Adam watched her stalk off towards the road, feeling as if some kind of tornado of will had picked him up and deposited him back on the ground.

Julia Shields could be a lot of trouble. But at least she recognised that he was needed by the community. This might be a positive thing.

Determined to look at the bright side of things, he began rehearsing his pastoral visit on his way back to the roadside. But first, he really was going to have to change those trousers.

One hour and a bowl of soup later, he crunched up the gravel driveway of the manor house, looking for clues in its lead-paned windows as to the depravity that lay within. But he could see none. To all intents and purposes, it was a handsome grey stone house with well-tended borders and a

15

scrupulously swept porch. Rather than red lights or displays of flesh, the windows revealed no more than vases of freshly cut flowers.

He rang the doorbell, then strained his ears for any sounds that might drift around the walls from the back garden. There was only the ruffled quiet of a springtime zephyr.

The door was opened by one of the girls he'd seen earlier – the pierced, purple-haired one. He hadn't been prepared for this, and his confusion and embarrassment were obviously visible because she shook her head and laughed.

'What's the matter, vicar?'

He tried to forget that he'd seen this girl naked and *in flagrante.*

'May I speak to …?' He realised Julia had not supplied him with the names of the miscreant purchasers.

The girl's smile began to fade.

'What can I do for you?'

'I wanted to speak to the new owners of the house.'

'Well, that would be me!'

'Oh … Really?'

'Yes. I'm Kasia. Would you, er, would you like to come in?'

'Well, yes, yes, I would. Thank you.'

She left him in a beeswax-smelling sitting room just off the entrance hall. None of its windows looked out on to the back garden, though a pair of French doors at the far end led to the tennis courts and pool at the side of the building. Feeling restless, Adam roamed the room, looking at the modern Ikea-kit furniture, so out of place in this wooden-beamed splendour. There were pale rectangles on the walls where Julia's family portraits must have hung. Any clues that the place was being used to make blue movies were nowhere to be seen. A large wedding photograph of Kasia – dark-haired instead of purple, but wearing a sumptuous scarlet corset dress – and her handsome husband stood on a glass-topped table by the giant TV screen, but apart from that, the room was impersonal enough.

Kasia reappeared, in the same ripped jeans and hoodie she had worn when she opened the door, carrying a tea tray with an open packet of biscuits – an expensive brand. A man followed her, the handsome groom in the photograph.

'Ah, we are honoured. You must be the new vicar?'

He held out a hand for Adam to shake. Adam thought about this for a few moments, then took it.

Shaking the hand of vice.

Adam felt as if his hand were covered in invisible slime for the remainder of the interview.

'Is this a social call?' the man continued, still making no move to introduce himself.

'It's a pastoral visit,' said Adam. The man and Kasia exchanged a smirk. Adam felt his cheeks heat up. Today kept dragging him further and further out of his depth.

'Pastoral? The good shepherd, eh? Well, do sit down and have a cup of tea and a biscuit. I'm Sebastian Hurley, and this is my wife, Kasia. As the village grapevine has no doubt disclosed, we're new to the place.'

'Thank you, but I prefer to stand. No, no, thanks.' He waved away Kasia's proffered cup of tea.

The pair looked at him, waiting.

'The fact is the village grapevine has had more than that to say about you.'

'Oh?' Hurley beamed, tossing his longish hair back from a high-domed forehead. He looked, Adam thought, the living epitome of the word *louche*.

'There is some local disapproval of your – new use for this building.'

'What use would that be?' Kasia blinked in faux innocence.

'The council passed our application for planning permission,' added Sebastian.

'I know nothing about that. What I do know is that you

are using these premises for – immoral purposes.'

'Immoral?' The pair gasped.

'Say it ain't so,' added Sebastian.

'It isn't true,' said Kasia. 'There is nothing immoral in what we do.'

'Pornography?' Adam thundered, suddenly feeling the fire of righteousness burn up his natural diffidence. 'Perversion? Fornication?'

'Wow,' breathed Sebastian. 'We should hire you. You'd be an amazing for that witchfinder script we were thinking of shooting.'

'I'll give you some advice,' said Kasia, her own indignation matching Adam's for strength. 'You stay out of our sex life and out of our legitimate business, and we'll stay out of your church. Is that a deal?'

'Legitimate business? Does the council know what you do here? Have you registered it?'

'Of course.' Sebastian sighed. 'There's nothing illegal here. We're a cottage industry. A film studio. We've filled in all the forms. We have a legal team. All performers are of age and consent fully to everything they do. And it's not the kind of porn you might be imagining. The kind you might have watched as a furtive, obsessive adolescent ...'

'I've never!'

'Well, maybe that's your problem. Anyway, as I was saying, what we make isn't the standard gonzo porn with blow-up blondes and increasing levels of misogyny and degradation. We hate that, don't we, Kasia?'

'Hate it,' she reiterated. 'We had a vision, Seb and I, of a different kind of erotic film. All about the woman's pleasure. All about what she wants. You know, this thing about women being less visual seems crazy to me. If I wasn't visual, why would I have all these tattoos?'

She pulled up her sleeve, revealing an intricate folk art design.

'It's Polish,' she explained. 'Like me.'

'You make perverted films about female – sexuality?'

'That's right.' Kasia patted him on the arm. 'Very perverted, mostly. You want to see one?'

'I want you to stop,' said Adam. 'This isn't appropriate. It's wrong. It's morally reprehensible.'

'I feel sorry for you,' said Kasia, turning to the tea tray. 'You are missing so much. But I think you must go now.'

'This is not the end of this,' Adam warned, calculating how best to make a dignified and emphatic exit. 'The village won't accept it.'

'Is that a threat?' asked Sebastian with a smile, taking Adam's elbow and steering him from the room. 'We don't like those.'

Adam shook the man off, almost sending him into a backward tumble.

'Do not touch me!'

He opened the door himself, then leapt back when he realised he had almost steamrollered a figure on the doorstep.

'Watch yourself, love.'

It was Evie, clothed now, in a pair of tiny denim hotpants and a gingham shirt knotted at her navel. Her hair hung down to her waist, crowned by a whimsical little garland of spring flowers.

Blood rushed to Adam's groin and he cowered like a wounded animal, standing aside to let her pass.

She ignored him, chatting to Sebastian and Kasia over his head.

'Won't be up to much tonight, sorry. Had a horny bastard of a day. Feel like I've shagged a shire horse. Do you mind if I stick with a bit of oral instead? I'll give, no bother.'

'We'll work with you, sweetie,' said Kasia, hurriedly drawing her away from the hall and into a side room. 'We're flexible.'

Adam looked after her wordlessly while Sebastian stood, arms folded, waiting for him to make his move.

'She's our star actress,' he mentioned once it seemed probable that Adam had suffered some kind of upright stroke. 'Evie Witts. Fancy her, do you?'

Adam's wits made a slow return to his head.

'What? Don't be – facetious.'

'You're probably the only man this side of Hamframpton that hasn't had her.'

'Don't speak of her that way.'

Why was he defending her, well, her virtue, when he knew she had none? She was the whore of Babylon, transplanted to Saxonhurst. Objectively he knew it.

But his crotch seemed to treat the knowledge with blithe disregard.

'You're right,' said Sebastian, holding open the door. 'I shouldn't belittle her. She's Kasia's heroine. A woman who likes sex and refuses to feel guilty or constrained by society. I admire her. Don't you?'

'You … It isn't too late. Repent, Mr Hurley. You can be saved.'

'I'll pass if you don't mind. Enjoy your evening.'

Adam swept through the door and down the porch steps without looking back. He hadn't achieved anything that would impress Julia Shields. But he had a mission now. A concrete and irresistible mission. He was going to save Evie Witts.

Chapter Two

Where were the flowers? At his last church, there had been fresh flowers every Sunday, organised by a committee of keen amateur florists.

St Jude's, Saxonhurst, was bare of such natural ornamentation. There was something else it was bare of too, that Sunday morning. A congregation.

No organist sat in the loft playing the introduction to the first hymn – they had last had one in 1962. Entering from the vestry, Adam launched into the opening verse of *O Worship The King*, his solo baritone echoing along the nave and up to the vaulted ceiling.

What a magnificent place this could be, if only the pews were full, the choir stalls peopled.

But his work lay before him, and he was hopeful.

So hopeful that he did not abandon the service, but continued doggedly, singing all the verses of the hymn, then moving on to the liturgy proper, leaving spaces for the responses that never came.

The neglected air was chill and damp on his skin, but he read the lesson regardless of its musty odour, enjoying the way his voice rang out across the empty benches.

The sermon he had prepared the night before, working at his desk until past midnight, would be wasted, but it would not be abandoned.

He closed the book on the lectern and struck his usual pose, a finger beneath his chin to signify curiosity, his crooked elbow resting on the ledge to suggest accessibility and modernity, his brow furrowed to bring the weight of profound thought to the ensemble.

'I wonder, brothers and sisters,' he opened, 'if we have lost sight of a simple thing, a thing so important to our forebears in this village, a quality that has suffered over the years from a kind of weathering, resulting in its erosion to something hardly resembling what our ancestors knew.'

He paused for effect. Leave the congregation some time to guess what he might be talking about, that was the advice he'd been given by his mentors.

'That thing,' he resumed after counting the requisite half a minute's beat, 'is decency.'

He looked up, all the way to the font, catching imaginary eyes with his frank and commanding gaze. Now they would be questioning themselves. Am I decent? Does he mean me?

He caught his breath when a figure moved at the back of the church, behind a stand containing unlit votive candles. It looked like her. Was it her?

'Decency,' he continued, in a lower tone than he intended, wavering slightly, 'used to mean something quite different. It has become a catch-all phrase that encompasses all behaviour of a generally moral nature ... Hello? Don't go.'

She had left through the optimistically open back door, a slight figure in a bright red dress, hair streaming gloriously down her back.

Adam looked about him, torn briefly between determination to see the service through and the urgent need to catch Evie.

Urgent need trumped professional determination, and he left the lectern and hastened along the aisle, robes billowing when he broke into a run near the arched exit.

'Evie,' he called. 'Evie Witts!'

But when he arrived at the porch, there was no sign of her.

The morning was bright and sunny again, another perfect

day in the ripening Vale, but here in this forgotten corner of the village it was shadowy and chill. Beyond the church, the graveyard was unkempt and overgrown, the lichened tombstones half smothered in vetch and cypress spurge. Valiant sunlight forced its way through a clump of yew trees lining the perimeter wall, but the fitful penumbras thus produced only intensified the sinister atmosphere.

Keeping to the weed-strewn path, Adam skirted the building, looking for a tell-tale scarlet flash, finding nothing until he came to the oldest part of the grounds, its uneven gravestones like lines of rotting teeth, the 16th century dates hewn upon them sealed up with moss.

He stopped, hugging his arms to his body, hearing at first only the breeze sighing through the leaves. Despite the unearthly calm, he felt that he was not alone.

Then he heard it. A sound that blended with the suspirations of nature and yet stood apart from them, heavier and more urgent. A human sound, panting perhaps. And then an unmistakable sigh of – of pain? Upset? Or base pleasure?

He had heard that same sound, from those same lungs, before.

'Evie!' he called again, angrily now. 'Where are you?'

He strode around the bell tower and then he saw her.

Lying on a flat granite slab, surrounded by a low wall and festooned with the only fresh flowers in the entire graveyard, was Evie. Her legs were bent so that the silky skirt of her red dress was rucked around her waist, baring her knickerless crotch to the gaze of any passer-by. She gazed up into the sky, one hand cupped around a breast, teasing its stiff nipple with a lazy thumb.

Her face was rapt, eyes glassy, and her back was arched. The flush of her cheek was just as it had been when he saw her the day before, taken by her string of lovers. She had been – doing something unspeakable – here in the churchyard.

23

For a moment, he could do no more than stare at her, his eyes drawn rudely to what was displayed between her thighs.

Then he took a long stride forward, reaching out for her arm to yank her off the slab. She anticipated him and rolled on to her side, ending up on all fours with her silk-encased bottom thrust up towards him.

'I've been a bad girl, vicar,' she said over her shoulder. 'Are you going to spank me?'

All self-control flying out of reach, he raised his hand to do exactly that. It wasn't until it had fallen, with a crack that sent the birds flying from the trees overhead, that he collected himself.

'Dear Lord, send me strength,' he muttered, staggering back until the stone of the bell tower supported his spine.

Evie put a hand on her backside, rubbing at the spot he'd made such impressive impact upon, then she rose and beamed impishly at him.

'That'll leave a mark,' she said, biting her lip. 'But I deserved it. I shan't tell anyone.'

He resisted the impulse to thank her, though he knew that his action could have spelled the end of his career.

'Yes, you deserved it,' he said. 'How dare you desecrate the graves of the dead in this way? You are brazen and sinful.'

'Just like her,' said Evie, casting her gaze down at the horizontal gravestone with its curlicued script. 'My great-great-great-grandma. There might be another couple of greats in there. I dunno.'

Adam stepped closer, reading the name.

'Evangeline Mary Witts. You're named for her?'

'Yeah, strange though, 'cos she weren't exactly a role model. We've got a lot in common, me and Granny Evangeline, if you know what I mean.'

'Do you think she'd approve of what you were doing on her grave?'

Evie looked as if she were struggling with some undefined emotion.

'I ain't looking for approval,' she said at last.

'That's obvious. But sometimes you get what you aren't looking for when you least expect it.'

'What d'you mean by that?'

'I mean, Miss Witts, that you are coming with me.'

She didn't resist when he took her wrist. He was both elated by and suspicious of her compliance, but he said nothing as he drew her along the path, through cobwebs and brambles, towards the vicarage.

'I was coming up here anyway,' she volunteered, in explanation for her lack of resistance. 'To see my aunty.'

'Who?'

'Your housekeeper. She's my aunt. I come up and have Sunday lunch with her sometimes.'

'Oh.' He fumbled in his pocket for the keys. 'Mrs Witts. Of course. I hadn't made the connection.'

'She's doing roast lamb today. Mint sauce. Roast potatoes. Carrots and stuff.'

'Roast lamb can wait. We have things to discuss first.'

'Do we?'

'Oh yes. Take a seat.'

He showed her into the living room, then went to find his housekeeper, who was peeling potatoes at the sink.

'I wasn't expecting you, vicar – that was a quick service. Ain't you meant to be going over to Little Minching before lunch?'

He'd forgotten his commitment to the late morning service in the neighbouring hamlet. But he still had half an hour before he had to be there.

'Yes, yes, that's all in hand. I meant to tell you, Mrs Witts, that your niece is here.'

'Our Evie?'

'Yes. I want to talk to her first. Could you make tea?'

'Talk to Evie?' Mrs Witts put down her peeler and

25

cackled. 'She ain't the religious type, I have to warn you.'

'Well, be that as it may ... Tea, please.'

'Of course. Biscuits?'

'I think, no. Just tea.'

He returned to the living room to find Evie running her finger along the bookshelves, letting it bump from leather spine to leather spine, over the gold leaf lettering.

'You read all these?' she asked idly.

'Yes.'

'You must have a lot of time on your hands. Don't you have work to do? Visiting the sick and whatnot?'

'Of course. I am a spiritual guide and mentor – which brings me to you. Please sit down.'

'You want to guide me?' She turned and let her lips slowly curve upwards. 'Aww, that's nice, love.'

'I said, please sit down.' Exasperation wasn't far beneath the surface of the cool, firm tone he had rehearsed to perfection.

'Dunno if I can, vicar. Got a sore bum, you see.'

He drew in a breath, waiting, trying to ignore the gathering tension in his trousers. She relented and plumped herself down on the sofa.

He subsided into the arm chair opposite and steepled his fingers, preparatory to making his first line of attack.

'Mind if I wash my hands?' She pre-empted him, her eyes alight with devilment. 'My fingers have been where a good girl's fingers shouldn't go this morning, if you catch my drift. S'OK, I know where the downstairs lavvy is. Wait a mo.'

She got up and scampered off, leaving Adam utterly disarmed and with an erection he couldn't do anything about.

He prayed silently, head in hands, until Evie's absence became conspicuous by its duration. Had she walked out?

Erection successfully banished by devout thoughts, he went to investigate.

He found her in the kitchen with her aunt. Both of them stopped talking the moment he appeared and looked at the floor.

'Evie,' he said, as sternly as he could. 'We haven't had our talk yet. Bring the tea things through, Mrs Witts.'

His second attempt began with a little more success. Once tea was poured and Mrs Witts dispensed with, he leant forward and gave Evie a long, hard look.

'What do you think I want to talk to you about?'

'Flowers? I'm good at flower arranging.'

'Not flowers. I'm worried about you, Evie. Deeply concerned.'

'You want to put me out of your head, vicar. I'm never going to be anything but what I am. I enjoy life, I don't hurt nobody, I don't start wars nor tell people what they can and can't do. I reckon that makes me OK.'

'OK? You, you're a pornographic ...' He couldn't complete the sentence.

She shrugged. 'I've fucked a few people on camera. Sorry, God. Please don't smite me now.'

He put down his tea. His hand was shaking too much to hold the handle steady.

'Do you truly see nothing wrong in what you do?'

'Wrong? Let me see. You tell me what's wrong with this. After I got to Kasia and Seb's last night, I got changed into a little bikini thing, all spangly it was, just a little G-string and the bra top had cut-outs where the nipples peeked out. We were doing a poolside scene, see.'

Adam thought, recognised, knew he should stop her. But the words wouldn't form.

'Now, I wasn't in no fit state for full-on shagging. You know why. Don't you?'

Adam spilled his tea, starting forward as if stung. She *knew* he'd been watching her at her cornfield orgy?

'Don't try and deny it, you dirty sod. Voyeur, that's what you are. But don't worry. I won't tell a soul. Just like I won't let on about you laying a finger on me in the churchyard. All your secrets are safe with me, vicar.'

She winked, watching him splutter and struggle to find a repudiation until she seemed to tire of the scene and continued.

'Anyway, my cunt weren't looking too clever, so we decided to do a girl on girl scene. Me and Bellissima – that's Kasia's girlfriend and co-star. She ain't really called Bellissima. Her real name's Shyanne and she's from Croydon. Artistic license, though. I call myself Angel Harp. Dunno why, just sounds nice.'

She laughed. He was having difficulty masking his horror and dismay.

'I know it's a bit inappropriate. An angel is the last thing I am. But it's pretty. Like me. Do you think I'm pretty, vicar?'

She didn't wait for a reply.

'Anyway, back to the poolside. Me and Bellissima were sitting on the edge of the pool, making out. She's got a pierced tongue and I love the way it feels when she pushes it all round the inside of my mouth. I like to flick the tip of my tongue over it, all smooth it is. So we were really getting into it, deep kissing, and we started feeling each other's tits, pulling down the bikini tops, though she didn't have to do that, what with my nipples poking out anyway. Can be a bit rough sometimes, Bel, and she was twisting them a bit, but I just stroked hers. Gorgeous, they are, really full, I think she's a double E cup.'

Adam uttered a bleat of "Stop" but it was so weak Evie didn't hear it. Or perhaps she pretended not to.

'They felt all heavy in my hands and I just wanted to squeeze. When Seb's filming, he likes to leave the action to us, let us take it where we want to go. We have directions that we know about before we start – like, we knew how the scene was going to end. But just for now, we were having fun, exploring each other's bodies. Her skin's so smooth and sleek, it's golden brown, you know, almost shines. Anyway, she was first with the hand down the bikini briefs. She took off her false nails before we started, thank God, so her hand just slipped in there, nice and easy. I spread my legs for her and she rubbed my clit nice and slow, still with her tongue in my mouth, frenching me for all she was worth.

'I started to feel like she was getting all the control, 'cos she can be a bit of a bossy bitch sometimes, and I wasn't having that. I wanted to be the dominant one in this scene. So I took her hand out and smacked it and pushed her down on the tiles.

'Her bikini bottoms came down and I threw 'em in the pool before she could grab them back. I made her spread her legs and I got between them and lay on top of her, dry humping her until she let me finish the kiss.

'Then I got stuck into her nipples, giving them a good licking, a few nips with my teeth. She's got big nipples, vicar, real dark, like bitter cherries. They taste gorgeous, she uses some lotion that smells of mangoes or passion fruits, not sure which, always get them two mixed up. She's not soapy, just a kind of sweet, salty flavour. I can't get enough of it. By then, I'd got my fingers into her cunt and believe me, she was wet. You could hear the sucky noise of it every time I put them in and took them out.

'I said a few words of dialogue, I told her what was coming to her. "You're gonna get fucked like a bitch, Bel," I said to her. "Like my bitch, on your knees with your arse up while I give it to you with my strap-on." That was her cue to start fighting me. I had to let her, it was in the script, but I didn't want to stop fingering her and sucking those fucking luscious nipples. Directions are directions, though, so I let her roll out from under me and escape into the pool.

'Their pool's lovely, vicar, just the temperature you want, like a warm bath. You'll have to go for a swim there some time. Anyway, I chased Bel around the water, but first I took off my bikini, 'cos who needs it? I dived in and got hold of her, but that took a while 'cos Seb couldn't get the shots he wanted. We had to do about eight takes. Finally he was ready for the big finish. I dragged her to the poolside and bent her over the edge. Gave her a few smacks on her wet bum – that hurts more, you know. Next time you spank me, remember that.

'Got her on her knees and spanked her again until she promised not to fight me. Then I whipped on the old strap-on and sank it right in. It's a big 'un, but she can take it. She stretched really wide, so I took it slow at first, made sure she was comfortable. Oh, you should've heard that girl, vicar. She's got one of those voices, kind of hoarse and throaty, you know. When she moans, she really moans. Fuck, she turns me on.'

'That's enough!' Adam forced the words out, the effort muffling them somewhat, but he accompanied them with a bold sweep of his arm.

'You all right, vicar? Your face is dead red.'

'What on earth do you think you're playing at?' He rose unsteadily. The phrase "Next time you spank me, remember that" flickered in and out of his mind, threatening his resolve and doing nothing to relieve the bulge in his trousers. 'Why are you spouting this –this – filth? In my living room? What are you trying to do?'

She widened her eyes and blinked, a classic faux-ingenue.

'I don't know what you mean, vicar. But if I was trying to turn you on, I reckon I've succeeded.'

She glanced down at the lump in his cassock, her lips twitching.

'I don't pretend,' he started stiffly, 'that I am not mortal. I suffer the temptations of the flesh, just like any man. But I don't yield to them. I don't let them rule me. That's the decent way, the right way. You need instruction in that way, Evie, or you are lost.'

'You want to teach me, vicar?' Her voice was soft and

breathy.

He knew she was toying with him, but this didn't deter him. There was a long journey to be taken, but it had to start with a single step.

'Yes. I think you should come here in the evenings and take instruction from me.'

'Learn the error of my ways? Correct my dirty habits?'

'It won't be easy.'

'I know. You can't make me do anything I don't want to, though, can you?'

'I realise that. I will rely on your – free will. Your God-given free will.'

Evie considered this for a while, sipping at her lukewarm tea.

The room seemed suddenly airless and oppressive to Adam, the birdsong outside deafeningly strident. The inward fight against his outward arousal reached its critical point. The visions of grabbing Evie and fucking her against the wall that threatened to tip into the broadest stream of his consciousness couldn't be repelled for much longer.

She broke the tension with a laugh.

'I like you, vicar. In a funny kind of way. You're interesting. All right, then. I'll do it.'

He was too surprised to move for a moment, winded by what seemed like vast and unexpected good fortune.

'You'll – study with me?'

'Yeah. Why not? Could be a giggle. Not every night, though. Call it Wednesdays and Sundays. Oh no, I guess you're busy Sundays. Mondays then. Wednesdays and Mondays. "Save Evie's Soul" – the challenge is on.'

'You must take it seriously.'

'Oh, I take you seriously, vicar. I take you very seriously. You're pretty scary in that black dress, you know.'

'Cassock. It's a cassock.'

'You're like a big old crow. From long ago.'

A knock on the door interrupted Evie's teasing. Mrs

Witts stuck her head round.

'Don't mean to interrupt, Reverend, but isn't it getting a bit late? They'll be waiting for you in Little Minching.'

'Oh! Yes. Yes.' He looked at the clock and sprang to life, gathering up books and papers for the service.

'You coming to the kitchen with me, Evie?'

'Yeah. Smells lush. Thanks, vicar. I feel like my spiritual life is about to begin. See you tomorrow night.'

She sailed past him with a wink, her scarlet silk dress swishing over her curves as she followed her aunt out to the hallway.

Once the door was closed, he sank to his knees beneath a wall-mounted crucifix and muttered prayers until the fever was past and he could embark on his trip in a pure frame of mind.

That night, he dreamed.

Evie sat at a desk, studying her Bible, but she was naked. Her hair spilled on to her round breasts and the nipples stood firm and proud.

He stood at the front of the room, a schoolroom. She inflamed him. He was powerless to resist. There seemed to be only one way to deal with the burgeoning heat in his groin, and she knew it before he even spoke.

She looked up at him and closed the book.

Lifting her hair and holding its heavy weight at the back of her neck, she rose, revealing a delicate covering of curls above her pubic triangle, though in reality he knew she was shaved there. Her body was healthily proportioned, blending pink and white, softness and firmness. She embodied fleshly temptation, sinful sensuality. Every move she made was a lure.

She walked to the side of the room and took from a cupboard a long willow switch. This she bore in both hands, palms upward, presenting it to him as an offering.

When he had taken it, she turned and wordlessly bent

over the desk, pushing out her bare bottom.

Next time you spank me ...

He looked at her sweet, white globes; unmarked, blank canvases. She wiggled her hips, as if impatient for him to begin.

He raised the rod and whipped it smartly down, exhaling along with the swoop of the lash, sighing as it made its crack of impact. A red line rose, beautifully contrasting with the pale skin it streaked. She made no sound. Before he stopped, she must beg for his mercy.

His arm powered back and forth, wrist flicking, switch falling over and over until that pert bottom was a criss-crossing welter of weals, bright red and raised. The endless giddy whoosh of the whip sang in his ears, the crack bumping along with his heartbeat. He made music, a flagellating symphony, and his blood fizzed with power. The girl was his. She submitted to his will, and through his will, the higher will.

He saved her with this switching. He saved her soul.

She spoke the words.

'Have mercy on me, a sinner.'

He put down the rod and put his palm to that subjugated flesh. How it burned. His mark was upon her, and she would bear it on her soul and in her memory even after it faded.

He unbuckled his belt.

The image faded and altered.

Evie disappeared.

Confusion reigned until he awoke to wet sheets and dry, feverish eyes.

'Have mercy on me, a sinner.'

But this time the words came from him.

Chapter Three

'We should begin at the beginning, shouldn't we, vicar?'

Evie pushed aside the *New Testament* and the exhortations of St Paul to the Ephesians.

'I think the most pressing issue for you is an understanding of how to live in a Christian fashion.' Adam disagreed.

He seemed to be disagreeing with everyone today.

He had disagreed with Julia Shields over the best way to go about banishing the pornographers from her ancestral home. She wanted him to make complaints to the authorities – the planning office at the local council, to begin with. But Kasia and Sebastian had registered the property's change of use in advance, and they were breaking no laws. They were paying their taxes like everyone else. "Render unto Caesar that which is Caesar's", he had told Julia. She had snorted and said Jesus didn't have to deal with skinflicks being made in his lowly stable.

'He wasn't living in a stable by then,' said Adam patiently, but Julia wasn't listening.

'Are you telling me that you are going to let them carry on with this? Right under our noses?'

'No, I'm not telling you that. I'm as against it as you are. But I think we need to get the village on our side. Why don't you call a meeting? I'm happy to give the church hall over to it. Leaflet the parishioners and get them on our side.'

And get them on to church premises, for the first time in their heathen lives.

With a little flutter of optimism, Adam saw an opportunity to make the church central to village life. If everyone joined in their crusade, he could make his services a key part of the fight. Bums on pews at last.

'Well, I suppose so.'

He didn't understand her dubious reaction. Surely this was the obvious path to take.

'Don't you think it's a good idea?'

'It's just, well, I'm not the most popular person in this village.'

'Oh.'

'Why don't you produce the leaflets? You're new here; they won't have any of their loopy peasant prejudices against you.'

He sighed. His head was going to be well and truly over the parapet. Trusting that the diocesan authorities would understand and approve, he assented.

So he'd leafleted each house in the village, calling a public meeting for the Thursday evening.

Of course, Sebastian had been straight on the phone.

'It's harassment, pure and simple,' he raged. 'Don't think I won't involve the police if it gets out of hand.'

'People have a right to express their opinions, peaceably,' Adam pointed out, though he was feeling far from peaceable at that point. The idea of storming the manor with flaming torches grew more appealing by the moment.

And now Evie, at her first tuition session, was taking a dim view of it all.

'I reckon God's all right with erotic stuff,' she said. 'Forget this St Paul bloke, let's do Adam and Eve. He gave them the Garden of Eden and I bet that was a sexy place. I mean, they walked around butt-naked all day long. God didn't seem that bothered by it.'

'Man wasn't able to handle his desires,' said Adam severely. 'Hence their banishment.'

Evie stretched out and yawned, her hand brushing

Adam's upper arm as he sat beside her.

'I reckon Eve gets a bad press. I would, though, wouldn't I? We've got the same name. I've always been on her side.'

'She was weak.'

'No weaker than Adam. I suppose you think he's all right, do you? It was him thinking with his dick got us into all this. And men ain't been no different since.'

'He disobeyed the word of the Lord, yes, but he wanted forbidden knowledge not – not, you know, sex. And so did Eve. They were both guilty.'

'But Eve got the worst out of it. Way the worst. Do you think that's fair, vicar? Adam had to chop a few logs but Eve had all the pain and the blood. I'd have swapped.'

'It was Eve who listened to the serpent, Eve who took the apple.'

'Apple.' Evie shook her head. 'Are we meant to believe that, vicar? Everyone got in all this bother just for the sake of a boring old apple? I'd understand if it was a Toblerone.'

With difficulty, Adam forced his mind back to St Paul, taking the book and shoving it down under Evie's nose.

'We are not talking about Adam and Eve,' he said firmly.

'Oh yes we are. When we're together, we're always talking about Adam and Eve.'

Oh Lord, she was right. How had this happened so fast and so fatally? Their dynamic already was one of tension, temptation, resistance, played out in infinite variations.

He had to be stronger than his biblical namesake, that much was clear. Whoever the serpent might be was doing a grand job of it.

Was it Sebastian? One of those village men in the cornfield? Someone had to be pulling Evie's strings. Who was it?

'What do you reckon the Garden of Eden was like?' she asked idly, pushing the *New Testament* away again.

He tried not to answer, he tried to resist her line of beguiling enquiry, made with such ingenuous lowering of eyelids, such provocative pouting of lips. But it was no use.

'A very beautiful place, of course. Scholars dispute over its geographical location –'

'Oh, I don't care about what it looked like. I mean, what was it *like*? What was it like to live there? What did Adam and Eve do all day?'

'Obey the Lord,' said Adam, a tad sulkily. 'And now -'

'What would you do all day? If you were in the Garden of Eden, starkers, with a beautiful woman?'

'This isn't relevant.'

'Yes it is. It's how it all began. How can it not be relevant? Imagine you're Adam and I'm Eve – not that much of a stretch, is it? You don't have to work. Everything's all there for you – food and warmth and so on. You can do anything and everything you want, all day and all night. What would you do?'

'I would pray. Now, when St Paul arrived in Ephesus … What are you doing?'

She had put her finger on his lips. She was so close to him and her hair smelled of meadows.

'I reckon it'd be like this. You'd be there, in the Garden of Eden, and once God had done that lecture about not eating from the tree and whatnot, you'd turn and see me on the grass beside you. And you wouldn't want to pray. You wouldn't want to stroll around admiring the rivers and the valleys and all that. You'd want to fuck.'

He took hold of her arm, wresting her finger away from his mouth.

'I won't hear that kind of talk in my home,' he rasped.

'I reckon the air in that garden was loaded with sex. You'd be at it night and day. And that's a good thing, vicar. While we're making love, we ain't making war. Don't you think?'

'There are other things to make, worthy things.'

'But right down at the root of it, we all want to fuck. Even you. Especially you. You want it right now, I can tell.'

'Get away from me!'

She did so, standing up and picking up her bag.

'Sounds like we're done for tonight, then. I feel sorry for you, Adam. What you need is a woman. Or maybe you're gay? Is that it? No, can't be, or you wouldn't fancy me.'

'Just leave me alone.'

'So, same time Wednesday?' she said breezily. 'I'll see you then.'

She turned and looked back at him just before she left.

'Oh,' she said.

He lifted his head from the desk and stared at her.

'You know about the May Fair, do you? On Saturday?'

He cast his mind back, vaguely recalling a notice on the village green.

'May Fair? Oh, right.'

'You'll come, won't you? It's so much fun. And you might learn a few things about us.'

She left.

He sat up eventually, bleary-eyed and thick-headed, still feeling drugged with arousal, but determined to stamp it down. He was a soldier of righteousness, and she was his adversary, trying to run him through with the lance of fornication. He let this metaphor run through his mind for a few moments longer, enjoying the image of himself in shining armour atop a fine steed.

He looked again at the antique writing desk that had formed part of the vicarage fixtures and fittings. Where was the key for that locked drawer? He'd asked Mrs Witts but she'd just given him her trademark bamboozled look and gone back to boiling asparagus. They had the best asparagus around here, elegant spears whose delicacy was famed across the country. In fact, all the fruit and vegetables grew in embarrassing abundance, nature's bounty blessing the Vale every year. Scientists had come to try and work out what made the soil so very fertile, but nobody had formulated a plausible theory yet. Chemically, it was no different to the neighbouring lands.

An image of Evie, taking village lad after village lad and performing those invocations to Robin Goodfellow sprang into his mind uninvited.

How preposterous. They probably believed that their barbaric little ritual was what made the tomatoes so very fat and red and the cucumbers so perfectly long and green. Idiotic superstitions.

He jiggled the drawer handle again, then gave up and let his head fall back on the polished walnut.

Evie in the cornfield. What made her the way she was? What kind of woman let herself be penetrated by a succession of men in pursuit of some ungodly tradition?

He sat up, rigid, his eyes wide.

Somebody was using her, making her the instrument of his will. Her conversation about Adam and Eve had been code, some kind of cry for help, maybe? She wanted him to save her from the serpent.

A force of evil, somewhere in the background, was decanting his foul lusts into the vessel of Evie's helpless body.

He would find out who it was. He would banish him, as God banished Lucifer from the chorus of the angels. This Adam and Eve would not fall. This Adam and Eve could ... Oh Lord, is that your purpose? Is that why you have brought me here? To show me my destiny, my, my, my *wife*?

Please. Let it be so.

'Evie, tell me about your ritual in the cornfield,' he commanded urgently the minute she had passed through his door on the Wednesday evening.

She looked surprised at his enthusiastic welcoming of her. Of course, she couldn't know that the very sight of her made his insides melt, his stomach churn, his skin prickle, his heart tighten. He longed to take her in his arms and tell her he knew her terrible secret and he could protect her, shield her even if it meant his death. But she wasn't ready for that, not yet.

'Evenin', vicar,' she said, dropping her handbag on the desk.

She looked luminous in a green halter-neck top and a flouncy white cotton skirt, like a ravishing village gypsy about to dance on her bare brown feet.

'The ritual?' he prompted.

'I thought you knew all about that, what with having a ringside seat for the last one.' She sat down, attempting a demure look that didn't quite come off.

'I know what you do, of course. But why do you do it?'

'For a good harvest. It brings the favour of Robin Goodfellow to the village.'

Adam raised his eyes to the ceiling and humphed in faux amusement.

'Robin Goodfellow? You really believe that?'

'I really believe that we have the best harvests around, every single year. So why wouldn't I? God, on the other hand, don't seem to do that much for us.'

'You need faith, Evie.'

'I need to eat, love. We all do.'

'Who started the ritual?'

'It's much older than I am.'

'When did you first perform it?'

'I was 18.'

'Who did it before you?'

She hesitated. She looked rattled. He was on to something here. Excitement swelled in his breast as her reaction seemed to fit with his theory.

'I dunno.'

'What? In a village this size? You must.'

She shrugged defiantly.

'How long has it been going on?' he persisted.

'Ages. Maybe 500 years, maybe more, how would I know?'

'Who introduced you to it?'

'Oi, vicar, I didn't expect the Spanish Inquisition.'

'They were Catholics.'

'Whatever. Can you lay off me, please? Unless you want to lay *on* me, know what I mean, Adam?'

She gave him a louche wink that immediately diverted his thoughts down to his trousers.

'Let's talk about the Ten Commandments,' he stammered.

'Oh gawd, let's not. Thou shalt not, thou shalt not, thou shalt not. What shalt thou? Is anything allowed?'

'Thou shalt have no other gods before me.'

'Before you? Sorry to break it to you, love, but you ain't no god. Not bad-looking, I'll grant you, but –'

He thumped the desk with his fist. 'Oh, for heaven's sake, Evie!'

She jerked back and looked up at him. The tiny tremor of fear on her face aroused him more than he had ever been before. Those eyes, wide, and those lips parted were maddeningly beautiful. He wanted to reach out, touch, kiss – but there would be time enough. He would pluck his pretty apple from the tree as soon as she was ripe.

She sat, quiet and subdued, through the rest of the lecture, hardly speaking at all except to answer questions in a sulky tone. He made it all the way up to "Thou shalt not kill" without encountering any resistance from her.

Before they could move on to adultery, though, and the speech he had prepared on how "adultery" technically covered all fornication including the things she got up to with the village lads and sundry porn actors, she stood and made an abrupt declaration of a prior commitment.

'Are you sure? You've only been here 20 minutes. I wanted to tell you so much more.'

'I'm a busy woman,' said Evie. The sly, teasing minx seemed to have disappeared, replaced by this stubborn alternative version.

Adam wasn't sure which he preferred.

She wouldn't be detained, and left him to tidy up his notes and reflect on the forthcoming village meeting.

That night he dreamed of her again, of a beautiful, naked Evie in his vicarage garden, lying on the lawn while blossom petals rained down on her luxuriant flesh. She was sleeping in dappled shade, the light playing on the curves of her breasts and hips.

He approached her, preparing to wake her, but before he could reach her a long, black snake streaked across the grass and alighted on her body, its glistening, muscular length winding itself around her helpless breasts and slithering lower. A jewel-red tongue darted in and out as it made its inevitable path to her sweet pink pussy.

Adam tried to shout out, to dive forward, but he could neither speak nor move, frozen and unable to prevent the serpent from gliding between Evie's soft lower lips and disappearing up inside her.

Aghast, Adam looked on, expecting Evie to wake in a paroxysm of terror, but she slept on, her lips moving slightly in exhalation, her face flushing pink. The exposed end of the snake lashed against her clit rhythmically and, to his horror, Adam realised that she was in a state of sexual arousal.

Her fingers curled and she arched her back, panting now, sighing for more. The snake hissed in triumph, knowing that it had her in its thrall. She rocked into orgasm, her entire body seeming to bloom in that moment of epic vulnerability, epic pleasure.

And now she was lost, belonging to the serpent, destined never to be his.

He woke up gasping and crying.

Out near the barn where the man had murdered his sweetheart then hanged himself, Evie ran along the path under a starlit sky. The moon was full enough that she didn't need a torch. She wore only a baggy cardigan on top of her gypsy skirt and halter top, and flip-flops on her feet, but she wasn't cold, despite the clear sky and the late hour.

Soon she would be warm enough.

She stopped by the overgrown wishing well, looking down into its dry depths. Then she stepped back, shut her eyes and took a moment to concentrate her mind.

Three times clockwise she circled the well, three times anticlockwise, then three more clockwise revolutions.

Kneeling at the tumbledown brick, she spoke some words in an arcane tongue, the meaning of which she barely knew.

She kept her eyes low and shut while the excitement danced figures of eight in her belly and the air grew fierce and hot around her.

She knew now to hold her nerve right up to the point where it seemed she would burst into flames. That was how long it took.

The critical point was reached and she met it head on without fear, without resistance. She was through. She had succeeded.

Gentle fingers tickled her under her chin and she fell into an embrace.

'Oh John,' he said. 'Oh, my love, he's here.'

Chapter Four

A passer-by would have seen nothing more than a beautiful woman on her knees in the dark by the broken-down mess of the old wishing well, but that wasn't what Evie saw.

She saw a man in a ruff and an embroidered cloak with thick, dark hair to his shoulders and a pointed barb of a beard. Strong, proud features were softened by the glow of adoration in his eyes and the fond curve of his lips.

She saw her one true love.

Her one true love who had been dead this past 300 years and more.

'The preacher?' he said, pulling her up and cradling her head against his shoulder.

'Yes. He has come.'

'And do you think …?'

'He is the one. I'm sure of it.'

'Is he inflamed by you?'

'Oh yes.'

John took her face in both hands, pinching the blushing flesh of her cheeks.

'As who would not be?' he said, bending to kiss the tip of her nose.

'Oh John, I miss you all the time …'

'Then miss me no more.'

The kiss drew them both into different worlds, a temporary resurrection for him, a return to age-old passion for her. So much more than a kiss – a communion and a transformation.

Evie felt it as strongly as she ever had done, through all the bodies that had replicated her soul and spirit down the years. His lips on hers brought her home to that battle-scarred land where they had first kissed. It had felt then, as it did now, like a resolution, the end of all unhappiness. In fact, it had only been the beginning of it.

But that wasn't on her mind now, while John's tongue probed in her mouth and his hands slid under the cardigan. Her mind blanked, overlaid with frantic desire. She fisted great handfuls of his hair and burrowed her way inside his jacket, rubbing at the cambric beneath, wondering at the heat of his body.

'You have kept me strong,' he murmured, laying her down on the ground. 'I feel stronger than ever tonight. How many did you take this week?'

'I've done it at least 20 times,' she said, grinning up at him, writhing on the grassy verge while he unbuckled his sword belt on his knees beside her. 'We did the fertility ritual and that helped.'

'Of course. All the power coming into your body from that has given me a new lease.'

'I can see it in you.' She put up a hand, stroking his forearm. 'You're almost your old self.'

'And I would do what my old self did, my girl,' he growled. The belt was off, discarded in a hedgerow.

'Be gentle,' she said, arching her legs so her skirt fell in a bunch around her waist, revealing an absence of underwear. 'Like I said, love, it's been a hard week.'

'It will not be long now,' vowed John, 'before you no longer have to do this work for me. Our time is near.'

Evie sighed as John's fingers dipped deep into her overexcited juices. He spoke on, playing with her clit, getting her wetter than she thought was possible.

'That time will come soon,' he said, crooking a finger inside her cunt. 'The time when no man's fingers but mine will gain access here. The time when my prick alone grants you your satisfaction, each night and many times in succession. Oh Evie, I will have you until you cannot walk or speak, my girl. I will have you for my own.'

'Do it, John. Please take me.'

She lifted her halter top and put a hand on her breasts, plucking at her nipples while John worked his fingers further inside, stretching her in preparation.

'Am I still the best?' he whispered, flexing them, finding her G-spot.

'Always, oh always, there's no one, oh John.'

A torrential orgasm threatened to drown her senses, then John's face loomed above her, his eyes glinting. He had torn off his jacket and the breeches were gone as well, only a long cambric shirt covering his broad chest and tight stomach.

'Thou and I, my village Eve, thou and I,' he said. 'It shall be so.'

She flung her arms around his neck and lifted her legs into the air, opening her cunt to him with instinctive urgency. She needed to feel his cock inside her, a part of her, bringing her to him.

The hard length pushed in, and it was as if the sting left by earlier invaders melted away in the face of this great and final conqueror. This was her true act of union.

'Now you are where you should be.' John's voice strained above her. 'My woman, on her back with her cunny filled. You shall feel this always, when we are together.'

'I long for it.' She dug her fingernails into his back and jolted her pelvis up, greedy for every inch of him.

'I shall wipe out all traces of what has gone before, placing my mark over them. You are mine, Evangeline.'

'And you are mine, John.'

He could speak no more, his throat taken up with the effort of controlling breath.

Evie settled into him, bereft in advance, knowing that this coupling could only be brief when she wanted it to be eternal. She wanted to be under him, on top of him, filled with him, at all times, in all seasons. Their bodies, like their spirits, were built to merge, her softness and his hardness complementing each other.

He moved into a fierce rhythm, as hard on her as he might be on his horse, each thrust a punishment for the situation he himself had put her in.

'Hurt me, John,' she sighed. 'Bruise me. I want those marks on me. Fuck me so hard I'll feel it every time another man's cock is in me. I only want to feel you.'

But he wouldn't hurt her. His power in reserve, he undid her with pleasure instead, three climaxes before he ended the fuck with his own spending.

They lay, entwined and sweating, on the verge, smelling of sap and juices, hearts hammering in time, floating half on the Earth and half off it.

'It'll be soon,' whispered Evie, clinging to him as if afraid he would disappear before her eyes. 'He's here. But I'm scared.'

'Take heart. Your work is almost done. Such a long, lonely job you've had. You have earned your reward.'

'What if he – knows?'

'How can he know? He's a mere human; he has no contact with his descendant.'

'There is something about him, John. He is so very like …'

She broke off and shuddered.

John squeezed her tighter, his arm protective.

'I warrant it recalls memories you would prefer buried, love. And I would it must not needs be so. But it must. There is no other path.'

'He is the one, John. Every time I'm with him I'm so scared. I have to try and chase the fear away by being cheeky.'

'You're good at that.' Lightly he tapped her wrist in mock reproof.

'Yes, but it's so hard. I want to kill him.'

'Well, you mustn't do that. That would finish us for good. The time is coming, and I am with you always, in spirit. Think of me when the fear is upon you.'

'I will. I'll think of you.'

'This week you have the May Fair, don't you?'

'Yes, on Saturday. I'll take as many as I can, John. I'll keep you strong.'

'Make sure you enjoy it, love.'

'I will.'

'The pleasure is what sustains me.'

'I know. Every time I take another man, it's like I'm with you. Because I'm doing it for you.'

Beneath the moon, they lay together, exchanging memories and kisses until John began to fade and Evie was left alone once more.

Adam was surprised to see Evie at the meeting.

'You want to protest against your, ah, employer?' he asked, cornering her by the tea table where Julia Shields was in charge of the kettle.

'No, just making sure both sides are represented,' she said. 'I reckon Seb and Kasia'll be along later too.'

'Well, they can't,' said Adam, somewhat agitated at this prospect.

'Why not? It's a free country, ennit?'

She picked up her plastic cup of tea and seated herself resolutely in the front row.

'The nerve of her,' hissed Julia, putting down the kettle. 'Little trollop.'

'I think perhaps she's more sinned against than sinning – in some ways,' said Adam.

'Good gracious, what on earth makes you say that? Nobody's forcing her to shag every man in the village. Oh, don't tell me you're another one.'

'Another one of what?' Adam turned to Julia, his heart

beating faster, as if he knew what she was going to say.

'Bitten by the love bug. Though it's more of a sex bug in her case. Are you, vicar?'

'What? Of course not! She's a parishioner, that's all. I feel responsible for her spiritual welfare.'

'Don't. That one isn't convertible. She lives to shag, and that's all there is to it.'

'Is it?'

Julia put her hands on her hips and glared.

'I think I'm going to need to take you in hand, vicar, if you're going to start getting romantic notions about Evie Witts.'

He looked towards the object of his desire, wondering if what he felt for her was romantic. It wasn't pure, and it should be. How could he make his wanting of her pure?

'Take me in hand?' he echoed, turning back to Julia with a perplexed smile.

'Save you from yourself.'

She sounded like he did when he reflected on Evie.

'I don't need saving,' he said. 'I'm the man who saves. Who tends. Who shepherds.'

'You need a flock for that,' said Julia acidly. 'Mind you, we seem to have a decent turn-out. I didn't think anyone would come.'

As it happened, a gratifyingly high proportion of villagers had not known what the manor was being used for, and weren't best pleased.

However, their objection didn't seem to be to the pornography per se.

'We don't like people coming in and making changes to the place,' one venerable old gentleman put it. 'Saxonhurst people like the village kept in the old way.'

'They ain't doing anything wrong,' said Evie. 'They bought the place fair and square.'

'Well, I'll admit none of us lifted a finger to help Ms Shields in her misfortune,' said a woman to Evie's left. 'For personal reasons more'n anything. But there weren't many of us happy to see the manor sold on. It should stay with Saxonhurst people. For that reason, I'd be happy to see these film-makers out of there.'

Adam looked on, feeling as if he'd been transported back in time. These villagers were so set in their ways and suspicious of outsiders – did they realise that the 21st century was here? And that Saxonhurst was unusual in its demographic; most of the neighbouring villagers were overwhelmingly occupied by commuters who'd moved out from the surrounding cities. "Local" people were few and far between in the modern Vale. Yet Saxonhurst heaved with them.

'So shall we organise a protest?' Julia seized on the mood of quiet hostility towards her usurpers, not wanting the meeting to dwell on its reasons for disliking her personally.

There was general assent to this. The protest was pencilled in for the day of the May Fair, in between the maypole dancing and the jam judging.

'I'll make some placards,' said Julia, packing up after the meeting.

'You won't get them out,' said Evie, stopping briefly on her way to the door. 'You don't have a leg to stand on. There ain't a lawyer in the land who'd back you up.'

'This isn't about the law of the land,' said Adam primly. 'It's about standing behind your principles. One day you might understand.'

She looked coldly furious for a moment, as if she wanted to hit out at him, but within seconds, the cheeky glint was back in her eye.

'People who are so scared of sex make me laugh,' she said, tripping off on the arm of a tall young man who'd appeared at her side. 'Don't you reckon, Joe?'

Adam's face twisted into an ugly snarl.

'Jealous, vicar?' asked Julia. 'I wouldn't be. I daresay she'd open her legs for you if you asked her to.'

'They don't like you, do they?' He rounded on her, stung. 'Why is that?'

'Because they're ignorant. That's why.'

She stalked off without another word.

That night, Adam closeted himself in his study with the parish records. The ledgers went back to 1566, but he decided to work backward, through the registers of weddings, funerals, and christenings, to see if he could gain any useful information about this baffling village from them.

The original documents were held at the county records office, but he seemed to have copies of everything he needed, neatly filed.

The first thing he looked for was Evie. Had she been christened here?

There was no sign of it. If she had been baptised, it had happened elsewhere. He searched before the year of her birth for any marriage in the name of Witts, but found nothing. A register office, then, or maybe her parents weren't married. These days, the village church was just a picturesque backdrop for an occasion, and even that role was being taken from it in favour of local venues with wedding licences. Records post-1960s were very sparse indeed.

He turned instead to a file from the early 19th century, curious about that earlier Evangeline on whose grave Evie had behaved so disgracefully.

Her funeral record showed that she had died at the age of 29, in childbirth. Her husband, one Alfred Witts, had predeceased her – by two years! The child was not his.

He checked the baptism records to see if he could glean any information about the child, but there was none, so presumably he or she had been stillborn. There was no funeral record, though. Perhaps the child was whisked away and placed in an orphanage. Or had gone to live with relatives in another village.

Tired of the inconclusiveness of his studies, he put the ledgers away and went to bed. Something told him that he would need plenty of rest before the May Fair.

Chapter Five

The maypole on the village green was the biggest Adam had ever seen.

He milled about between stalls, avoiding the Morris dancing display, searching for Evie, but she was nowhere to be found. Julia Shields and her placard-wavers were gearing up for their protest. Julia was fielding questions from a local journalist, getting herself nicely aerated in readiness.

The jingling of bells and banging of sticks came to an end and Julia marched around the green at the head of the protest before lining up in front of the manor house and blocking the gates.

"PERVERTS OUT!" read one placard.

"SAXONHURST, NOT SEXONHURST!"

"SAVE OUR VILLAGE!" was by far the most popular though. Village politics were a strange thing, Adam thought, especially here. As long as the pornographer was born within the village bounds, presumably their activities would be smiled upon. It was lucky for him, and for Julia, that Sebastian and Kasia weren't children of Saxonhurst.

He stood at the head of the placard wavers, playing it up for the benefit of the cameras from the local TV station – Julia hadn't warned him they were coming – until some kind of kerfuffle behind the gates caused him to turn around.

They opened mechanically, and a parade of exotically dressed people poured forth, dividing the protesters into two groups.

At their head, Sebastian and Kasia were dressed in top-to-toe rubber, carrying whips and placards of their own. "FREEDOM OF EXPRESSION!" it read.

A bevy of oiled, muscular men in thongs and curvaceous women in similar followed, chanting and smiling, inviting all to join in their procession. In the centre, held aloft on a kind of chair on poles borne by four strong men, was Evie.

At first, Adam thought she was completely naked, but closer inspection revealed that she wore little wreaths of strategically placed flower petals on her breasts and between her legs. A bacchanalian Queen of the May, her locks flowing from beneath her crown of cherry blossom.

Adam dropped his placard in dismay.

'Sweet Lord!'

He ran alongside the chair, begging her to come down and get dressed, but she laughed down at him and waved, then turned to wave at everyone on the green.

The cameras kept on rolling, despite the film crew's reservations about being able to show this on the pre-watershed news bulletin. Julia's protesters chased the caravan, shouting abuse, but it soon became clear that the procession had more support than hostility from the village in general, and defeat had to be admitted.

'Give us a twirl, Evie!' bellowed a village lad into Adam's ear.

She stood, wobbling perilously, on the chair seat, and spread her arms in a gesture of universal beneficence. The pert cheeks of her arse were bisected by a cunning little twine of greenery, firmly wedged in her crack and continuing below to hide her pussy from view.

'I love you all!' she shouted. 'I love my people! Free speech and free love for all!'

The children of the village were being hustled home by their parents. The mood was changing from one of bucolic innocence to something darker. The jam judging was cancelled. A crowd built up around the maypole, muttering, swigging cider, under a lowering sun.

Adam wondered why some dancing round the maypole was building up so much tension in the air. Then he watched the crowd divide as Evie, down from her chair, was led on to the green by two of the musclemen, each drawing her forward by reins made of threaded flowers, the colours striking, ravishing, against her bare skin.

'What is this?' he asked the person next to him, his hackles rising, stomach churning with a kind of exhilarated dread.

'Maypole, ennit? Saxonhurst tradition. Oh, you're in for a treat, vicar.'

Adam watched as the musclemen placed Evie with her back to the maypole. She raised her arms above her head, and one of the ribbons was wrapped round and round her wrists until she was bound in position. Another ribbon performed a similar function around her waist. Her hair hung loose over her petal-strewn nipples and her face was ecstatic, beatific. She reminded him of depictions of female martyrs. What on earth was she doing this for?

Before he could move forward to try and intervene, the Morris dancers had surrounded Evie in a tight circle. They began to jig around her, their bells jingling and sticks clanking while a man played an accordion and the villagers clapped in rhythm. The sun dipped lower, sinking under the horizon, and the dance got faster, the music wilder. Once the red-streaked skies had turned purple and then inky blue-black, the Morris dancers abandoned their performance and Adam found himself caught up in a free-for-all as villagers surged forward, eager to grab themselves one of the maypole ribbons.

He was almost knocked over and staggered sideways. By the time he'd steadied himself, 16 villagers stood hanging on to the multi-coloured strands, over which there had been a few angry exchanges and even a slap.

Now an equal number of men and women had succeeded in taking a position and they stood, facing inward, waiting for something to happen.

But what?

The accordion started up again and the villagers began to dance, ribbons criss-crossing, forming a different pattern with each move. At one point each one of them wound their ribbon around Evie until she resembled a more colourful version of an Egyptian mummy, then they were individually unwound again and she was once more a beautiful, nearly naked woman bound to a maypole.

The music ended once all the ribbons were unravelled and an expectant tension rippled through the crowd.

'Go, Evie!' yelled one man, prompting a little wave of encouraging shouts.

A man Adam recognised as the owner of Saxonhurst's biggest fruit and vegetable growers came to stand beside Evie. Anthony Farren was his name; he was a broad, brash man, given to vulgar displays of wealth.

'May our first bearer of tribute come forward and worship your queen.'

Queen? Adam narrowed his eyes, frowning as one of the maypole dancers, a woman, approached Evie.

She dropped to her knees, lifted Evie's right ankle in her hand and began, quite slowly and deliberately, to suck her toes.

Evie giggled and squirmed with infectious delight as the middle-aged farm worker held her foot in rough hands and flicked her tongue into the grooves between her toes. With thick fingers, she caressed Evie's instep, causing her to scream out loud, and covered her red-painted toenails with kisses. Only when every inch of Evie's little feet had been smothered with attention did the woman stop.

A man was next, and he gave Evie's calves, shins, and knees the same treatment. She fussed and wriggled when he took his time kissing and licking the sensitive backs of her knees. Adam noted how flushed her face was and how her eyes rolled back with pleasure. Something told him he should stop this from going any further. Something else prevented him.

A second woman had stepped up, and she was sucking on Evie's fingers, one by one, then putting a few of them in her mouth at a time. Fervently, she kissed the knuckles and let her tongue lick a trail in the creases of her palms.

The second man was in charge of wrists and forearms and inner elbows, while the third woman took over the upper arms, even going so far as to bury her face in Evie's exposed armpits.

What was coming next? Adam wondered, transfixed.

Another man took the woman's place. He worshipped Evie's stomach and hips with his tongue and his hands, circling her navel for a good, long time while she threw back her head and moaned.

It was up to the next woman to untie the sash around Evie's waist and turn her to face the maypole. She massaged Evie's shoulders and back with a touch that looked sensuous but firm. With a jolt of shock, Adam recognised the woman as Mrs Witts, his own housekeeper and Evie's aunt. Was there no end to the barbarity of this village?

She patted Evie's side and said something in her ear before turning her back around to face the front once more and retiring.

The next man seemed to signal a new phase in the action. He kissed Evie from shoulder to neck on both sides, then set to sucking at the tender flesh there until it was marked in several places. Evie's eyes closed in rapture, and when he withdrew, her nipples were poking rudely through their petal covering, pink and stiff.

The fifth woman took Evie's face in her hands and subjected her to a passionate and thorough kiss, tonguing her so that the crowd could see how deeply Evie's mouth was taken. The young women smooched until Evie was rubbing herself against her embracer's pelvis, rubbing her legs up and down the other girl's jeans.

Adam tried to look away, but it was the most gorgeous and sensual sight he had ever seen and he felt light-headed, his throat and mouth too dry to attempt speech.

Oh, Lord, if that could be me, please let it be me.

The young woman released Evie from that epic kiss and had her place taken by the fifth man. He gently unpicked each petal from around her left nipple before fondling it, squeezing the breast, tonguing and sucking its pert pink tip for a long time; perhaps it was five minutes. The crowd did not seem to tire of the sight, egging him on to keep up the pressure. Evie's hips bucked wildly and she tried to capture the man by hooking a leg around his waist, but he maintained his severe focus on her left breast, leaving her pussy unfilled.

The sixth woman repeated this process with Evie's right breast until the maypole-bound girl sobbed with desperate lust.

'Touch me down there, please, please.'

But the woman's only response was to nip at Evie's right nipple so that Evie sucked in a breath.

'I know I'm a bad girl,' groaned Evie. 'I know I shouldn't ... I wish you could just touch me there.'

'You'll have to wait,' teased the woman before resuming her tormenting task.

Evie was panting, her breasts heaving up and down on her ribcage, by the time woman number six retreated.

There were still five villagers waiting to pay their tributes. How much further could this go? Adam stumbled forward, half-intending to say something, to try and stop it, but the crowd pushed him back again, linking in front of him to prevent his further ingress.

The sixth man turned Evie back around again, revealing the succulent curves of her back and bottom, before accepting a handful of sappy green willow wands, tied at the end with a red ribbon.

The crowd, already vocal, began to roar their

encouragement, cheering wildly when the young man drew back his arm and applied the first of several firm strokes to Evie's quivering bum. The word "Stop" died in Adam's throat the moment he saw the faint pink tinge the willow switches conferred to her skin. His fantasy made flesh. All he could do was gawp, eyes swimming, throat tight, heart pounding.

The willow wands were young and supple, bending and flexing as they swished through the air. Evie's little mewls of protest could barely be heard under the baying of the villagers, but Adam could just catch each yelp. He should be rescuing her but instead here he was, a voyeur in her moment of fleshly subjugation, enjoying it.

The man hesitated after 11 strokes of the switches and Evie's hips wiggled, then she pushed out her bottom, as if begging for more.

Adam thought he would swoon. She *wanted* it.

The final stroke fell with vicious efficacy, striping the lower portion of her bottom with marks that would last a few hours, by the looks of them.

Evie sighed some incoherent words of thanks, and her flogger retired, flinging the switches to the ground. They were seized as trophies by several of the nearby viewers and brandished in the air.

The penultimate woman turned Evie to face the crowd again. Her eyes were shut, her lip swollen and bitten. She writhed almost continually, as if trying to force herself on the woman, who maintained a strict distance until Evie behaved herself and calmed down.

Then the woman dropped to her knees and put her hands on each of Evie's inner thighs, gently parting them as far as they could go. Once she was spread and on show for the whole village, the woman ducked her head closer and began to massage Evie's vulva and clit with deft, sure fingers.

Within half a minute, Evie was jerking on her floral chains, face bright red, clearly in the throes of orgasm.

But the woman did not stop there. She gave Evie a moment to subside into passivity, then she slowly and deliberately inserted two fingers inside her cunt and began to lick her clit.

Evie moaned and protested that it was too much, she couldn't, she needed a rest, but the woman's fierce absorption in her task made Adam wonder if she'd even heard the girl whose juices she was scooping out with her tongue. He watched Evie's stomach ripple and squirm above the girl's head – who was she? Was every villager in Saxonhurst perfectly content to perform depraved acts on each other at a moment's notice? It certainly seemed like it.

After five minutes with her face buried in Evie's pussy, the woman struck gold again, and Evie came a second time, almost sobbing, trying to yank her wrists free of their bonds without success.

The woman stood back up and turned to face the cheers of the crowd. Her mouth and chin shone with Evie's juices, which she tried to wipe away with the handkerchief she waved in victory. She ran back to join her friends, who hugged and kissed her, as if eager to get their own little taste of the wanton maypole captive.

Now Anthony Farren pulled a sturdy wooden stool from the side of the green and placed it in front of Evie before calling up the seventh man.

He climbed up to kneel on the stool, unbuckled his belt, unbuttoned his jeans and introduced the tip of his cock directly to Evie's lips. She opened them and her pink tongue darted out, drawing a feathery circle around the cock's bulbous head, licking up the pearly drops at its end. The man pushed his shaft further into Evie's receptive mouth, holding it tight, breathing hard, while everyone watched her lips stretch to accommodate their invader.

Her tethered wrists meant that she couldn't get a hold of him, but she did her best to swallow as much of his length as she could, then he began to thrust. His balls swung against her chin and all Adam could see was the very root of his cock, shoving back and forth, fucking Evie's beautiful face until tears began to stream from her eyes. Once again, he tried to step forward. This time, he was tripped up and he fell back on his arse in the dust. The crowd's roar signified that the man had ejaculated into Evie's throat.

By the time Adam was on his feet, she was licking her lips, grinning like a Cheshire cat as the man she had just blown righted himself.

Only two villagers were left now.

What on earth could the final woman have lined up? Was Evie going to lick her as she knelt on the stool? Adam couldn't work out how that would be possible, given the angles involved, and indeed, it seemed that this was not the plan, for Anthony Farren removed the stool and replaced it with a much lower one.

From his little box of tricks, he produced something Adam had never seen in his life – a kind of leather harness, from the front of which protruded something unmistakably rude and phallic.

The woman buckled it around her waist and through her crotch, over the top of her spray-on jeans, until it seemed that she was blessed with an erection of her own, albeit a shiny black latex version.

She turned to the crowd to give them a few suggestive hip thrusts, making them roar and whistle, then she stepped onto the low platform and pushed the end of the dildo between Evie's pussy lips, circling until it was wet with her juices.

She clung to the back of Evie's thighs, pulling them forward so that the dildo slipped into the shallow basin behind her vulva and butted its tip in the opening of her vagina.

Evie moaned.

'You ready for this?' shouted the woman, her voice as penetrating as a military drill sergeant. 'Your cunt nice and wet for me, is it?'

'Yes, yes,' whispered Evie.

'I can't hear you, slut. Tell me your cunt's fucking hot and wet for me, and when you talk to me, you call me ma'am, right?'

'Yes, ma'am.'

'Go on then. Say it.'

'My cunt's so wet for you, ma'am, real wet and juicy. It wants a good fucking, ma'am.'

'It's going to get one, slut. Take this.'

Adam winced as the long, curved phallus entered Evie in a swift stroke.

'Have 'er, Gill!' yelled the woman next to Adam. 'She took your man. Get 'er back!'

He felt his hackles rise and a strong instinct of protection kick inside him. Evie was being revenge-fucked by this scary specimen of a woman. Somebody should stop it.

But Evie was submitting readily enough, moaning as the woman grabbed and squeezed great handfuls of her bum cheeks while she slammed into her cunt.

'That was a good   hipping' you got,' gasped Gill. 'You deserved more, though. Didn't you, eh? Little slut.'

'Yes, ma'am.'

'You ever cross me again and I'll be givin' you more than that. Get those legs wider, go on. Get that cunt proper stretched.'

She banged on in a frenzy until Evie began climaxing in a high-pitched whimper, her head flailing from side to side. The violence of it both shocked and aroused Adam, and when Gill completed her hard shafting with a smart slap to Evie's face, he doubled over and squeezed his thighs hard, only too conscious of his erection.

Gill yanked the dildo out of Evie so swiftly that her legs buckled and she seemed to hang there, all her weight supported by her poor bound arms, until she found her feet again.

Gill put her face to Evie's cunt, taking a good long look at it.

'That's been well fucked,' was the verdict. Then she unstrapped and flung the harness aside, marching down to the green's edge like Joan of Arc in battle.

Adam was on his knees when the final man took his place.

The vicar covered his eyes. Surely Evie couldn't take another pounding up there, so soon after that barbaric Gill had done her worst.

But when he peeked between his fingers, he saw that the man had turned Evie around again and was spreading her bum cheeks, stroking gently around her exposed little rosette. Evie was twitching and flexing up and down on tiptoes. The man's attentions to her arse seemed to be ticklish and she wriggled and giggled as he got closer and closer to the target.

He was going to take her there.

Adam couldn't look. He knew it would inflame him over the edge and no woman was going to make him disgrace himself on the village green in full view of his entire parish.

The commentary from the surrounding audience was more than enough to undo him, though.

'Ooh, he's got a finger in there, see?'

'Rather 'er than me.'

'Nah, she loves it. Look at 'er. Most every man in Saxonhurst has had her up the bum before now. She's well known for it.'

'She's well known for everything.'

'That's true. Oh, he's getting her lubed up now. Nice and shiny.'

'Big cock too, our Jase.'

'You used to go out with him, didn't you, a few years back?'

'Yeah. He's got a lovely one. Used to get a bugger of a face-ache, though, when I blew him.'

'Ah well, swings and roundabouts, ennit?'

'Yeah. Oh, he's got his cock between her cheeks. Steady on, Jase. Nice and easy does it.'

'Did he used to have you up the bum, then?'

'God, no, not me. Not my thing. He tried a few times, mind, the dirty bugger.'

'Dirty bugger's about right. Look, he's getting right inside her arse now.'

'That's gotta hurt. Especially where you can see where she was whipped. Must be sore.'

'She loves it. Look at the whore. She's pushing back for more.'

'We'll have good luck this year. Good health, lots of new babies in the village. Gotta hand it to her, she does a good job of it. You wouldn't do it.'

'I suppose. She doesn't have to be such a fucking man-stealer, though.'

'Goes with the territory, I s'pose.'

'Yeah. God, look at that. All the way in. Right to the hilt. She can't go nowhere.'

'Can you come from anal sex then?'

'Dunno. Let's see if she does. Ooh, look at it! Big fat cock going in and out. I don't get how it fits up there, but it does somehow.'

'Look at the dirty bitch. She loves it.'

The conversation degenerated into catcalls and insults, mingled with shouts of encouragement for the sodomiser.

'Do her!'

'Fuck her whore's arse!'

'She loves it!'

'Oh my God, is she coming?'

'I think she is.'

Adam lifted his head to see Evie kicking and thrashing in a frenzy, filled to bursting with the man's thick cock, which continued to piledrive into her while she sobbed out her climax.

He turned around and crawled through the legs of unidentified dozens, hearing the cheery voices of the girls who'd commentated for him asking each other if they fancied a cider.

There was a move en masse towards the pub and he managed to get to his feet and hobble the few yards to the church grounds without being stopped.

Back in the vicarage he threw himself on his bed and bucked against the mattress, still fully clothed, until he came, long and hard and miserably, in his pants.

This was no good.

He had to get out of here. Soon.

But he wasn't leaving without Evie.

Chapter Six

Mrs Witts looked somewhat alarmed when Adam burst into the kitchen the next morning before breakfast, and well she might.

He had not shaved and, after a sleepless night, he imagined he must present a somewhat wild aspect. He ran a hand through unbrushed hair and asked her to sit down.

'What's this about, vicar?' She paused in the search for a frying pan from the cupboard and leant against the work surface, a picture of reluctance.

'Please, sit. I want to talk to you.'

She sat at the farmhouse kitchen table.

''Bout what?'

'Evie.'

'Ah. Our Evie.'

'That – thing yesterday at the maypole. What was that?'

'Village tradition. Every year, the May Queen has to accept the tributes. It's for luck, you see.'

'I don't see. At all.'

'If she is generous with her favours, then so will Mother Nature be.'

'What utter …' Adam lowered his forehead to the table and knocked it a few times before sitting back up. 'This is what Saxonhurst is, then? Flagrantly pagan? You seem to have no – shame.'

'What's to be ashamed of? We don't harm no one.'

Evie's old refrain.

'You harm your immortal souls!'

'Oh, them.' Mrs Witts shrugged. 'We don't know about them, do we? Who sees them? Who knows they're really there? No. What's really here is our bodies, vicar, and our minds and everything around us. That's what's real in Saxonhurst.'

'But why the incessant fornication?'

Mrs Witts laughed out loud.

'Why not, love? Life's short and full of pain and trouble. We must take our pleasure where we can.'

'I don't think you're a suitable person to be working in a vicarage.'

'Now don't you think about sacking me! I'll have you at a tribunal faster'n you can thump your Bible, mister. You can't discriminate on the basis of my religion – or lack of it.'

He took a moment to calm his mind and accept the wisdom of the Holy Spirit, which counselled against taking this woman by the scruff of the neck and hauling her out of the front door. Besides, he hadn't asked the crucial question yet.

'Where does she live?'

'Who, love?'

'Evie.'

'Why? You want to ask her out?'

'I want to know where she lives.'

'In the village.'

'Where in the village?'

'Out at Witts Farm, just a little way up the Parham road. There's a sign for the farm shop right out front – you can't miss it.'

'Thank you.'

He turned to leave.

'What about your breakfast?'

'I'll forego it this morning. Thank you.'

He got his bicycle out of the shed and set off on another fine, warm May morning through the sleepy roads.

After the excesses of the May Fair it seemed everyone

was sleeping in, their curtains still drawn against the sun. The hedges were strewn with discarded streamers and on the green the maypole still stood, its ribbons now tightly wrapped around it.

It seemed like some grotesque erotic dream now and Adam almost wondered if he'd hallucinated it all. Maybe there was something in the Saxonhurst water.

Then his front wheel squashed over the abandoned clutch of willow wands, and he knew it was real.

The cottages thinned out on the road to town and Adam found himself freewheeling through lush green and yellow until he rode past a chalkboard offering a range of pick-your-own fruits and vegetables at Witts Farm. He slowed down, spotting a cluster of buildings a few yards further on that must be the place.

A hand-painted sign advertised the farm shop, selling eggs, honey, free range chickens and every kind of fruit or vegetable known to grow in the valley. Asparagus was popular at this time of year, and the strawberries and other soft fruits were just coming into their own.

He turned left into a small gravelled car park and hopped off his bike, looking about him at the well-kept farmhouse and its collection of outbuildings, including a whitewashed single-storey cabin that must act as the shop.

It was closed, but he could hear frantic clucking from the back of the house, indicating that chickens were being fed.

He walked around to the back yard and found a woman in a headscarf flinging grain at a large collection of different poultry. He watched their mindless pecking for a while, waiting for the woman to see and acknowledge him.

When she looked up, she started, then walked over.

'The new vicar, isn't it?' she said.

She didn't sound pleased to see him.

'Adam Flint,' he said, offering his hand.

'I won't,' she said, indicating the basin of chickenfeed. 'Bit dusty. What's this about?'

'Pastoral visit,' he said. It sounded unconvincing as soon as the words passed his lips.

'Pastoral? We don't keep sheep here. This is arable land.'

'But my flock is human.'

'Oh, right. I still don't really understand what you're doing here.'

'Excuse me, but are you a relative of Evie Witts?'

'Yes, I'm her mother.'

'Would you mind if I came inside and spoke with you about her? Is she here?'

Evie's mother waved a hand at one of the curtained upstairs windows.

'She won't surface till midday. Out for the count, she is.'

'I can't say that surprises me. So?'

The woman grunted ungraciously. 'S'pose. I'll put the kettle on. My husband's out in the fields or I'd get him in too.'

He followed her across the yard, dodging bantams that squawked and ruffled their feathers in his path, then passed through a door curtain into a rather old-fashioned kitchen, all exposed brick and white wood cupboards with catches. In a huge Belfast sink, an array of blackened pots and pans were stacked up. A bluebottle buzzed around an open jam jar and the place smelled of dog food and grease.

Perhaps, thought Adam, such domestic laxity had sunk into Evie's soul and morphed into sexual licentiousness. A dirty mind begotten by a dirty house.

Her mother hauled a kettle of water on to the range and found some clean cups from a dusty cupboard.

'Were you at the maypole last night?' Adam opened, watching the woman fuss with teabags and milk bottles.

'Me? No. We goes to bed early here. I know what our Evie gets up to and, not saying I disapprove, but I don't much want to watch it.'

'How can you bear it?'

The words came out so emphatically that Evie's mother

wheeled around in surprise, drops of milk spilling from the jug she'd been pouring it into.

'Bear what?'

'Your daughter – your precious child – used in that way by all and sundry?'

She shook her head.

'Listen, vicar. There's a reason none of your kind has lasted long around here, and you're giving a good account of it right now. You don't understand our ways, and you don't try to understand them. You can't change us. We are what we are and we're happy with that. Milk? Sugar?'

'Er, a drop of milk,' he said after a pause. 'How long has she been – like this?'

'There's been a wild Witts girl every generation of the family since the 1600s, Mr Flint. It's in her genes. She can't help it no more than you can help having dark hair.'

'You expected this?'

She sighed. 'I thought long and hard about marrying Jim Witts, truth be told. In a way, it's a bit of a curse. You know it's going to happen. You try and protect her but as soon as she hits 18, there's nothing you can do to stop it happening. She's a grown woman, Mr Flint. And she's happy. That's all I care about. As long as she's happy, I can't complain.'

'So you put all this down to biological determinism?'

'Biological whatamism?'

'You think it's inevitable that she will have an ungovernable sex drive? It's part of her DNA?'

'It's her heritage.'

'When did all this start?'

'Same as with her grandmother, and her grandmother before her. She was fine as a child, just a happy little soul like any other. Then, when she finished her GCSEs, she got this wild eye for the boys. I tried to keep her in, tried to stop her hanging around the village bus stop at all hours, but it was like she was mad for them. And she's such a beauty, they weren't going to ignore a girl like her, were they?

69

Funnily enough, that's when her gran started to settle down. About time too, coming into her 60s.'

Evie's mother folded her arms under her bosom, shaking her head.

'So your mother-in-law …?'

'She was just the same. Settled down now, mind, with an insurance salesman from Parham.'

'Are Evie and her grandmother close?'

'Thick as thieves, always were. Peas in a pod to look at too.'

Adam took the mug of tea that had been thumped down in front of him, looking for clarity in its muddy depths. Evie and her grandmother, and the Victorian Evangeline Witts – all these madly sexy women in one family. It was like a sick, twisted fairy tale. What was the meaning of it?

It made more sense to assume that Evie had been heavily influenced, to the point of being led astray, by her wanton grandmother. That seemed to hold more water than her mother's bizarre theory of genetics.

'Where does she live?'

Evie's mother shifted in her seat. Her evasive body language irritated Adam.

'You know I can always ask your sister-in-law – my housekeeper.'

'She's on holiday right now. Not back till the end of the month. But she lives at Honeysuckle Cottage, if you must know. By the green.'

'Thank you. Mrs Witts … I wonder if I could ask a favour of you?'

'Depends what it is. We've always got eggs to spare if you're short.'

'No, I don't need – eggs. Would you try to influence your daughter away from her excessive lifestyle? At least talk to her about it …?'

'There's nothing I can do, vicar.'

Mrs Witts' face was stony.

'She's your daughter.'

'*Nothing* I can do. Now if you'll excuse me, I need to open up the shop.'

The tea was vile anyway, and leaving it undrunk was no hardship. But Adam wondered why his parishioners were so intractable and mysterious. What was all this "Saxonhurst way" nonsense he kept hearing about?

On his way round the farmhouse to retrieve his bicycle, his attention was caught by the rattling of a sash window and a voice calling to him from upstairs.

'Morning, vicar!'

Evie's head appeared beneath the sash, hair wild and unbrushed, a broad smile all over her sleepy face.

He stopped beneath her, looking up at the apparition.

'Evie.'

'To what do we owe the honour?'

'I wanted to speak with your mother.'

She yawned. 'Sorry. Heavy night. I'm aching all over, you can't imagine. What did you want with our mum?'

'I worry about you, Evie.'

'Oh, don't fuss your head. I'm fine. Are we still on for tonight?'

'On? For …?'

'Bible study. Don't tell me you forgot. Don't you love me no more?'

Her raucous laughter mocked him all the way to where he'd left his bicycle. He rode it through flapping, clucking chickens, scattering them across the forecourt until he was away from that fetid-smelling place and back in the pure country air.

Honeysuckle Cottage was indeed empty, the shutters closed and a build-up of advertising bumf visible through the porch window on the mat. Adam spent a few moments looking around at the garden, which was somewhat overgrown and tangled, before heading back out of the front gate, only to

71

bump straight into Julia Shields.

She was in the company of a good-looking young man with an expensive camera around his neck, talking so animatedly to him that she didn't notice Adam looming in her path.

'Oh! Vicar!' she exclaimed. 'You might want to help us with this.'

'With?'

'This is Trevelyan. He's an investigative journalist. He's come up from London to try and get a story on the pornographers in my ancestral home. We're going to make it into a big story, national exposure, maybe get it into one of the high circulation magazines like *Tea Time* or *Isn't It Crazy?*'

'So you're going to – interview them?'

'No, no, we're going through the hedge to get a few decent shots. Or rather, indecent shots.' Julia's laugh was like a polite bray.

'You're going to trespass?'

'Yes, like you did. Remember?' She wasn't laughing now. She looked furiously determined.

'Do you think they'll be filming after last night's extravaganza? I imagine they might take a break.'

Julia's eyes narrowed.

'Good point. Let's change plans. Trevelyan, why don't you go and doorstep them – try to get a couple of quotes. We'll do the photographs when Miss Evie Witts has recovered from the maypole.'

'Recovered from the maypole?' Trevelyan looked intrigued.

'Never mind,' said Julia hastily. 'Go to the manor and try to get an interview with the filth-mongers. I'll be waiting for you in the Fleece. There's unlimited drinks for you if you get them to say something scandalous.'

'Unlimited? Right.' Trevelyan sauntered off towards the manor house leaving Adam and Julia behind.

'Tell me about Saxonhurst ways,' said Adam, watching the young man's behind disappear along the distant driveway.

'You're finding them out for yourself, aren't you? None of the other vicars ever stopped to watch the maypole. Some of them tried to stop it. But you just stood there gawping like a child in a sweetshop.'

'It's some kind of tribute to pagan gods of fertility?'

'In essence. Throughout the hard times, the droughts, the poor harvests, Saxonhurst has always continued to produce abundantly. Perhaps it's nothing to do with the rituals, but would you risk finding out now, after all these years?'

'Why must all this fall on to Evie's shoulders?'

Julia hee-hawed again. 'Does she look as if she minds?'

'I mind,' said Adam vehemently. 'And so should we all.'

'God, it's so tedious. She only has to look at a man … Anyway, I'm getting the drinks in at the Fleece. Are you coming?'

'No. No, I have – a sermon to write.'

'Keep telling yourself that,' said Julia with derision, striding away up the village street.

Chapter Seven

Evie showed up at Adam's door in a pair of the tiniest cut-off shorts imaginable and a bikini top. She had a jewelled ring in her navel and ribbon-tied espadrilles on her feet.

'Evening, vicar. So, what am I in for tonight? Revelations?'

She sashayed in, moving straight past him so he had to follow her. The abbreviated shorts showed the lower portion of her bottom, on which the fading marks from the willow thrashing she had received the night before were still highly visible.

Adam swallowed, trying his hardest not to look, but her hips swayed and she pushed her bum out as if inviting his eyes.

In the study he shut the door behind him and said, 'Take a seat.'

'I don't know as I can, vicar,' she said, all doe eyes and pouting. 'My bum's so sore today. I know I shouldn't be such a bad girl, but I can't help it somehow. I'm always getting spanked by someone or other. Do you think I deserve it?'

In an agony of desire, he managed to cough out the word, 'Yes.'

'If I was thinking straight, I'd have put on a nice loose dress today, but somehow I wanted to wear these instead. Pulling 'em up over my bum was agony, though! And now I've got tight, rough denim rubbing over those marks, making 'em sting all the more. It feels so hot and uncomfortable.'

She put her hands on her buttocks and stroked them slowly up and down while Adam watched transfixed.

'Tell you what, vicar, have you got any cream? E45 or similar? Just I'm not going to be able to concentrate with this burn behind.'

'Right. I'll have a look.'

He darted out, relieved to be away from her, and went to check the bathroom cabinet. When he returned with the tube of salve, he waited outside the study door for a moment, gathering himself, imagining a giant obscene orchid standing in the middle of the room, radiating toxic scent that would overpower and knock him out. That's what Evie was. A beautiful flower with monstrous properties. He needed to be on his guard.

He opened the door and held the tube out to her, but she shook her head, hair hanging over her eye coquettishly.

'Oh, vicar, I was hoping you might do the honours. Can't really reach down myself, or see where the marks are. Would you mind?'

Already she was unbuttoning, then she turned her back to him and eased the shorts with infinite care and gentleness over her rounded bottom, revealing her thong and the angry reddening welts the denim had aggravated back into full throb.

'It's not ... I can't. I'll leave you to it.'

'Please.'

Her heartfelt purr undid him. He uncapped the tube and smeared some of the pale cream on to his fingers, then moved towards where Evie had bent herself over his desk, soft globes presented, perfect legs pressed together.

'Look, Evie ...'

'Oh, it's so sore, please put some on me.'

As if his fingers were magnets heading for the field of attraction, he placed his fingertips at the end of one particularly cruel-looking criss-cross of marks and pressed the cream in. It felt so hot. The cream evaporated instantly, turning to colourless grease that made the red patches shine.

'Oh yes, that's nice, more please.'

He began to treat her welts in earnest, gently circling her buttocks with cream-tipped fingers, waiting for each treatment to soak in before applying more.

Fatal weakness travelled from his fingers through his wrists and up his arms as if her allure had entered his bloodstream. He caressed each raised red line with infinite care, wishing beyond everything that he had been the man to inflict them, that he was performing this act of tenderness after beating the devil from her, and that she was bent over now sobbing with remorse and eager to make amends for her sin.

How magnanimous he would be, how protective and nurturing of her newly minted virtue. She would accept his proposal and become the model vicar's wife, baking Victoria sponges in a floaty dress with flowers in her hair.

They could be happy. God would show them how to be happy.

Evie coughed and looked over her shoulder.

'Hello? Vicar? Are you with us?'

He came to with a start, realising that he had paused in his ministrations and his hands rested on Evie's bottom, as if warming themselves on a radiator.

'Oh! Yes. I, er, had an idea for my sermon. Sorry.'

He removed his hands and rubbed the shining grease into his palms.

'That was lovely,' said Evie. 'Real lovely. You've got such a nice touch. Wasted on the church, it is. You should be a masseur or something.'

Or your husband.

'I'm not sure God has called me to the massage parlour,' said Adam dryly, then, 'For heaven's sake, pull those shorts up.'

'What's wrong? Temptation? I've got two apples – not

just one. Eve's got nothing on me.'

She pulled the shorts up, still unable to contain a wince, but claiming to be much more comfortable now.

'So what are we up to tonight, vicar?' she asked, leaning against the desk, still unwilling to sit. 'The Ten Commandments again? I've broken most of 'em. Especially the one about coveting my neighbour's ass. I covet my neighbour's ass all the time.'

She giggled and Adam wanted to grab her and shake the profanity out of her. He would do it. That day would come.

'I want to discuss your conduct,' he said stiffly.

'That ain't in the Bible.'

'No, but there are exhortations to chastity and condemnations of fornication that you would do well to heed.'

'Are there?' She blinked. 'I'll take your word for it, since I understood about three words of that.'

'You are ruining yourself. Do you set no value on yourself at all?'

Evie pursed her lips. 'This again? I think we'll have to agree that we have different ideas of what that value is. My self-worth ain't tied up in my fanny and I don't know why you think it should be. If you carry on with this, you and I are going to fall out. Now, let's do some proper Bible stuff. Some of that's quite interesting. Can we do the bit about Sodom and Gomorrah?'

But Adam made her sit down and squirm over the first letter of St Paul to the Corinthians instead, with particular reference to chapter seven.

'It is better to marry than to burn,' he quoted, looking Evie directly in the eye.

'He had some funny ideas, that St Paul,' she said, but her voice was soft, lilting. She held his gaze, never looking away, until Adam's hand trembled on the page.

'What he means is, if you can't control yourself, you should get married. Then it doesn't matter. You have a person available to satisfy your – needs.'

'He thought everyone should live like a monk. He sounds hung up to me. Where does he think the next generation of Christians is coming from?'

'Look at it, Evie – he accepts not everyone is cut out for monastic life. That's why he recommends marriage. It channels the sinful urges into a productive outlet.'

'Yeah, very productive. All the kids those poor cows had to churn out.'

He essayed a weak smile. 'Well, things are bit different now ...'

'No thanks to St Paul. He's the type to think contraception's wicked.'

'He was a man of his time, Evie.'

'Yeah, well, his time sucked.'

'But many of his ideas, many of his recommendations hold good today.'

'Like marrying off the girls like me?'

'"The unbelieving husband is sanctified by the wife, and the unbelieving wife is sanctified by the husband."'

'So if I marry a, I dunno, a godly man – I get saved. Is that it?'

'It's what Paul implies.'

'Why are you looking at me like that, vicar?'

'I'm not aware that I'm ... Like what?'

'Like a man with a plan. You know I'm beyond redemption, don't you?'

'Nobody is beyond redemption.'

'Shit, is that the time? I've got to go. I've got a date down the pub. Thanks for the cream, lover. Ciao for now.'

Her escape was so rapid that Adam almost reached out to stop her, but she had gone before he could rise from the desk.

He sat rigid and sweating, for a long time. His moment had come and he'd let her ruin it. Still, the idea was there, a seed planted in her mind. He had pointed out an alternative path to her. Now he had only to convince her that reformation was in her best interests, and that he was the man for her.

But what of this date?

He got up, seized his jacket and headed out.

The sun was setting and there was a smell of barbecue smoke in the air. From the Fleece, at the far side of the green, came the sounds of laughter and outdoor carousing.

He was obstructed in his path by a prostrate figure, clutching a gate post and groaning faintly.

Crouching down to investigate he saw that it was Julia Shields, very much the worse for wear.

'Julia,' he said, putting a hand on her upper arm. 'Julia, are you all right?'

'Wassit look like? Don't go drinking with journos, I tell you. You'll lose.'

'You've been in the pub since I saw you this morning? Hold on to me. Up now.'

He managed to pull her to her feet and supported her swaying figure along the lane to the small new-built flat she now rented on the outskirts of the village.

She fumbled for her keys for so long that eventually Adam took her handbag and extracted them for her. She collapsed on to her sofa, face in the cushions.

'I'll get you a glass of water,' said Adam. 'Then I'll leave you to sleep it off.'

'Don't go,' she mumbled.

'Sorry?' He placed the glass on the coffee table. 'I can't stay, Julia.'

'You on a mission again?' she slurred. 'That's you. Mr Missionary. Go on, stay with me. I think you're …' She hiccupped and subsided back into the cushion.

He tiptoed away, then stopped by a bookshelf, his attention captured by a huge, leather-bound volume entitled *Saxonhurst: A Village of Secrets*.

He turned to the almost insensible Julia.

'Do you mind if I borrow this?'

But her only reply was, 'Awful cute,' followed by another hiccup.

He held the book to his chest and left.

The Fleece wasn't terribly busy – yesterday's May Fair lingered in the livers of the villagers – so Adam was easily able to find a secluded alcove table in the snug. He set down his bottle of tonic water and his book and peered around the sparsely populated room. No sign of Evie. Had she been lying about her date?

His fingers drummed nervously on the hand-tooled cover of the book he'd borrowed. Only the village's most dedicated imbibers could be seen propping up the bar. Perhaps she was in the garden.

He strode over and peered out of the door. A large group of middle-aged people, non-villagers, possibly walkers, sat with their pints of real ale at the favourite tables. Other than that, there didn't seem to be anybody out there.

Oh no! Oh, what was that? At the top of the children's climbing frame, two people all wrapped up in each other, snogging fit to wipe each other's faces off.

He sidled closer, taking care to remain at an angle that wouldn't be visible from the play area. The girl's legs were bare, in ribbon-tied espadrilles, and that mane of curls gave her away immediately. It was Evie all right.

But who was her beau? He looked familiar. Clothes you'd never see the village lads dead in – a fitted blazer, very tight jeans, a fringed scarf round his neck. And an expensive camera at the top of the slide! It was that London journalist, Travesty, or whatever his name was.

Adam kept out of sight, sipping the tonic water in the gathering dusk, avoiding the attention of the walking group as best he could. It would only take one villager's cheery cry of "Oi! Vicar!" and Evie would know he was stalking her.

He pretended to take an interest in his book, but read the frontispiece over and over again until, half an hour later,

Trevelyan and Evie slid down the slide, entangled and shrieking, and picked themselves up at the bottom.

'You staying here, then, Trev?'

'Yeah.' He was obviously enormously pissed, but he held it better than poor Julia Shields. He was able to walk and his speech was only marginally slurred. 'Nice room. You wanna see?'

'Too right, babe. Is your bed comfy?'

He laughed and swung her around in a bear hug.

'Come and find out.'

Eyes narrow with rage, Adam watched them enter the pub. For a moment he stood looking after them, trembling, drawing some low-voiced comments and laughter from the walking group.

Then he turned his eyes back to the climbing frame and saw the camera, still there, hanging from the frame by its strap now.

He retrieved it and made his purposeful way to the pub staircase, finding nobody on duty to stand in his way.

At the top he paused to look around. Which of the four old oak doors would lead into Trevelyan's room?

A sudden earthy sigh and a thump had him scurrying straight for the furthest door. He had to bend his head in order not to bump into the low-slung beams. When he reached the door, he knelt and tried to look through the keyhole.

He was in luck. The key wasn't in the door.

He could see the edge of the bed. Evie was bent over it, her face buried in the covers, presumably unwilling to put her bottom in contact with anything potentially frictive. Trevelyan had removed her shorts and was kneeling on the floor, her legs over his shoulders, his eager mouth breathing alcohol fumes on to Evie's spread pussy.

Adam saw Trevelyan's tongue reach out and lick the upper portions of Evie's thighs, then he buried his face in them, snuffling like a stupid fashion-victim dog.

Evie's gorgeous tanned flesh jiggled, the bottom he had touched only a couple of hours previously now in the hands of another man. It was unbearable.

His urge to burst in and disturb them battled with his urge to keep watching Evie's mesmerisingly beautiful body. What if he never saw her naked again? What if this was it?

He held his breath, waiting for Trevelyan to start licking Evie out properly. It was torture, knowing what she looked like undressed, knowing how she fucked, knowing what she sounded like when she came, yet never having done anything to her himself. When would he be the man to make her whimper? When would he be the man to make her eyes roll back in her head?

What did this bastard journalist have that he didn't?

Trevelyan fitted his tongue into Evie's groove, licking sloppily and without decorum.

He isn't even sober. I would never go to her drunk. I would see that I was fully aware of what I did to her.

Evie's limber legs kicked and flexed over Trevelyan's shoulders.

'Ohh, keep going, lover,' she said softly. 'Lick me nice and slow.'

Adam watched, shaking as if in a fever, until Trevelyan had been feasting on her juicy cunt for five long minutes. Then, just as Evie began to make those tell-tale sounds he'd heard so many times as she writhed under other hands, he knocked loudly at the door.

'Fuck!' he heard them both exclaim.

He smiled, despite the obscenity, his heart gladdened by the ruin of their moment.

'What?' shouted Trevelyan. 'Who's it?'

'I have your camera.'

'Adam? Is that you?' called Evie.

Through the keyhole he saw her slide under the bedclothes and bury herself in them.

'Who's Adam?' Trevelyan asked. 'Better not be your

82

husband or, y'know, shit like that.'

'He's the vicar,' Evie mumbled from under the duvet.

Adam straightened up, abandoning the keyhole when Trevelyan's shambling body filled the view.

The door opened a crack and a bloodshot eye looked out.

Adam held up the camera.

'It was on the slide,' he explained.

He heard Evie's feet patter up behind Trevelyan.

'It is you! What you doing here, vicar? Getting wasted?'

'I was just passing. And, while I'm here, perhaps I should call you a taxi.'

Evie hooted with derision.

'Taxi? In Saxonhurst? You'll be lucky. They have to come all the way out from Parham, and they don't like it.'

Trevelyan opened the door wider and took the camera.

'Saw you earlier, didn't I?' he said, squinting. 'With that one – wassername – you know her.'

'Ms Shields. Yes.'

'Shit,' he said, urgently, backing away from the door. 'Gonna puke. Bye.'

'Didn't realise I tasted that bad,' Evie called after him, then she took his place in the doorway, an unfriendly look on her face.

'You been following me, Adam?'

'As I said, I was …'

'Just passing. Right.'

'Why do you want to stay with him? He's incapably drunk.'

'When I could be at home doing embroidery?'

'Evie, you are worth so much more.'

'Save it, vicar. G'night.'

She slammed the door in his face.

For a moment, he contemplated thumping the door even harder, refusing to leave until she accompanied him. But, on reflection, that was a good way to get himself arrested. So he took his big book of Saxonhurst secrets and went home, his loins tight and his heart heavy.

Back at the vicarage, he brewed himself some strong coffee and betook himself and his book to the most comfortable armchair.

'The village of Saxonhurst,' he read on a page overloaded with illuminated script, 'nestles in that idyllic corner of England known as the Vale of Parham. Abundantly fertile and green, this lush land grows much of the fruits and vegetables that fill the baskets of the nation. It is noted for its fine Norman church and an ancient hostelry that draws visitors interested in heritage. But there is another side to Saxonhurst, and it is this side I endeavour to explore in this volume.

'For Saxonhurst has secrets.'

Adam took a sip of his coffee and muttered, 'Oh, you noticed that, did you?'

He looked again at the front cover. The author was one J. E. Lydford. He had heard that name before. Where?

He shook his head, unable to make the connection, and turned back to the book.

'This picturesque village gives the modern visitor no clues to its violent and dark past. It is one of many places laying claim to the title of Most Haunted Village in England.'

Not just the most godless, then, noted Adam.

'Now, in the mid-20th century, an array of ghostly figures are said to walk the quiet streets of this sleepy hamlet. At the crossroads, a spectral coach and four thunders past on moonlit nights, while a white lady is abroad at the manor house.'

Adam raised his eyebrows, wondering what effect a white lady might have on the village's resident pornographers. He couldn't imagine she'd approve of what was going on.

But ghosts aren't real, he told himself sternly.

'In the churchyard, the figure of a hanged man has been

84

spotted swinging from the branches of an old yew tree.'

What rubbish. What sensational nonsense. Whoever wrote this was counting on an influx of gullible tourists to swell the coffers of the pub and tea-rooms.

'But Saxonhurst's most unpleasant secret concerns the ruined barn on the edge of the fields.'

Adam shut his eyes, remembering that fateful day at the aforementioned edifice, Evie in rut, her naked body glorying in its lascivious degradations. She had bewitched him that day. Perhaps something unearthly did dwell amongst those rotting spars. He read on.

'To fully understand its gory history, we must go back 300 years, to the time immediately after the English Civil Wars, when Royalist Parham had been comprehensively trounced in battle by the forces of Parliament. Cromwell and his Puritan followers were never popular in Saxonhurst and its environs, and the village traditions were threatened by the arrival of missionaries, bent on changing everything.

'In this solemn time, everything was banned. Maypoles and dancing on the village green, drinking at the inn, even the convivial suppers villagers had enjoyed on quarter days – all were frowned upon under the new regime. But Saxonhurst did not take well to the Puritan yoke, and resistance was mustered. This core group of rebels were led by one John Calderwood, a gentleman of the village, thought to have practised law in Parham.'

Calderwood? Adam racked his brain to think of any villagers of that name, but he couldn't. Either the man had no descendants, or they had long since left the area. Before he could return to his studies, the phone rang.

The conversation with the Archdeacon about parish affairs and plans and the next Diocesan Council meeting drove the book out of his head.

He went up to bed, leaving it open on the coffee table, forgetful of its presence.

From his bedroom window, he could see the Fleece and

he tried to make out the window of Trevelyan's room. A chink of light shone through the curtains, but surely nothing could have happened between Evie and the journalist, especially considering the state he was in. No, Trevelyan would be snoring, fully clothed, in his bed, and Evie would have given up in disgust and gone home.

She was at home. She was asleep, in her bed, curled up, eyelashes dark on her cheeks ... She was not with a man.

He would never sleep if he thought she was with a man.

The coffee had been a bad idea, on reflection, and he tossed and turned in his lonely bed, jumbled thoughts crowding in his head and refusing to clear. The maypole, Evie leaning over so he could rub cream into her bottom, the haunting of Saxonhurst, that Trevelyan character, Evie's family, the order of service for next Sunday ... It went on and on, turning unexpected corners, coming back to the same places, like Alice's looking glass world.

He must have fallen asleep at some point, because his bedroom became a different place, with an open fire crackling in the sealed-up fireplace and plain white walls. Dark beams crossed the ceiling overhead, and outside in the churchyard he could hear unholy shouts and wails.

He rose from his bed and padded to the window. The uncovered floorboards were splintery and rough on his bare feet. He opened the casements, then pushed aside the wooden shutters. Outside, in the churchyard, there was a small bonfire made under the yew tree, and villagers were dancing and carousing around it.

The heathen spawn of the devil! In the house of God too.

He felt himself overcome with rage and he bellowed through the window at them to put out the fire and go to their homes.

They wore masks, so he could not identify them, and their replies came in the form of rude gestures.

This was the village he was meant to save. What chance did he stand?

He lit a candle, pulled on his clerical garments and hastened down the stairs, ready to disperse them with threats of calling the soldiers from the garrison at Parham.

When they saw him bustling down the path, they disappeared, leaping over the gate with catcalls and laughter. He tried to give chase, but only one of them was slow enough to be caught.

He whipped off the mask and found a girl, a young woman, a beautiful vision with dark curls and glowing, impudent eyes.

Evie.

He knew it was her, and yet she was a stranger and this their first meeting.

In the light of the dying fire, he held her by the shoulders and harangued her.

'What means this? Why do you seek to desecrate this place?'

'We want our village back from the likes of you. We want dancing and cider and Christmas. We don't want your rules.'

'The rules are not mine, they are Cromwell's, and they are enforced for the sake of your immortal souls.'

'We won't have it.'

'Who is "we"?'

'You'll know. Let me go!' She struggled free of his grip and hared away, vaulting the wall with energetic ease.

He looked after her, knowing that his soul was under threat, but not knowing quite how.

He extinguished the fire and returned to his bed.

Puritans were on Adam's mind when he dressed the next morning. His own manner of dressing was reminiscent of those severe pilgrims, always in black, always simple yet striking. It seemed his 17th-century precursor had just as difficult a job in inculcating virtues into the people of Saxonhurst as he did.

After a light breakfast, a whim took him into the church, to see if he could find the name of that vicar whose flesh he had seemed to inhabit in his dream.

On the board in gold lettering, he found the name Tribulation Smith, incumbent between the years 1647 and 1651. As he pondered the terrible crimes of nomenclature committed by those God-fearing souls, another name caught his eye and drew it down the board. J. E. Lydford, the author of the book, had been vicar here in the 1950s. That explained the sense of familiarity he'd had.

Pondering this, he returned to some administrative tasks in his study, but he found it hard to concentrate with the book calling to him from the living room.

He was about to give in and sneak in an hour's reading when the doorbell rang.

On the step, he was mildly disgusted to find a pale-faced Trevelyan, in the company of an even paler Julia Shields. No sign of Evie – with any luck, she had seen sense and gone home.

'Vicar, I wonder if you could do us a favour.' Julia dived in without preamble. 'Trevelyan needs somebody to show him how to get into the manor estate, but I simply must dash into Parham this morning. Hospital appointment, you see. Could you possibly show him to the gap in the wall?'

'Can't he find it himself?'

'He'll need someone to keep watch.'

'Oh no. No, no. You can't ask me to do this. I don't approve, for one thing. This is your crusade now, Julia. I don't discourage it, but I can't have my name linked to it.'

'They're filming Evie today,' said Trevelyan thickly. 'Big scene. She's the star.'

Adam's stomach lurched. He looked from Julia to Trevelyan, eyes narrowed in suspicion.

'Did you tell him to say that?' he asked Julia abruptly.

'Of course not. I didn't know. He's the one who spent the evening with her. I suppose she told him herself.'

'Yeah,' Trevelyan confirmed.

'And does she know you're planning to sneak up with your telescopic lens and take candid pictures of her?'

'No,' Trevelyan admitted. 'She thinks I'm here to do a picture story on arable farming.'

'You lied to her, in other words.'

'Needs must when the devil drives,' said Julia in clipped tones.

'I'm not sure which of you is the devil,' muttered Adam. 'Possibly all of you.'

'I'm just doing my job,' said Trevelyan with a yawn.

'A job that involves sleeping with and betraying the local women?'

'Look, if you don't want to come …'

'I'll come. Give me a minute.'

'Thank heavens for that,' said Julia, rolling her eyes. 'Right then, I'm off. Good luck. Hope you get your exclusive, Trev.'

'Yeah, cheers,' he drawled, waving vaguely before turning back to Adam. 'You ready?'

Adam looked pointedly at the camera slung around his neck. 'Just as well you've still got that,' he said.

'Yeah, yeah, thanks, Monseigneur. Let's go, shall we?'

Adam followed him along the path.

'Reverend,' he said. 'Not Monseigneur. I'm not Catholic.'

'You're all the same to me,' he said.

'What do you think Evie will think when she finds out you've plastered her naked body all over the celebrity magazines?'

Trevelyan stopped and stared at Adam. 'Are you serious? She'll fucking love it. Pardon my French. I'd put money on her having her own low-rent reality show by this time next year. Girl's got star quality.'

Adam thought about Evie, carried off to London, the new sex symbol for the nation. Nausea gripped him.

They were careful to avoid being seen as they crossed the road and slipped into the woodland that surrounded the manor's walls.

'So,' said Adam, trying out a bluff man-to-man tone that didn't quite come off, 'what's your angle going to be?'

'My angle?'

'This story. Are you in Julia's pocket or do you have a different story to tell?'

Trevelyan exhaled deeply.

'Well, I don't know, to be honest with you. It depends who wants to pay me the most money for the story. I can make it shock horror or I can make it a lighter piece about saucy goings-on in the village, you know? I know Julia wants the full-on *Daily Mail* hands-in-the-air, what's-to-become-of-us? But I don't have a personal agenda. What about you? I guess you disapprove?'

'I don't approve of pornography, no. But I think Julia is seizing a moral high ground she doesn't really occupy for her own ends. She wants the house back, by hook or by crook.'

Trevelyan stopped dead.

'Did you hear that?' he whispered.

Adam heard nothing but crackling twigs and chirping birdsong.

'No.'

'Listen.'

Adam heard singing, a sweet, almost ethereal voice. The softness of it led him to believe it must be close by, in the trees. They were close to the break in the wall now, but was it safe to go through?

'Is this it?' Trevelyan whispered, squeezing himself through, shaking the hedge as he tried to elude its stiff twigs.

'There's someone nearby. Perhaps we should wait.'

'No, come on. It'll be fine.'

He held out a hand to Adam, who took it with misgivings, unwilling to be caught red-handed, as it were, in the middle of a porn set.

They tiptoed through the dense copse, the singing voice always nearby, until Adam caught a glimpse of a bright red scarf and ducked back.

Trevelyan, however, had not seen it and he blundered onwards. It must be the singer.

Seconds later, Adam heard Evie's voice.

'Trev! What you doing here?'

Chapter Eight

'Oh. Hullo.'

'And you've brought your camera. I think someone's got a naughty plan.'

'I just wanted ... You know, just for personal use. A few shots.'

'Wank material? But you need everyone's consent for that, love. Didn't you know?' She raised her voice. 'Oi, everyone! I've found a stray photographer in the wild.'

'No, no, I'll go back, don't ...'

'Come on, love. Come and have a look at what you wanted to see. Come with me.'

Adam allowed himself a moment of Schadenfreude. The odious Trevelyan had had his plans scuppered. But he supposed he ought to go and keep watch over him, in case the situation turned ugly. He edged forward, slowly and carefully, following the sound of cracking branches and footsteps ahead.

Soon he had his view of the lawn at the back of the manor, the pool in the distance. In the immediate foreground, camera crew and actors milled around, putting on make-up, drinking coffee and chatting. Into the midst of this, Evie pulled Trevelyan along as if leading a recalcitrant dog on its lead. She was wearing a tiny black dress accessorised with the bright red scarf Adam had caught sight of.

'See! You've got real wildlife in your grounds, Seb,' said Evie, stopping in front of the Lord of the Manor.

Sebastian looked the journalist up and down. 'Who the fuck are you? And where have you come from?'

Adam could just make out the remark above the murmur of chat, which was dying down as people began to take an interest in the little scene.

'I'll leave,' offered Trevelyan. 'If you want. But I can get you some press interest, if you'd like that.' He held up his camera. 'Do you fancy it?'

Seb's lip curved upwards.

'You're a journalist?'

'Yeah, freelance.'

'Why didn't you approach me directly instead of creeping around in my bushes? You want to make trouble for me, don't you?'

'No, no, seriously, no. I don't.'

Sebastian sat in his director's chair and considered the situation for a while. Adam saw Trevelyan look around himself anxiously, checking for escape routes. He ducked down further, not wanting to be discovered himself.

'I've got a story for you,' said Sebastian suddenly. 'It's a good one. You'll be able to sell it to a lad mag or a top-shelf version. *My Day As A Fluffer.* What do you think?'

'What? You mean …'

'You know what a fluffer is, don't you?'

'They, uh, they get the performers – ready.'

'Ready, yeah. Hard. You can suck my actors' dicks for them before they fuck their colleagues. What do you think?'

'Um … I'd rather not. Not really.'

Sebastian tutted and shook his head. 'No nose for a story,' he said.

'You wouldn't mind doing it with your hands, though, would you?' suggested Evie. 'It's ever so easy. And you could help us girls too. I could do with a hand with my vajazzles. And he could do all the lubing.'

'That sounds – acceptable,' said Trevelyan weakly.

Adam clenched his fists. He didn't know what vajazzling

was, but he didn't want Trevelyan doing it to Evie, that was for sure.

'Fine,' said Sebastian. 'We have a runner. Oh, but you aren't taking the pictures. I'll do that. Hand over the camera.'

'I'd rather not ...' Trevelyan saw that he had little choice, though, and the camera was taken from around his neck and relinquished.

'Good. Now, I think our Evie needs some ornamentation. Would you be so kind?'

Evie grinned impishly and dragged Trevelyan by the arm over to a chair. Sitting down on it, she raised her skirt and spread her legs without a word, revealing everything within to whomever cared to look. Then she reached down to a big compartmentalised box at the side of the chair and drew out some little sparkly gems on plastic backing.

Adam watched Trevelyan taking instructions from her and decorating her shaved pubic triangle with the tiny multi-coloured gems until he had successfully depicted an unfurling rose bud.

It was some measure of Adam's infatuation that he did not look away once, even when an enthusiastic threesome scene was filmed a few metres away from Evie's chair.

The groaning and grunting washed over him, the cocks plunged unseen into their corresponding cunts. All that filled Adam's world was that tiny sparkling inverted triangle and the parted lips beneath.

He watched, barely breathing, as Evie pulled off her dress and scarf and allowed Trevelyan to dress her in a crotchless latex catsuit. This took some time, a great deal of talcum-powdering, followed by an heroic struggle of tugging and yanking. Eventually, she was second-skinned in shiny black and ready to have Trevelyan fasten her thigh high boots.

His next task was to scrape back her mane of unruly hair and fasten it in a severe bun. He required the help of the onset stylist for this, but seemed to relish taming it with quantities of gel and hairspray.

Evie wasn't Evie any more, thought Adam. This foreign creature in her intimidating black with her sharply accentuated cheekbones wasn't the girl he longed to take under his wing and keep from the wicked world.

She *was* the wicked world.

But it was a role, he told himself, a part she had to play. And he still maintained that she had found herself in this situation by default, rather than seeking it out. He had to believe it. Evie's entire persona was a role – the outrageous, sexually flamboyant animal-girl. She had been groomed for it, by this mysterious grandmother of hers. What chance had she stood?

Trevelyan handed her a whip, a thing with an ornate, jewelled handle and many strands of braided black leather.

Adam shook his head. His Evie was no dominatrix. She taunted him so because she wanted him to tell her where to stop. She wanted him to raise his hand and say "Enough" and take her for his own. She wanted this. Why else was she coming to his Bible study lessons?

All the same, he was intrigued at the figure she cut, striding around, flicking the whip so it swooshed. Trevelyan stood well back, afraid of catching a tip across the cheek.

Kasia, in a ballet skirt and glittery pasties and little else, came running out from the house, her expression perturbed. She had some bad news, Adam thought.

'Seb, just had Cal on the phone. He can't make it. Rugby injury – he needs to see a physio.'

'Shit,' said Sebastian, and Evie's face also fell.

'I ain't put this thing on for nothing, have I?' she demanded, trying to pluck at the latex, but finding it unpluckable.

'I don't know,' said Sebastian. 'Without Cal, you can't play this scene.'

'Why not?' said Evie. 'What about him?' She pointed at

Trevelyan with her whip.

'What?' Trevelyan looked up from lubricating another girl's anus, his shock of hair dishevelled.

'You can be my sub, love. What do you think?' She sauntered over, caressing the underside of his chin with the strands. 'Can't deny you deserve a whipping, can you? Leading a girl on like that last night. You played me for a fool.'

'I ... It was just a bit of fun,' he said. Adam relished the rapid rise and fall of his chest, thinking he might actually enjoy watching the idiot get his comeuppance.

'No fun for me,' pouted Evie. 'You was wasted. I had to go home without a proper orgasm. 'Cept that one you gave me with your tongue, but that don't count.'

'I'm not into pain,' he wailed.

'I won't hurt you, sweetie,' she said with a beaming smile. She reached a false-nailed hand up to muss his already-mussed hair. 'It's not proper pain, anyway. It's pleasure-pain. Try it. You'll see.'

'He's not an actor,' objected Sebastian. 'He doesn't have the paperwork.'

'He don't have to act. He just has to get whipped and – stuff. He doesn't have to put his cock in anyone either, so we don't need the medical. Oh, go on, Seb.'

'I'm tempted ... We can't force him, though. It's assault.'

They both subjected Trevelyan to the full force of their persuasions, Evie wheedling, Sebastian cajoling until he agreed to take the place of the injured submissive.

'Just think what a story you'll have,' said Sebastian, smiling, as Trevelyan began to shed his urban hipster uniform.

Adam's sense of Schadenfreude grew to monumental proportions as he watched Trevelyan buckled into a harness and collar, then oiled by an enthusiastic Evie.

She rubbed the sheeny lotion into Trevelyan's pale

buttocks, giving him a running commentary.

'You're nowhere near as fit as Cal,' she told him, gratifyingly for Adam. 'He's got a fucking amazing body. Yours is average.' She frowned. 'At best. But you've got a lovely little bum, really soft and tender. It'll mark better'n Cal's, I bet. I have to whack seven bells out of him before I get a good stripe.'

'You don't seem the type,' said Trevelyan with a fearful laugh.

'What, the mistressy type? It's fun, that's all. I can dish it out and I can take it. I'm lucky like that.'

'Which do you prefer?'

'Depends who's the other half of the equation,' she said thoughtfully. 'Totally depends on that.'

Kasia came over, waving some script notes.

'OK, guys, we need to be clear on what's going to happen. Evie, you take this guy, I can't pronounce his name, for a walk around the garden on a leash. You give his bum a good whack every now and then, right? Then you make him do doggy tricks – sit, lie down, that kind of thing. Can you handle that?'

She stared hard at Trevelyan, who nodded.

'We'll do that, then move on to the next bit. So, here's the leash ...' She attached it to Trevelyan's collar, handing the looped end to Evie. 'You start from the cherry tree over there. Take your places. Oh – you forgot the cock ring.'

'The what?' yelped Trevelyan.

Adam laughed to himself, watching Evie squeeze a tight circle of rubber over the tip of Trevelyan's hardening cock.

'That squeezes!' he complained.

'Gets you hard, though, don't it? Come on, Trev. You need wood, love.'

She cupped her small hand around the journalist's burgeoning prick and the laughter died in Adam's throat. Evie's palm exerted gentle pressure on her target until he grew, stiff and proud, to the full length.

97

Only then did she tug on the lead and pull him over beneath the flowering cherry tree, the pair of them standing amidst the fallen blossom like a hellfire depiction of Sin in the Garden of Eden.

A clapperboard snapped into action and Trevelyan contorted his features immediately into what he must have considered the closest approximation to a submissive expression. His tongue hung out like a dog's, with forlorn eyes to match.

'Lassie, come home,' muttered Adam scornfully.

'On your knees!' said Evie coldly, her local burr subsumed by a heavily faked approximation of Received Pronunciation.

Trevelyan sank to the ground, looking up at his mistress.

'Do you dare to look at me?' she said, giving his face the lightest of slaps then grabbing his hair and forcing his chin downwards. 'Look at that instead. That shameful erection. Who's that for, boy? Eh?'

'For you, uh, mistress.'

'Yes, for me. Do you know what that tells me about you, boy? Do you?'

'No, mistress.'

'It tells me that you are a miserable little piece of filth who loves to be abused and humiliated. The more I do it, the more it turns you on. You can't deny it, can you?'

'No.' Trevelyan looked stunned, as if an epiphany had just been delivered. Perhaps, Adam thought, this was his natural bent and he had simply never discovered it.

Evie lashed the whip over his curved back.

'No *what*?'

'No, mistress.'

'Good. Now, crawl for me, around the garden, towards the post.'

Trevelyan fell forward on to all fours and began to move slowly over the grass. Every so often Evie yanked at his collar so that he yelped, or laid the whip across his bare buttocks.

'That's just a taster,' she yelled, disturbingly sergeant major-like.

Adam could not decide whether he found this new version of her palatable or not. On the one hand, she certainly poured well into the latex. On the other, her stentorian bark, with its ersatz clippedness, did little to lure him into sinful imaginings. Which was a mercy, given the frequency with which they plagued him these days.

He watched as poor – or was it poor, given his flushed cheek and bright eye? – Trevelyan was whipped around the lawns, gasping and barking, his cock straining inside its ring in a way that looked painful to Adam.

When they reached 'the post' – an X-shaped piece of wood, cemented into the ground – Evie yanked on Trevelyan's leash and ordered him to kneel up.

'Sit up and beg,' she said.

He lifted his chin and extruded his tongue, panting hard, putting out his hands before him like paws.

'Good boy,' purred Evie, sounding more like herself. 'Now roll over.'

He fell sideways on the grass, his cock in full view of the camera.

'Lie down. No, idiot, on your stomach. Dogs don't lie on their backs, do they?'

Trevelyan crouched on the grass, his belly low, his legs and arms bent. His back and bottom bore faint lash marks.

'That's good, boy. I think you've earned yourself a treat. On your knees again.'

Sebastian shouted 'Cut!' and Trevelyan flopped down, breathing deeply.

'You know what comes next, Evie?' called Kasia.

'Yeah. Read the script last night, once Flopper 'ere bailed on me.' She prodded Trevelyan's thigh with a pointed toe. 'You're getting your comeuppance for that,' she told him.

He shut his eyes, in a kind of rapture, but his interlude

didn't last long.

The clapperboard intruded once more, and Evie dragged him to his feet by his upper arm.

Before long, he was bound to the wooden cross, facing outwards, his arms and legs tightly tied inside lengths of stout rope. Harnessed and collared, he had no way of accessing his cock, which was harder than ever.

Adam held his breath, watching Evie creep closer to her helpless victim. When she bent and blew a sweet breath on Trevelyan's cock head, Adam felt his own tool swell in sympathy. Perhaps submission was not so alien to him after all.

He exhaled, his face stretching in agonised desire as he watched Evie's tongue tip dart out and lick a zigzag trail up Trevelyan's shaft. At the top, she pushed it into the frenulum then gave the purple bulb a catlike lick, around once, before breathing on it again and drawing back.

Trevelyan looked as if he might die.

'You'd like me to suck it for you, wouldn't you, boy?'

He nodded, as far as the constraints of his collar would allow.

'Bad luck.'

She took up the whip and he yelped in alarm, but all she did was draw its knotted strands up and down, from his thighs to his belly and back, stroking him.

Then she held it the other way, using its blunt handle to push against the creases of his thighs, massaging them firmly, then moving it behind his testicles and manipulating the tight little sacs until he was crimson-faced and gasping.

'Please,' he wailed.

'You're getting this up your arse later,' she said, and he sobbed. 'That's after I've worked it over your bum cheeks. Shit, sorry, Seb. Lapsed.'

'It's OK, we'll cut that line and re-do it with the proper accent later. Carry on.'

'Cheers, mate.' She turned back to Trevelyan, her voice

once more sculpted ice.

'You'll feel it up there,' she said. 'Have you ever been buggered, boy?'

'No, mistress.'

'I expect you're looking forward to it, then?'

There was a loaded silence. Adam swallowed. He knew what he would say and it would be emphatically negative.

Trevelyan's admission came out as a whisper.

'Yes, mistress.'

'Oh, I'm so pleased to hear it. Good boy. You deserve doggy treats.'

She wrapped her latex-gloved hand around his cock and began to tug at it, without finesse, but Trevelyan was past caring about subtle technique.

It took no more than a few jerks of his swollen cock for his semen to spurt out, covering Evie's gloves with trails of pearly white.

Trevelyan's head fell forward, his hair plastered to his brow, his eyelids lowered.

Adam shut his eyes tight against the blasphemous visual comparison forming in his mind. No, he must not think it. He must never think it.

Evie's ferocious yell caused his eyes to fly back open.

'Not even a word of thanks for your mistress?'

Poor Trevelyan tried manfully to raise his head and utter some broken words of gratitude, but it was never going to be enough for Evie.

She flicked the whip with vicious accuracy across his flank and he moaned and gasped.

'I'm going to have to punish you for that, you realise? Where are your manners? We'll have to work on them, won't we?'

She released Trevelyan from his bonds, only to turn him the other way and re-tether him. Now his back and buttocks were perfectly presented for the chastisement Evie had in mind.

'You ever been whipped before?' she asked him gruffly.

He shook his head.

'OK, I won't go in all guns blazing. But it'll hurt. If it gets too much, you say "Pax", OK? Repeat it after me.'

'Pax,' he said.

Evie went to stand a little way away from the cross, swishing the thongs this way and that, rehearsing her aim.

'Right,' she said. 'Ready? It's a sound thrashing for you, my lad. This'll be a bit more than a kiss.'

Fascinated dread coursed through Adam's veins as Evie drew the whip back, preparing for the first stroke. It was as if he experienced Trevelyan's anxiety by proxy.

The lash fell with a swoop and a fierce snap and Adam winced at Trevelyan's bellow. Angry waves of red rose on his body, soon joined by more as Evie found her stride and plied the whip with a will.

Snakes of scarlet crept across Trevelyan's skin, sometimes intersecting, sometimes rising in welts. Soon he was sweating and shiny and the strokes must have hurt more, that salty emission sinking into the sting and doubling it.

But he didn't call "Pax", even when his bottom and back were more red than white.

Eventually Evie's arm tired and she paused for breath, her latex-covered breasts rising and falling.

'Boy's got stamina,' she said to camera. 'I think he's found his niche.'

Amid ribald laughter, she tiptoed up to Trevelyan and put an arm around his waist.

'Are you all right, lover?'

Adam's insides tore with jealousy. Why was it not his ear into which she murmured words of sweet concern? The hateful Trevelyan got to experience pleasure even when she avenged herself against him. How had he earned this luck?

He must have given her some kind of green light, because she stepped back and picked up the whip again.

Surely she was not going to subject him to more flogging? She must have come close to breaking his skin as it was.

But no. She collected a bottle of lubricant from the

sidelines and set to work pushing her rubber fingers, coated in grease, between Trevelyan's twitching buttocks. She worked slowly, the cameras on zoom, making sure that they got plenty of shots of his spread cheeks and exposed anus before sliding a finger inside.

Trevelyan rutted compulsively against his wooden prison, grunting like a man possessed. Evie continued to work on him until finally she judged him ready to accept the oiled whip handle. Carefully, inch by inch, the shiny black handle disappeared between Trevelyan's parted globes. His hips twisted and his legs struggled to kick but the object continued in its inexorable journey until it was seated to the strands, then Evie began to thrust.

She shoved and rotated and manipulated the whip handle inside Trevelyan's back passage until he began to twitch and utter hoarse expletives.

'Going to come with a whip up your arse, are you, boy?' she asked sweetly. 'Going to show everyone what a dirty little slut you are?'

He roared and sobbed.

Adam put his hand to his crotch, horrified by his own level of arousal.

Evie laughed, softly but triumphantly, and kept up the pressure until Trevelyan was no more than a weeping mass of orgasmic flesh.

She pulled out the whip handle, threw it to the ground and circled his hips with her arms.

'Bloody good for a newbie,' she said, kissing his shoulders and neck. 'You done a great job, Trev. I'm proud of you.'

Again, the words cut Adam like knives.

He almost broke his cover and strode on to the set, but remembered his sanity just in time. How on earth would it profit him to expose himself as a hopeless voyeur? It would only consolidate a reputation already held.

Trevelyan was untied from the cross and showered with food, drink and praise. It was time for Adam to get away from here. Julia Shields wasn't going to be best pleased with the turn her little exposé had taken, but he could hardly be blamed for it.

Chapter Nine

According to J.E. Lydford, the amount of pagan practices thought to flourish in Saxonhurst after the Civil War merited the appointment of the most hardline clergyman available, one Tribulation Smith. This austere preacher was charged with the mission of bringing Saxonhurst to Puritan virtue. Judging by the way the modern village carried on, he had met with little success, Adam parenthesised.

The tragedy by the ruined barn was precipitated by a love affair.

'Oh,' said Adam, shaking his head. ''Twas ever thus.'

Tribulation Smith had called the local witchfinder to the village to assist him in flushing out the agents of Satan in their midst. The witchfinder had pointed out one Evangeline Lillie as suitable for burning atop a pile of faggots, but it seemed Smith had disagreed and refused to allow her death.

Instead, he had married her.

Adam closed the book, his mind whirling. Always these Evangelines, sewn up in the chaotic history of this village. Evangeline the witch, whose spell had even fallen on a Puritan preacher of the severest tendencies – he felt uneasy at the parallel with his own infatuation.

Three weeks after Trevelyan's pornographic debut, he was no closer to achieving anything. Evie remained maddeningly just out of reach, seeming to come close to him during their Bible sessions, then withdrawing, teasing, always full of excuses and apologies.

He had organised and advertised a number of church

events – a youth group, a ceilidh, even a bingo night (despite his own disapproval of gambling) – but nobody seemed to take the remotest interest.

At least he had a congregation now, even if it was only Evie and Julia Shields.

But as he shut his book and put it on the bedside table, he felt the acuity of his failure. This village threatened to defeat him. Even worse, it was impacting on his faith. It was a poisonous place, a well of corruption. What chance did he stand?

He prayed in the dark until consciousness slipped away, and then he was somewhere else, somewhere that was still Saxonhurst, and yet so very different.

The low, thatched cottages with their warped-looking beams still stood around the green, but on that green were stocks and a pillory, and in the pillory was a man, a young and handsome man, but Adam sensed a strong antipathy towards this character without knowing why.

He stood at the edge of the grass, watching while villagers threw rotten vegetables rather half-heartedly.

'With a will!' he suddenly roared. 'Go to it. This man is godless and ye should shun his example.'

The villagers didn't want to pelt the softening fruit, but they were scared of something. Of – him?

They wore jerkins and leggings and dirty-looking linen shirts, as if taking part in a historical re-enactment.

As Adam watched, he became aware of another man standing beside him. The man turned to him.

'And these women of whom you spake? Where shall I find them?'

'They inhabit a cottage at the fringe of the village. Three crones and a younger woman. But there is a maiden there also, whom I believe can be saved if the corrupting influences are removed.'

'Think ye so? That is for me to determine, Reverend.'

'They are all in thrall to one John Calderwood, who is in

hiding, fearing his satanic alliances will be unmasked.'

Adam and his guest walked along the sun-bleached track to the village edge, arriving finally at a cottage Adam had not seen before, yet seemed to recognise.

It was a squat dwelling with only one shuttered window, rough and dilapidated. Outside, a tethered goat bleated fiercely in a scrappy chaos of overgrowth.

'Aye, a coven, you can be sure,' said the witchfinder with relish.

They hammered at the door, which was eventually answered by a very elderly lady, crabbed and bent, the epitome of the conventional imagining of a witch.

She stared at Adam and his guest, before calling behind her, ''Tis the preacher and another.'

Another woman, perhaps in her 40s, hair streaming from beneath a filthy bonnet, appeared behind the crone.

'We have not called on your services,' she said. 'Leave us be.'

'Know you not who I am?' asked the witchfinder in sonorous tones.

'Indeed I do not. Good day.'

He stepped between the women and the door, holding up his hand.

'I have a warrant for the arrest of all who dwell here, on charges of witchcraft.'

The crone wailed deeply, then flung her hands over her mouth.

'Come out, one and all.'

Curious villagers had gathered by the fence to observe the sorry little group of women who emerged from their smoky hut.

Three elderly, one younger, and one … Oh. Evie. The girl who had danced by the fire in his earlier dream.

'Not her,' he found himself saying, urgently, to the witchfinder. 'She is not one of them. They seek to take her soul, but it is still intact.'

106

As before, the witchfinder brushed his words aside.

'She must be tested. She dwells in a coven, Reverend.'

'I will attend the testing.'

'No, that is not necessary. I shall take them to the manor house where I am staying and conduct my enquiry there.'

Adam followed the witchfinder and his mournful victims to the manor house, but he was not permitted past the gates, which were fastened firmly against him.

Evie looked over her shoulder at him as she trooped up the path at the back of the line, eyes wide and frightened.

He clutched at the gate bars.

He had to save her, even if it meant risking his own skin.

Looking back to make sure nobody could stop him, he climbed over the gate.

Adam woke up in a cold sweat.

Evie's grandmother.

Tomorrow, he would visit Evie's grandmother.

Honeysuckle Cottage showed more signs of life than it had done on his last visit.

The curtains were open and the postage stamp-sized lawn had been mowed.

Adam's determined rap at the door was quickly answered by a dopy-looking man in glasses. The insurance salesman from Parham, no doubt.

'Vicar?' he said, squinting. 'Collecting for something? Only I'm all out of cash.'

'No, no. I was wondering if your, uh, your good lady was in?'

He laughed rumbustiously at that.

'Don't think I've got one of those, vicar. But if you mean my wife, she's out the back. Just a moment.'

He turned and called out along the passageway.

'Lyn!'

Lyn, thought Adam, *not Evie, or Eve or whatever.*

The woman who came to the door could not possibly

have been Evie's grandmother. She looked no older than forty, her hair big and bouffant and her face reminiscent of Sophia Loren's, with dark almond eyes and feline cheekbones.

'A man of the cloth,' she said huskily. 'We are honoured. Do come in.'

Insurance-man peeled off into a side room while Adam followed Lyn along a narrow passageway to a sunny back kitchen, considerably more pleasant than that of her daughter-in-law at the farm.

'Do excuse me, I've just been baking. Hence the apron. Do you like walnut and banana loaf?'

'Oh, I've just had breakfast, thank you.'

'But you'll have a cup of tea, won't you?'

'Thank you. That would be – nice.'

He took the seat she offered at a neatly laid kitchen table.

'It's a long time since I had any dealings with a vicar,' said Lyn conversationally, plugging in the kettle and taking mugs from a tree.

'You weren't married in the village church then?'

'Dear me, no. Register office job. Second marriage for both of us, you see.'

'You're divorced from Mr Witts?'

She turned around and stared at him, perfectly plucked eyebrows raised.

'Mr Witts is dead this nine years come September. Why would you mention him?'

'I know you're Evie Witts' grandmother. I've come to talk to you about her.'

Lyn poured boiling water into the teapot with expert care, then put on the lid and the cosy and placed it on the table.

'Yes,' she said. 'I know you've been taking an interest in our Evie.'

Her lush lips were pursed, pressing layers of high-shine gloss together.

'A pastoral interest.'

'I'm sure.'

'She is a –' He halted, casting around for something that wouldn't sound lecherous. 'A very interesting young woman.'

'Yes, she is.' Lyn poured the tea. 'Interesting and talented and, what's more, what's *everything* in this world, she's free.'

'Her mother says you've always been close.'

'That's right. She's the apple of my eye. I won't hear a word said against her, vicar, so –'

'I haven't come here to speak ill of her. Not at all. But I wonder what has made her what she is.'

'That's easily answered, vicar. It's her blood. She's an enchantress who can captivate men and women alike with a click of her fingers. It's hard to believe, looking at me now, but I used to be like that.'

'Not hard to believe at all,' said Adam truthfully.

'Well, bless your gallantry, but all that's behind me now. I live peacefully and I keep myself to myself. Ken and I appreciate our quiet life.'

'While Evie's taken on the carnival and chaos that you bequeathed her.'

'I can't make bequests,' snapped Lyn. 'I'm not dead.'

'All the same, Evie's proclivities seem to have skipped over a generation, directly from you to her. Lyn, don't you think she's damaging herself? Don't you worry that she'll – burn out?'

'Better to burn out than fade away,' quoted Lyn snarkily. 'Our Evie's a beautiful beacon of light in this world. If she chooses to spread that light around, good for her. That's what I say.'

'But …'

'But nothing, vicar. It's perfectly plain what your agenda is. You're besotted with her and you want to snatch her from the world and hide her away. Just like … Oh, never mind.'

'Just like who?'

'It doesn't matter. Have you finished that tea? I've got to go to Parham for an eye appointment.'

'You misunderstand my intentions –'

'Ken! Have we got petrol in the car?'

Adam conceded defeat, drained the tea, made polite goodbyes and left under the baleful eye of Lyn.

Julia Shields almost fell through the open door of the post office as he passed.

'Mr Flint!' she barked at him, rustling her copy of the local newspaper. 'Did you know about this?'

'About ...?' He took the paper off her. "Reversal of Fortunes", he read. "Ancient manor house used as pornographic film set". Underneath was a condensation of Trevelyan's article for a top-shelf magazine, leaving out anything unsuitable for a "family newspaper" but still somehow managing to be heavy on the salacious detail.

'That little bugger,' seethed Julia. 'He duped me and used my tip-off to get himself a nasty little reputation in the seedy film industry. If I ever see him again I'll ...'

'You've got your publicity,' Adam pointed out.

'And where were you when all this – filth – was going on? I thought you went there with him.'

'Oh, I just kept watch by the wall,' said Adam hastily. 'Didn't see a thing. Had no idea what he got up to in there.'

'It's not good enough. Not at all good enough.'

She accompanied him down the lane, brooding all the while, until they reached the lych gate.

'I don't know about raffles and suchlike,' she said abruptly, her eye caught by Adam's bright red advertising poster. 'But what you should organise is a day trip.'

'A day trip?'

'Yes, you know. Take the villagers back to the old days of the charabanc to the seaside. They're always reminiscing about that kind of thing.'

'An excursion?'

'Yes. You can get them to sing a few hymns on the

coach, just to keep the God angle in there. Set them loose on the candyfloss and cheap beer while you listen to the Sally Ann band on the seafront. Doesn't that sound like a good plan?'

'Actually ... It does. I like it. Thank you, Julia.'

'Don't mention it.'

The screams guided his footsteps, drawing him through the darkened house towards the back.

Adam knew, even in his dream, that he was looking for Evie, to save her. If he didn't find her soon, she faced the noose, or worse.

At the end of the passageway, candlelight issued from a half-open door, but it was no welcome glow. Instead it was a sickly yellow thing, redolent of torture and suffering. The stench of sweat and blood and burning flesh assaulted his nostrils as he put his hand on the door and, steeling himself, pushed.

The witchfinder stood with his back to him, in his hand a long red-hot poker. The oldest crone lay insensible on the floor while the other two wept in each other's arms in a corner.

Evangeline Lillie sat, tethered to a chair with rope, her chemise torn down over her breasts, above which the witchfinder brandished his weapon.

'Now speak, witch, or you will find those pretty dugs in close communion with my brand.'

Despite her fear, Evangeline's chin was thrust forward, her eyes afire.

'I have nothing to say to you,' she spat.

The witchfinder's elbow moved. Adam leapt forward, the element of surprise working in his favour. After wresting the brand from him, he threw it aside, into the grate.

'No!' he said forcefully. 'She is not to be treated like the others. She is innocent.'

'So you keep saying,' snarled the witchfinder. 'I think

her spell has worked on you.'

'You will leave her be,' retorted Adam, untying Evangeline and lifting her into his arms, then again, on reaching the door. 'You will leave her be.'

'You are bewitched!' the man called after them, but Adam was beyond reasoning with.

Swiftly he made his way out of the manor house, hefting Evangeline over the wall and running with her to his little cottage in the church grounds.

He laid her on his bed and turned to the water jug, pouring her a cup.

'What has he done to you?' he asked, kneeling beside her, putting the water to her lips.

'I didn't ask for rescue,' said Evangeline, every bit as obstinate as her modern counterpart, it seemed. 'I want to go back. Back for my kinswomen.'

'Back for a taste of his red-hot poker?'

'I ain't scared of him, Mr Smith. I ain't scared of no-one.'

'But look at you – you're bleeding. Let me dress the wounds.'

There was something infinitely blissful to Adam about having the opportunity to touch her gently, to tend to her. Evangeline allowed him to wash the cuts and grazes and to soak up the blood with old linens. His hand drifted down the slopes of her breasts, touching that flesh he yearned for, bringing it relief.

'Why did you come for me?' she asked.

'You know why,' he said.

'Witchfinder'll just come back. With reinforcements.'

'He can't take you if you're my wife.'

She sat up, wincing.

'Your what?'

'Evangeline, marry me. I can protect you as your husband.'

'I can't marry you.'

112

'Why not?'

'You ... I can't marry a preacher. Not being the sort of girl I am.'

'The sort of girl you are is exactly why you should marry a preacher. You will stray no longer and return to the fold, where you will be happy, Evangeline, happy and cared for and so much loved ...'

He broke off, choking.

Her eyes seemed to burn into him, her face still sheened with the sweat of torture and fear.

'You are unfair,' she whispered. 'You offer what I cannot take.'

'But you can take it, my Eve, my only love. You can.'

She swallowed then, and reached for his face. What ecstasy in her fingertips as they travelled along his cheekbone. He put his hand over them, holding them against his skin.

'If you have lived wickedly,' he murmured, 'it is because you suffered evil influences to flourish in your life. You did not act against them, and that is your sin. But it is a sin capable of redemption. Allow yourself to be redeemed. Come to me.'

'You've a pretty face and you speak pretty words,' she said. 'I could almost ...'

'Consent. And you will be protected.'

'I will live,' she whispered.

'I promise it.'

'And my kinswomen?'

He hesitated, wanting those inconvenient crones out of the way, but he was so close to having her, how could he let them ruin it?

'I will do such as I can,' he said.

'Then I shall say yes.'

A potent amalgam of happiness and triumph beat in his veins. He leant towards her, breathing in the scent that lay beneath all the blood, sweat and tears – her unique

113

Evangeline Lillie fragrance, that which had driven him wild since he arrived in Saxonhurst.

His lips touched hers, and the flame of desire streaked through him. How she bewitched him, and yet her witchcraft was of a kind he felt he could not live without.

The kiss moved quickly from a tender brush to a raw and salty clash of mouths. Adam felt he could never get enough of her taste, of her warmth, of her tongue. Finally, his increasingly desperate prayers had found their answer, and the answer was yes.

He awoke to find himself snogging the pillow, one hand wrapped tight around his erection. Oh, no Evie after all, no full lips, no slip of tongue, no breasts bared to his eye. But the imprint of her remained on his memory for as long as it took him to bring his cock to complete engorgement.

I should let go. I should turn my mind to other thoughts.

But Evie's hold on him was absolute now. She had slipped past every moral defence, to place herself at the centre of his world, which was no longer a world of cool ascetic pursuits but one of thunder and blood and lust.

He thought of her underneath him, her curves and smoothness, her careless eroticism, her joy in the act of sex. He had to have her, had to, had to.

He came hard, and afterwards, for perhaps the first time, he didn't feel guilty.

Adam was surprised at how many villagers had signed up for his seaside trip. Standing at the coach door with a clipboard on a flaming day in early June, he ticked off each new passenger as they hauled themselves up the step.

Lyn and Ken, Julia Shields, Sebastian and Kasia all rolled up for the pleasure trip. But where was Evie?

'Just five more minutes,' he said anxiously to the coach driver, who sat with the engine running, checking his watch.

The villagers grumbled and fanned themselves and opened packages of sandwiches while Adam peered up and down the lane.

Finally, she appeared, a vision in a huge straw hat and sunglasses of similar size, tripping along the road in a halter-neck sundress and raffia wedges.

Adam's mouth watered. Here she was. His future wife. His past wife. His only wife.

'You waited for me,' she said with a flirtatious smile. 'You're so sweet. Sorry I'm late, Giles from the cricket team kept me up all night.'

Adam's mouth dried out immediately and he clenched his hands. The clipboard fell to the floor. Evie swung herself up on to the coach as he bent to retrieve it. For one split second, he got an uninterrupted view up Evie's voluminous skirts. She wasn't wearing knickers.

She looked over her shoulder at him and winked, flitting away to the back seat where the more disreputable members of the cricket team were already opening cans of lager.

The only available seat was next to Julia. Adam took his place, craning his neck down the aisle to where Evie sat on some yokel's lap, giggling and being fed Pringles. This was not how he had envisaged things.

But there might be a chance, once they reached the coast, to steal her away from her companions and take a walk on the beach, the two of them alone. Every minute brought him closer to his declaration, after all.

'Murray Mint, vicar?' Julia cut into his thoughts, proffering an open bag.

'Thanks.'

'You've got a good turnout. Told you they'd go for this.'

'Yes. I should hand out my leaflets.'

Adam had printed a cunning little booklet, which masqueraded as a selection of word games and activities, but was laden with religious references and even the odd Biblical text, snuck into the margins in Comic Sans. On the back were details of church services and times. He passed them around the coach, then returned to Julia, who greeted him with one of her rare smiles.

She looked young and a little bit wicked when she smiled, though actually, Adam thought, she had an ageless quality. She was one of those women who looked the same at 50 as they did at 15. Trying to take his mind off the riot breaking out at the back of the coach, he decided to talk to her.

'Have you always lived in Saxonhurst?'

'Of course. You know I have. The ancestral pile and all that.'

'Are your parents still alive?'

'No. Well, yes. Yes, they are.'

What a strange answer. Adam waited for her to expand.

'They're in a home,' she said shiftily. 'They aren't really all there, mentally, you know.'

'Alzheimer's?' he asked sympathetically.

'No, no, they've been there since I was a child.'

'That must have been hard on you.'

She shrugged. 'Things seem normal, don't they, when they're part of your childhood.'

'Who took care of you?'

'My aunt Cordelia. We lived in the house together until she died five years ago. That's when things started to get ropey for me. She did all the accounts. I'm afraid I've no head for figures, none at all.'

'Maths wasn't your strong subject at school?'

'I didn't go to school.'

'Oh?'

'I went to a few. Got expelled from them all. Cordie gave up the ghost and said she'd educate me herself. Except she didn't really, except in horses and dogs and things of that sort. Animals were her great love.'

'I can't picture you as the school troublemaker. What did you do?'

'Oh, I was a little shit, pardon my French, vicar. But I was. I liked to frighten people. I lived to scare them out of their wits, in fact. And I was very good at it. So good that nobody wanted to share a building with me.'

Adam found himself looking more closely at Julia, at her aquiline features and her cool, challenging eyes. Her dress was always understated, her manner aloof – she was, in so many respects, Evie's complete opposite. But something about her drew him in today, and he couldn't put his finger on what it was.

'I suppose after what happened with your parents – you had some emotional difficulties,' he surmised.

'If you say so. You're a very interesting man, you know,' she said suddenly, homing in on him.

'Oh, I don't think so,' he floundered.

'I do. I'm intrigued by you. You seem so – hardcore. And yet you have this ridiculous weak spot. More like a weak crater, actually, miles wide. For that little tart at the back of the bus. What is it about her?'

'Please don't talk about her like that.'

'Why not? She opens her legs for all and sundry and makes no secret of it. Is that what you like about her?'

'I won't discuss this.'

'It must be something,' she persisted. 'She's pretty, that can't be denied, but there's more than one pretty girl in Saxonhurst.'

'Change the subject.'

'Oh, all right. When did you last have a girlfriend?'

'Not that one.'

'Oh, Adam, don't be so tight-lipped. You look furious! It's a reasonable enough question. I want to know about your past.'

'I can't think why you would. I'm a vicar. I trained as a vicar. I got ordained. I came here.'

'This is your first parish?'

'No.'

'Why did you leave the last one?'

'Julia, are you a Catholic?'

'No, of course not, why do you ask?'

'You seem to have had training from Torquemada.'

'Goodness, so cagey. So Adam Flint has no past, no relationships, no previous job. How interesting. What a challenge for an enquiring mind.'

'I'm really very much as you see me. There's no great mystery.'

'I refuse to believe it. I'll work you out yet. See if I don't.'

He strove, with some effort, to drive the conversation towards the history of Saxonhurst.

'Was there always a member of your family as lord of the manor?'

'Oh yes, we go back centuries,' she said. 'There's a Shields in the Domesday Book, you know.'

'No, really?'

'Indeed. We presided over this village through thick and thin and we always chose the right side. Stephen over Matilda, Yorkists over Lancastrians, Parliamentarians over Royalists. We had the best connections and we made sure they counted. When Saxonhurst was a rotten borough, a Shields was the MP. We were bulletproof. We even got away without a single plague sufferer.'

'So what happened?'

'I've told you.' Julia's face, eager for once, closed immediately. 'The misfortune of my parents, my own financial incompetence.'

'And there isn't a single spare Shields who can come and take the reins of the dynasty.'

'I'm last of the line.'

'You never married?'

'Oh, I'd tell you mine if you'd tell me yours. But you won't, will you?'

And there the conversation ended, signposts for the seaside having been sighted on the motorway, to rousing cheers from the back of the bus.

*   *   *

The villagers had scattered so rapidly and randomly once the bus was parked that Adam had missed his chance to try and ascertain Evie's movements.

He found himself alone on a crowded promenade, a lonely black-clad figure in a sea of lobster-red skin and fluorescent nylon. What should he do with himself? Have his fortune told by Gypsy Rose Petulengro? Hardly appropriate for a man of the cloth. Have his portrait drawn in charcoals? Who would ever want such a thing? Take a ride in a flight simulator? No, all the amusements ranged around him failed to amuse.

He wanted Evie. He wanted to find her and take her away from her pernicious influences, just as Tribulation Smith had done before him. But where was she? If he looked in all the seafront pubs, he would draw unwanted attention to himself. Perhaps she was innocently eating candyfloss on the pier. Yes, the pier.

Without questioning it too deeply, he let his footsteps tend in that direction. He walked on through a garishly painted arch, on to the wooden boards, and spent 50 pence on looking through a telescope, out to sea and the cliffs that bordered it.

'You won't find her out there,' said a voice behind him.

'Julia,' he said, removing his eye from the lens and turning to find her proffering an ice-cream cone with a chocolate flake.

'Spotted you moping about on the prom. Thought you looked as if you needed cheering up. Come on. Walk along the pier with me and I'll tell you about my lovers.'

'Julia, my interest wasn't prurient …'

'Of course it wasn't.'

She winked – a most un-Julia-like gesture.

'Come on,' she wheedled. 'Have the ice-cream. Live a little. God knows, you need it.'

He took it and walked with her past the faded ballroom

and the clapped-out funfair to the end of the structure, where beaten-down fishermen sat all day with rods and lines.

'I met him at the seaside, actually,' she said.

Waves rolled in and under the boards, sea spray kissing the metal spars that held them up.

'Your husband? You had one?'

'It was a short-lived thing. A whirlwind romance.'

'You don't have to tell me.'

'I want to. I was in one dodgem car. He was in another. He wouldn't stop ramming me – rather metaphorical, really. He drove me to the side of the ring and I couldn't out-manoeuvre him. He said he'd let me out again if I went for a drink with him. He wasn't my sort really – a jack the lad, all charm and flash, no class. But sometimes you get so tired of having to measure up class, don't you find? You want to throw it all aside and get to the heart of things, to the lusts and desires that drive them.'

'I couldn't say ...' Adam feared he might be blushing.

'After one gin and tonic with Darren, my legs felt like they wanted to open wide and stay that way for ever. He could do what he wanted with me. He wasn't even that good-looking, but he had charisma, that certain Pied Piper thing that makes people follow and fall for him. It was in the way he looked at me, as if he could see me naked. And the way he dropped his voice to talk to me, and the way he used his smile, and his eyes. I was a goner, then and there.'

'You got married?'

'I haven't got to that part yet. Don't rush me. That gin and tonic was the only drink I had that day – unless you count Darren's semen.'

'Julia!'

'We never made it back to the bar. We went straight behind the pub toilets, this dirty little outhouse in this nasty little gravelled car park, and I let him lift up my skirts and put his fingers right up me. And then I let him lift me up and hold me against the wall and fuck me the way I'd never been fucked in my life. Properly, for the love of it, for the need of it.'

'Why are you telling me this?'

'Because of the way it roughens your voice and reddens your cheeks. Because it's what you need. You need a Darren.'

'I'm heterosexual.'

'I'm metaphorical.'

The bold challenge of her eyes should have driven his own sideways, or upward, or somewhere that wasn't Julia's face, but it didn't. Somehow he couldn't look away from her.

'What is it with the women in this village?' he muttered.

Julia put her hand on his upper arm, then, when he didn't shy away, she moved it to his face.

'It's not wrong, you know,' she said gently. 'It's not healthy to keep it all in.'

For a horrible moment he wanted to cry, the way he did as a child when somebody was teasing him in the playground for his uncool trainers or poor prowess at Sonic the Hedgehog. *It's not my fault,* he used to yell. *It's not my fault I'm not like you – any of you.*

Julia offered him an opportunity to be normal, to be a card-carrying citizen of the 21st century, just for that afternoon – and it was almost too cruel of her. How could he accept it? He loved Evie and love had to be pure and unselfish and not driven or derailed by base lusts and ...

Julia kissed him.

Her lips were slightly dry, cracked and salty-tasting, and yet the word that flashed into Adam's head was *manna*.

She was taller than Evie and her touch was cool where Evie's was feverish – in his dreams, at least. She was like the moon to Evie's sun, pale and remote but no less desirable for it.

There was a mad second during which Adam vacillated between hysterical repudiation and continuation of the kiss. The second passed and the incipient panic died away, replaced by a profound and almost reassuring pleasure.

Julia's kiss, so sure and confident, made him feel that everything would be all right. This was good. This was fine. The saints did it – well, some of them.

His hands wavered at her side for a moment or two, then, as their embrace deepened and the roar in his ears drowned

121

out the roar of the sea, he put them to the sides of her head, mussing her immaculate coiffure. She didn't seem to mind.

Against his clerical black shirt, her silky blouse slipped and slid, the pearl buttons bumping about his chest. Their arms stretched and wrapped around one another, their hips and pelvises met, their thighs pressed together. She was so slight, almost insubstantial in his hands, that he felt he had to cling to her to prevent her slipping away from him like a vapour. But her mouth was full and lush and promised him the earth, especially when she made use of her tongue.

The fishermen forgotten, Adam shut his eyes and let himself be beguiled. It was a moment of relief, that was all, a break to recharge the batteries of his virtue before he put them to work on the claiming of Evie Witts.

Julia's tongue flicked along his lips, one of her hands massaging his neck while the other dropped lower, creeping with manicured fingernails down his back until it reached his bottom and gave it a cheeky squeeze.

He wriggled his hips involuntarily, panting into her mouth, feeling the dragging weight of his balls and the uncomfortable tightness of his trousers.

I shouldn't, he thought foggily. *I shouldn't, but ...*

She found his testicles and gave them a rub through his trousers.

Now is the time to stop this, if I'm ever ...

Her palm closed on his erection.

She broke the kiss.

'I know a good hotel. A friend owns it ...'

'Oh God, forgive me,' he whispered in agony.

'He will. That's his job, isn't it?' She put her head to one side and stroked his cheek pityingly. 'Poor love. You need it so badly. Come on. Come with Julia.'

He allowed her to lead him by the hand.

A lamb to the slaughter.

Chapter Ten

The funfair was riotous, the lights flashing and the sirens blaring. Further on, in the faded ballroom, something was even rowdier, a huge press of men with plastic pints of lager spilling out on to the boardwalk, whistling and catcalling.

From somewhere inside, louche music played.

Adam saw Julia peer inside, then look sharply forward and step up her pace to a near-run. Intrigued, he pulled her back, wanting to know what had caused her change in demeanour. A pin-thick gap between sweating beer guts gave him the glimpse he needed.

He let go of her hand and barged through the crowd.

Evie was pole-dancing on a stage, apparently participating in some amateur competition. She had exchanged her sundress for a skimpy bikini and the raffia wedges were replaced with diamante stilettos. Her routine was so blatantly suggestive the other competitors whispered behind hands or sat watching with milk-souring expressions. She was more popular with the men, though.

Adam had never seen tongues literally hanging out until now.

Every man in the place wanted to take her from that pole and fuck her raw.

The very air swam with sex and violence.

It smelled of sweat and stale beer.

Adam fell forward on the carpet and retched over some huge tattooed hulk's shoes.

He looked up to apologise, only to see a fist descending

at speed and from a great height. He shut his eyes, resigned to unconsciousness, but the fist was halted by a flailing, kicking dervish who proved, once Adam had groggily come to his senses, to be Julia Shields.

'*Get off him*!' she shrieked.

The pole-dance music stopped.

Somebody took Adam by the arm and dragged him away from the hulk, then handed him a paper tissue to wipe his mouth.

In the meantime, the hulk had stepped back from Julia and was being calmed down by a group of friends.

'Come on, Adam,' said Julia gruffly. 'You need a lie down.'

Evie leapt off the stage and stood with a hand on her hip, staring fiercely at Julia.

'What's your game?' she demanded. 'What are you doing with him?'

'I don't have a game,' said Julia haughtily. 'You're the one with the agenda. We all know what it is. Well, I don't think he deserves it.'

'Get your hands off him!'

'Come on, Adam.'

Adam, unsteady on his feet and with black spots floating in and out of his field of vision, followed the most soothing voice. It happened to be Julia's.

He wove through the mob in a dark-edged dream, his stomach in revolt, his brain furred up with equal measures of revulsion, despair and, behind it all, a confusion of lusts. For Evie, for Julia, for flesh, for sin, for forgetting – any or all of them boiled within him as his feet trod an unknown, careless path.

Greasy smells of frying onions and burnt candyfloss and engine oil mixed with the sea salt, swimming past him, with the noise and the press of heated bodies.

He came to his senses on a bed, sprawled out where Julia had pushed him. She had loosened his collar and taken off his boots.

He opened his eyes slowly, taking her in as she hovered above him with a tooth glass of water. Her fair hair shone like a halo.

She sat down on the side of the bed and stroked his brow. He couldn't hold back any longer. He laid his head in her lap and burst into tears.

'There, there,' she said, and every caress of her fingers, mopping up his tears, was like the re-establishment of some long-lost bond.

'What's happening to me?' he pleaded. 'Why is it happening to me?'

'Darling, I imagine this has been a long time coming. You're tired. You've used up too much energy denying your nature and masking it with this old-time religion of yours.'

'What do you mean, my nature? You don't know me that well.'

'I know you very well, Adam. You and all who came before you.'

'What are you talking about?' His lament came out as a strangulated bellow. 'What is going on in this village? Julia, I have dreams – such dreams. Dreams of being a Puritan preacher who takes a witch for a wife. What does it mean?'

'It means you're the last in a long line, my love. And so is Evie Witts.'

'What line?'

'I shouldn't say. The village secrets aren't mine to disclose.'

'Oh, for God's sake! Forgive me, O Lord. I'm leaving. I resign.'

'You won't.'

'How do you know?'

'Evie won't have it. You won't leave here without her. And she'll never leave.'

Adam contemplated this. Julia was right. Except he would make Evie leave. He would make her come with him.

'Tell me why you came here,' said Julia in a low, persuasive voice.

'Nobody else would take the post,' moaned Adam. 'And I couldn't find another. I have a reputation – for being a bit too hardline. I'm an embarrassment to the church, this stupid soft-centred namby-pamby church of ours. Where are all the muscular Christians now? That's all I want to be.'

'I think you're a very muscular Christian,' said Julia soothingly, putting a hand on his upper arm and squeezing it. 'You have the soul of a missionary. In fact, one of your predecessors had been a missionary. A Victorian chap, came to us from Congo. A rather unsuccessful mission, I gather. He bore some interesting scars.'

'What are you talking about – my predecessors? You keep coming out with these bizarre statements, speaking as if you were 400 years old yourself.'

'I need to mind my tongue, don't I? Thank you for telling me about how you came to be here. Now, how about the girlfriends?'

She smiled roguishly and ruffled his hair.

He shut his eyes and whispered, 'Nothing to tell.'

'What? You've never had a girlfriend? Is that what you're telling me?'

'The risk … Too much.'

'Risk? What risk?'

'Risk of temptation. Temptation of the flesh.'

'Adam, you aren't a monk!'

'I wanted to save myself. I wanted to be pure.'

'You're a virgin?'

'Yes.'

'You don't kiss like one.'

'Thanks, I think.'

'You weren't born for the celibate existence, my love. You need more than that.'

'My flesh is so weak …'

'Don't think of it as weakness. It's another way of being.

It's not wrong, it's not right. It's how God made you.'

'God would not make me a – fornicator. It's His way of testing me, the hardest test He could give me. I don't care for drink or gambling or money or anything like that. But Evie Witts … Oh, Evie Witts …'

'Never mind her. She'll never be any good to you.'

Julia's fingers had strayed to his loosened dog collar, at which she pulled gently.

'I've always wanted to take this off you,' she whispered.

'No, you can't,' he whispered back, but there was no firmness in it, no purpose. She pulled it free of his shirt, exposing the lower part of his neck, which she bent and kissed.

'Poor Adam,' she crooned. 'So intense, so full of fire. So desperate for a fuck.'

She let one finger move down Adam's chest, gliding between his pectoral muscles, dipping down into his abdomen. His capacity for resistance was gone. He was floating somewhere in a place where his moral compass didn't operate, a badland. A badland that was good, that felt good, as good as Julia's fingertip tracing his waistline before grasping his belt and sliding it through the buckle.

The memories of Julia's kiss and Evie's pole-dance had left him semi-erect even through the unpleasantness that had followed. Julia's sudden statement of intent, in removing his belt and unbuttoning his trousers, brought him to full engorgement straight away.

'Nobody has ever done this for you?' she said, still disbelieving, pushing his trousers over his hips and thighs to release his cock. 'Except yourself, of course.'

'I try,' he gasped, 'not to. I try to think of – other things …'

'It's killing you,' she said. Her hand closed around his testicles. 'Feel that, Adam. So tight, so pulsing with need. You must be awash in sexual desire, 24 hours a day, with nowhere for these little swimmers to swim to, except when you dream. You do dream, don't you, Adam?'

'I told you,' he gasped. 'I dream. All the time. Vivid dreams. Sinful dreams.'

'Your only outlet. Your brain and body conspire in your sleep, Adam, to get the release they're so desperate for. You deny them, you deny yourself. You aren't made for abstinence. Your unconscious has spoken.'

'Don't say that, don't say that. I can resist ...'

'You can't.'

He arched his back and gripped at the sheets as Julia's fist found his cock, wrapping itself perfectly around its rigid girth. The feel of her clasp, of his enclosure in it, tipped him over an edge. He couldn't turn back now. This was his fate, for good or ill.

'You shouldn't,' she said, and her hand moved up, moved down, weakening his spine. 'Why resist it? It's what you want. Fear is not a virtue, darling, and it's fear that holds you back. That's not strength. That's not muscular Christianity. That's craven cowardice.'

The pep talk, coupled as it was with a slow jerking back and forth of his foreskin, didn't really sink in. But he was absorbing the gist, letting it settle into his consciousness together with the divine sensation of being touched intimately by a woman, so that the two would always be inevitably linked.

She made me do it. Already his bargain with his maker was being stored up for rehearsal. *She has a serpent's tongue.*

He wondered, in his delirium, if she really did have a serpent's tongue, and if so, how that would feel, licking and flicking around the sensitive underside of his glans.

But Julia did not need to perform any manoeuvre more extravagant than her perfectly judged handjob to take Adam to that higher plane of pleasure. He was already too close, caught in the grip of her elegant fingers and her seductive whisperings. Behind his eyes, bright colours burned while every muscle tensed, every string pulled tight.

'Julia,' he panted. 'Julia, I ...' The words tailed into a low, suffering sigh. His abdomen and Julia's fingers were smeared with ejaculate, rapidly cooling where it lay.

He could no longer feel his bones and his thoughts drifted into a place of repose, of sleep, of forgetting. He didn't even last long enough in his post-orgasmic wakefulness to look into Julia's face.

When he came to, she was lying naked in the bed beside him.

'Oh God!' he cried, once an initial sensual, sleepy warmth had given way to hard reality. 'What have I done? What's happened to me? Julia, why are you …?'

'Oh sweetheart, please calm down. You've done nothing. You've rather been done to, though. Don't you remember?'

'Yes, yes. So that was – all?'

'Wasn't it enough? I was hoping you might have rallied a little, after your nap.'

She bent her head to kiss him, but he struggled and pushed her off.

'Julia, this is, this is – oh God – wholly inappropriate.'

'Holy? There was nothing holy about it.'

'Not holy! Oh just, just, just … What's the time?'

Julia yawned. 'About four-ish.'

'We have to leave in an hour. Get up, get dressed. Oh God.'

'Oh, must we?' she purred with a wicked smile that made Adam feel suddenly much less resolved. 'It's so long since I shared a bed with an attractive man. Now I've got one next to me, I think it would break my heart to let him go.'

Adam bent his legs and hid his face in his knees.

She was sent to test me. I failed.

He rose heavily, still in his black shirt, which had ridden up to his nipples, his trousers rumpled around his ankles. His black boots had never been removed, and his stomach was tight with flaking dried semen.

He was thirsty and there was a vile taste at the back of his throat.

As soon as he registered it, he thought of Evie, and the huge surge of longing and guilt and tenderness and exasperation and loving hatred almost knocked him back on to the bed.

'Adam, don't be like this.' Julia sat up, ran fingers through her hair.

'Like what? We have to go. The driver'll be waiting for us.'

And so will Evie.

He pulled up his trousers and buckled his belt. He left the room without a backward look.

In the car park, the villagers milled, many the worse for an afternoon spent in the seafront pubs.

''Ere 'e is – the reverend 'imself.'

Laughter of a not particularly charitable nature greeted Adam as he hurried across the car park, still beset by an urge to vomit. No sign of Evie.

'You look rough, Rev. Too much communion wine?'

Adam shook his head and tried to smile, but the nausea was stronger than ever.

It was another five minutes before Julia appeared, looking as immaculate as ever.

She hoisted herself on to the bottom step of the bus with a feline smile and a flash of leg and left Adam to his clipboard.

What if she said something? What if she spread it round the village that they had …?

But the return of Evie broke into his worries. Back in her halter dress, she tripped through the cinder car park as merrily as if she had just returned from a picnic in a fragrant meadow rather than a pole-dance competition in a tawdry dive bar.

Drawing close to Adam, though, her placid expression soured.

'Where's your girlfriend?' she hissed.

'I don't know what you mean.'

'Yeah, you do. Your fancy piece. Nice bit of aristo fanny you've landed there, vicar. Congrats.'

'Evie, there's nothing –'

'Oh, don't bother about me. I know when I've been outclassed.'

She flounced on to the bus, with that same flash of knicker-free bottom she'd given him on the outward voyage.

He had to throw up into some scraggy weeds on the other side of a low brick wall before they set off again.

Chapter Eleven

Three times around the old well Evie skipped, then three times in the other direction, then the final three revolutions before she sank to her knees and spoke the words of the spell.

'I feel your strength tonight.' The spirit spoke, after their long embrace of greeting. 'How many did you take?'

She shrugged. 'A few. Won a pole-dancing contest. Got lots of offers from that.'

'What is this pole-dancing whereof you speak?'

'Don't matter. Thing is, love, we've got a problem.'

'Evangeline.' He seized her hands and she felt the flame that still burned in him, despite his phantasmagoric appearance, warming her to her core. 'What is amiss?'

'Her ladyship. She's taken it upon herself to save him from me.'

'The woman Shields?'

'That's the one.'

The spirit seated himself on the well wall and gazed abstractedly at the stars.

'She has ever been a thorn in our flesh, has she not? Her ancestor it was laid open the manor for the witchfinders' use. What is her purpose?'

'She says she doesn't think he deserves what's coming to him. She knows what we mean to do – of course she does. Over the centuries, there ain't been a Shields that's bothered their heads about our business. They've let us get on with it. Too many troubles of their own. But she ... I dunno. I think she's fond of him.'

'He is loved?'

'Oh, I wouldn't go that far. She just fancies him, I reckon. But if it goes any further ...'

'Is it like?'

'Well, you know, I think I've got him well enough hooked in. At least, I hope I have.'

'Hope isn't enough, Evangeline. Hope will not bring me back to glory. There are still three months until the harvesting. You must keep his blood up and his thirst high for you. There is no other course.'

'I know it. God, John, it's hard, though.'

He drew her on to his lap and cradled her head in his shoulder. His snowy ruff tickled her cheek in that comfortingly familiar way and she felt herself reassured.

'There's no other girl in the whole of England could win him,' whispered John. 'No other girl in the whole of England can make a man's heart pound louder and his cock stand prouder than my Evangeline. You are my sweet and wicked little miracle.'

His hand pulled up her skirt in bunches, drawing the fabric slowly over her sun-kissed thighs. She stretched out her legs, assisting him, and laid back in his arms until her neck tipped and coils of her hair trailed in the tufty grass. He kept an arm braced beneath her spine, holding her firm while she began to raise one leg.

'This has done fine work for me,' said John, patting the spreading slit between her legs that was exposed by her actions. 'This saves me a little more each time it is filled. Fill it again, Evangeline, fill it endlessly. Let your greedy cunt be my salvation.'

His fingertips nestled in the wet channel, strumming Evie's clit while she let her leg point up to the stars.

Now, here, with his hand upon her, she felt a different order of pleasure than she did in her everyday dealings with village lads and passing fancies. Those were playthings, to

132

be used, to be enjoyed and discarded once the orgasm had been gained. This was a deeper connection, a rooted thing, the fruit of ancient seeds.

She and John had history spanning three and a half centuries – she continued her line and, she hoped, she would end it. The time was approaching when all the efforts of her ancestresses would be realised. John would return and they could enjoy the togetherness they were never granted in life. Oh, she longed for it.

Her clit vibrated with her lover's touch. She felt the strength of it, making her cunt quiver with need for his cock. She shoved the triangles of fabric that covered her breasts roughly aside, exposing her hard nipples to the evening air. With her own skilled fingers, she twisted and tweaked them, working in concert with John to bring her body into a state of possession. Possessed by pleasure, desire, and love, she whipped this way and that in her lover's arms until her orgasm had its way with her.

And then it was John's turn. Tipping her from his lap, he pushed her on to her knees and had her leaning over the old well wall with her skirts about her waist.

'Who's had you here today?' he enquired gruffly, piercing her cunt with three long fingers.

'Three village lads and the man who owned the pub where I won the contest.'

'Is that how you won?'

'No, it was fair and square! But I gave it him afterwards, in the tap room.'

'I see. And here? Who's had you here?'

One finger nudged at her anus. She shivered and tensed it, even as a slow smile spread across her face.

'None today, lover.'

'None yet. Spread wide your cheeks, my wench.'

Evie obeyed, her fingers pressing into the soft, firm flesh as they pulled apart her buttocks. She felt the drift of air along the crack, then John dipped his cock into the plentiful gush of her pussy juices and rubbed it, thoroughly and with stately pace, until it was completely slick and coated with them.

'Keep yourself open for me.'

She gripped tighter as John's blunt cockhead travelled across her perineum and into the lower reaches of her arse. When he settled himself against her anus, she did her very best not to let the muscles contract, despite her natural inclination.

She felt her breasts squashing into the mouldering brick and breathed in the damp, peaty air of the well, but nothing could overpower that singular sensation of John's cock pushing against her most intimate orifice.

That first nudge forward always earned a whimper from her as she worked hard to keep herself spread and accessible. She trembled through the first few inches, the familiar burn, the panic-inducing sense of over-fullness, the fear that she might split or tear, and then that moment was over and John was snaking up inside her, filling her bottom in the rudest, crudest possible way.

'This makes you mine,' he rasped in her ear. 'This is how I have you. I know you let the other boys do it to you, but in my mind, this makes you mine.'

'You're the only one who makes me feel it this way,' she said. 'You're the only one who puts his stamp on me.'

'I'm all the way inside you now. I'm going to fuck this sweet, tight arse for all I'm worth. Hold it wide and say a prayer.'

Evie didn't feel the chafing of the brick against her skin, nor the strain of her thigh muscles, nor the pitiless jolting of her stomach against the edge of the well. All she felt was her arse being well and truly buggered, hard and fast, by the man who owned her soul. She knew he took a kind of revenge this way, a kind of assuaging of his masculine pride for the uses he put her to, but she knew it was only because he loved her that he did it, only because he found it all so unbearable.

But soon it would all be over. Soon they could be together.

She sobbed out an orgasm of immense proportions, then clenched him tight within her, milking him of his seed.

He rolled her over and over in the dusty grass, kissing her until her lips were sore and almost numb.

'I have to go, my love,' he whispered, and she saw his strength fading, his image losing its distinctness. 'Keep him close. Keep him in your sights. Love me.'

'Always.'

Adam was surprised to see Evie the following evening. In his miserable confusion over Julia's behaviour on the outing, he had quite forgotten that it was Evie's Bible study night.

'Oh … Evie,' he said, standing at the door, watching her stomp in, curls flying. 'Yes, you're quite right.'

'Forgotten me already?' she said, hand on hip at the study door. 'It's all Julia, Julia, Julia now, I s'pose? My charms don't stand up to hers.'

'What's she said to you?' Adam felt the blood drain from his face. All day he had been wrestling with the horrible dread that Julia might spread the tale of their little seaside interlude all over Saxonhurst and beyond.

'Nothing. She don't need to. You and her was thick as thieves yesterday. Where'd she take you, after you did your spectacular puke at the pole-dance contest?'

'Nowhere, nowhere. Just – some public lavatories. To clean myself up. Then for a cup of tea. Nothing special.'

Thou shalt not bear false witness.

'She's got an eye for you.'

Adam opened the study door and ushered Evie in.

'Oh, nonsense, Evie.'

'She has. What she said …' Evie trailed off.

'What did she mean by that? About knowing your game,

and how I didn't deserve it? It didn't make much sense to me.'

'Just raving. She's like that. You know her.'

Adam contemplated Evie's shifty eyes and guessed she was equivocating. He pulled out a chair for her and motioned her to sit.

Standing over her, he asked, 'So, what *is* your game, Evie?'

For the first time since arriving in Saxonhurst, he felt at an advantage over this tormenting minx. Something about the – thing – with Julia had lent him a certain confidence that had been lacking before. He wasn't sure why, but he intended to make the most of it.

She looked up at him coquettishly.

'Game? I don't play games. I'm a straightforward kind of a girl. What you see ...' She stretched out her long, bronzed legs from under the denim miniskirt she wore and crossed them at the ankles. 'Is what you get.'

'What I see is what I get?' Adam swallowed, staring down at her. 'Are you sure about that?'

'Positive. Keep looking, vicar.' Her voice was soft and she bit on a finger. 'That's what you get.'

Nobody breathed for a good half a minute, then Adam inhaled hugely.

'The Sermon on the Plain,' he said, plucking a Bible from the shelf.

'Not the Mount? That a different one, is it?'

'Yes.'

'Pity. I like a nice mount.'

'A plain is just as good.'

They were deep into the teachings of Christ when Adam's phone rang – an unexpected event in itself, causing him to wonder aloud who on earth would be calling him.

The voice on the other end was brisk.

'Adam. We need to talk.'

'Ah, yes.' He looked furtively at Evie, wondering if she

could hear Julia's voice from her corner of the room. 'I'm with a parishioner at the minute. Perhaps I could call you back.'

'No you bloody well couldn't. "A parishioner". Any money says it's Easy Evie.'

'Yes, well, that's a diocesan matter, of course, and I'd refer you back to the bishop.'

'I refer you back to the handjob I gave you yesterday afternoon. Regarding which, I expect to see you here at my place in about an hour? Yes?'

'Oh, I understand the bishop's very overburdened just at the moment. Possibly the archdeacon, then? In any event, yes. I'd say, yes.'

'Good. See you then.'

'Thank you. God bless. Goodbye.'

He put the phone down, excused himself, and went to stand in the vestibule for five minutes to compose himself.

Julia and Evie.

Was it possible that he, Adam Flint, fire-and-brimstone virgin of this parish, was at the centre of a love triangle?

He stuffed his mouth into the sleeve of his hung-up coat to stifle a wave of hysterical laughter.

'Where you been?' demanded Evie when he was master enough of himself to return to the study.

'Parish business,' he muttered.

'Parish business? You ain't got no parish. Your parish is me and the widow Shields.'

He double-took, his fingers skidding over the book he had been about to open.

'Widow? Julia's a widow?'

'Yeah.' Evie seemed to enjoy the impact her words had made. 'Didn't you know? Came to a bad end, he did, old Darren Frensham.'

'Frensham?'

'She never took his name. Why should she? Don't suppose I shall, when and if I marry. I'm a Witts and I'm proud of it.'

'What was this bad end he came to?'

'Well, there's the thing, vicar. It's all a bit of a mystery. He had a bit to drink, went out walking to the barn to clear his head, and never came back.'

'Never came back? So ...?'

'Oh yeah, he's dead. They found the body, right there, in Palmers Barn.'

'What – did he die of?'

'Seemed like a heart attack.' Evie shrugged. 'Something scared him, p'raps. He ain't the first to die out there, after all.'

'You're talking about ghosts. Please don't. Perhaps some animal? Or he was attacked?'

'Not a mark on him. There's those as suspects our precious Ms Shields put something in his drink. You see, they weren't getting along so famously – it was common knowledge in the village.'

'Don't be ridiculous.'

'She married beneath her, for love. Or something like it. More like lust, I think. He was a charmer, was Darren. But he was no good. Gambled away most of her money and drank the rest. That's why she lost the manor.'

'Oh.'

'It was repossessed the week he died.'

'Oh.'

'She weren't best pleased.'

'No.'

'There's a substantial school of thought in the village that she had something to do with his death.'

'And that's why she's unpopular here?'

'That's about it. The black widow, they call her.'

'Imaginative.'

'Yeah, not really. You do like her, don't you? Darren was very well liked, especially around the pub. He was one of those blokes – you know he's no good, but you can't help but want to be in his company. He weren't faithful to her neither. And she knew it. Everybody did.'

'Did you and he …?'

'No, he weren't my type. I know, I know, you'll say everyone's my type. But Darren weren't a Saxonhurst boy, so he was pretty much off my radar.'

'So Julia married a wastrel …'

Evie laughed. 'I love the way you talk sometimes. You're so old-fashioned. You're just like …' She broke off. 'Don't worry about it.'

'Julia married this Darren, who broke her heart, lost her money and her home and then left her a widow in the most unpleasant circumstances – and yet nobody in this village feels any sympathy for her?'

'Well,' Evie shrugged. 'She ain't likeable, is she? Aloof and snooty, thinks she's better than us.'

'Yet a gambling, womanising – piece of worthless rubbish – is mourned here. Never has my challenge in this parish been more starkly illustrated.'

'I reckon that's life,' said Evie.

'Yes. Yes, you're right. And thank heaven for the one that follows this and is to come. If it weren't for that, why should any of us behave decently?'

'See, you're angry now. Don't shoot the messenger. I just told you what happened. I bet she'd've kept it close. You'd never have heard it from her.'

'It's her private business.' Adam felt intensely defensive of Julia, despite her alarming behaviour at the seaside. Or perhaps because of it. He couldn't really explain it himself.

'Don't you get mixed up in it,' warned Evie. 'Stay with them as cares about you.'

Adam stared. 'And who might they be? Nobody in this village, as far as I can make out.'

'I do, Adam. I care about you.'

'Then why, Evie, why do you … Oh.' He threw up his hands, waiting for another pert answer. But this time it

139

didn't come.

Evie was silent for a while, and she seemed to be struggling with something – was it tears?

When she spoke, her voice was low.

'I'll never be able to explain to you why I act as I do, Adam. But I'm asking you to believe that there is a reason, and it ain't just my nature. Though I do love to love, and be loved – that's like breathing to me. There's other forces at work behind it, and I just want you to – I dunno – look out for me. Is that too much to ask?'

'Forces? At work?' Adam's mission of salvation rushed back to his emotional foreground, all thoughts of Julia's plight pushed behind it. It was true. Evie did not want to spread her legs for every oaf who winked at her. She needed him.

His body burned as if in fever at her admission.

'I can't tell you,' she said, and a tear fell.

He made a dive forward, snatching at his handkerchief to wipe it away. With one hand gripping the back of her chair, he crouched close beside her, breathing in her rich, animal scent, mingled with some cheap musky perfume from the supermarket. All his blood rushed to his cock.

'Evie, let me help you. I just want to protect you.'

'I wish you could. But the time ain't right. I have to wait. Wait for me, lover.'

What had she just called him?

'Oh my darling,' he breathed. 'How long? How long must I wait? I don't think I can.'

'I've got things to finish this summer. Things I can't let drift. But when the harvest moon comes round, then I'll be free.'

'And you will come to me?'

'I will come to you. I promise it.'

'Oh Evie.' He took her face in his hands and swooped forward, but she turned her head swiftly.

'Not yet. You mustn't kiss me. Not yet.'

'How can you say these things and ask me not to kiss you?' Adam was in agony, and yet ecstasy was laced through it at every point.

'Don't question me. It's how it has to be. And now I should go, before …'

'Before?' He swiped at the empty air where she had been sitting.

But she was on her feet, gathering her bag.

'You only have to wait,' she said softly, standing by the door. 'That ain't so hard, is it?'

She must know that it was the hardest thing of all, thought Adam, surely she must.

But he looked after her as she hurried, head down, through the churchyard, and then he could do no more than sit in the seat she had recently vacated, staring into space, in a profound rapture, for the rest of the evening.

Chapter Twelve

Her wedding gown was no more than a shift with a coarse peasant dress over the top. In her hair she wore a garland of flowers. He didn't approve of such ornamentation, but since she was a bride – his bride – he decided to let it pass.

Few guests attended the event, the sole witnesses being Sir Henry Shields of the manor and his wife. Previously, the good preacher had thought the changes to the marriage laws and the introduction of banns a good thing, but this past three weeks had had cause to differ. If he could have married Evangeline sooner, his influence might have saved her kinswomen. As it was, they had been hanged in a trio at Parham, just the week before.

But Evangeline survived, and Evangeline was the important one.

Even in her grief, she was beautiful. Her tears didn't redden her nose or dim her eyes like they did with other women. Instead, they made her soul shine through the defiance and the lack of refinement. She was a living thing; she breathed and felt.

He might have postponed the wedding to a less inauspicious time, but it seemed the witchfinder snapped at his heels, eager to come back and bag the final female of the quartet. Even if it was not so, he felt it must be.

His ring on her finger, he bore her away to a frugal breakfast at the manor, courtesy of the Shields, and then they returned to his abode.

'Good wife,' he whispered, as soon as they were through

the low door. 'There is but one duty left me to perform.'

She raised her face to his and accepted a kiss. She was always so passive, never responding in kind, yet never recoiling from him either. It was, he supposed, a maidenly modesty within her, which knew the meaning of sin and avoided its active commission. But now, within wedlock, there was no sin in this. He sought to remind her.

'Dearest love, we are wed. Such as it pleases us to do will also please the Lord. We act in good faith and with the blessing of the church if we ...'

He reached for the neck of her shift and made to lower it, exposing the upper slopes of her breasts. Again, she merely tilted her neck to one side and let him, her eyes half-shut and distant.

'Do you love me?' he asked.

'No,' she replied.

He held his hand where it lay and stared at her.

'You say no? You do not love me? I, who have saved you?'

'You did it for your own base reasons. If my mother had taken your fancy, she it would be who stood here today.'

A great anger arose in him. He tore the shift to the hem of her bodice and held her close to him, their faces touching at the nose tips.

'You would prefer to have swung? You would prefer to burn?'

'No, sir, and that is why I am your wife, and each day I chide my own weakness. Yet I will not bear you love. I will never bear you love.'

His vision flushed hot red and the blood thumped in his ears. Seizing her by the shoulder, he flung her on to the bed that lay in the corner of the single-roomed dwelling.

'If you will not bear me love, then you will bear me obedience,' he vowed.

In his ears rang her screams, and for ever more he would never forget her fearful eyes, her whispered curses, the thin, mean pleasure he drew from his transgression.

And the other thing he would never forget was the stain on the sheet afterwards.

No blood, only his own issue.

'You have another lover!' he bellowed, beside himself, on his knees before the crucifix that was the room's only embellishment. 'You have duped me.'

'You won me by false means,' she wept. 'I have always loved another. I feared to tell you.'

'Who is he? Tell me his name.'

'You will do him harm.'

'I will find it out, Evangeline. It will be known to me.'

Adam awoke in a cold sweat. He was still in the desk chair and his muscles ached from the unforgiving wood. But the physical discomfort was as nothing compared to the unfolding pain in his head.

He, as Tribulation Smith, had raped Evie. It was a dream, yes, it was not a substantial crime, and yet he felt as guilty as if his own body had violated hers. It made no sense, but it was so vivid that he felt again the retching nausea that had overcome him at the seaside.

He sank his head on to the desktop and groaned with anguish.

The groan was still not fully discharged when an indignant rapping at the door interrupted it.

'Oh Lord, have mercy on me,' he whispered, deciding to ignore the late-night caller. Even Evie would not be welcome at this time, surrounded as she was with these disturbing ghosts and presences.

But within a minute, a dark shadow loomed by the window and knocked on it. Adam leapt from his chair and moved towards it. The shadow was slight, almost wraith-like. With a shock of yet more guilt – this variety from a different source – he recognised Julia.

He gestured towards the front door, indicating that he would go and open it for her. When he did so, she streaked inside like a cat, flattening herself to pass him and head straight for the living room.

She was already sitting, like an enthroned queen, on the best armchair in the house when he entered. He stood uncertainly in the door frame for an instant, too out of sorts to know how to speak or act.

'Why didn't you come?' she asked. 'What are you afraid of?'

Two very separate questions in Adam's mind. He decided to tackle only the first.

'Evie was here. I lost track of time after she left, fell asleep in the chair.'

'She makes you lose your mind. Ah well, perhaps it's too late after all.'

Julia chewed moodily on a knuckle, looking sideways at the bookshelves. J.E. Lydford's history of the village caught her eye.

'That book's mine, isn't it?' she said, stalking over to inspect it.

'You lent it to me.'

She narrowed her eyes. 'Why don't I remember it?'

'You were – well, you'd had a drink or two.'

'Oh, that sodding journalist. Yes, well, you shouldn't have taken advantage of me.'

Adam burst into a mirthless laugh.

'The irony,' he said.

She came closer, close enough for him to smell her, if she'd had any scent except an anonymous floral perfume. He tensed.

'You were asking for it,' she said, softly. She reached for the book. 'I'll have this back, if you don't mind.'

'I haven't finished reading it.'

'It's codswallop, start to finish.'

'You seem very sure of that.'

'An interesting man, Joss Lydford. He was vicar here, half a century or so ago.'

'I know. I've seen his name on the board in the church. What happened to him?'

'He went mad.'

'That's a pity.' Adam felt a pull of the most heartfelt sympathy for his predecessor. It would be very easy, perhaps the easiest thing of all, to go mad here, in this role, in this horrendous parish. He shut his eyes for a moment, wondering with distant horror if that might not be what was happening to him.

'Yes, isn't it? The thing is, he got too involved. Too drawn into the village and its secrets. Which simply won't do. It's a sure-fire route to madness.'

'You know these secrets, or so you keep intimating?'

She pursed her lips.

'I know a lot of secrets, Adam. Some of them would benefit you. Some of them wouldn't. Do you want me to show you?'

She put a hand on his shoulder.

He flinched, thinking of Evie, swallowed and shook his head.

'Julia,' he said in a hoarse whisper, 'what happened on the excursion ... It was ... I think you meant well. But it can't have a sequel. It can't happen ... I'm not free ...'

'Not free?' Her fingers closed around his shoulder, bony and hard. 'What do you mean? What's happened?'

'I can't change the way I feel,' he said. 'Especially if she feels it too.'

Julia retracted her hand and used it to smite her forehead, groaning.

'Dear God, she's got you. You're doomed. Well, now I need to rethink. Somehow or other, by hook or by crook, I'm not letting this happen. If I can't tempt you with a shag, then I need to come up with something else. Watch this space.'

She swept away, taking the book with her.

Adam sank down into the armchair. His brain was a fog

of alarming information. How Julia's husband had died, the fate of J.E. Lydford, his horrifying dream and, most of all, the fact that Evie might, after all, come to him and be his.

It was too much. For the first time in his life, Adam found himself craving brandy, or at least a little something to dull his senses and let him drift easefully into dreamless sleep. But there was no brandy in the house and he sat up, hour after hour, until finally, just before the dawn, the relief of oblivion was his.

The village cricket match against Hamframpton had been going on all day. On and on and on, in fact, if you asked Adam, who was no great fan of the sport. But he had volunteered his services as umpire, in his endless quest to grab some kind of foothold in village life, so he stood under an unforgiving late June sun in a white coat a size too small for him, his face smothered in clown-thick sunblock.

Saxonhurst were winning. In fact, according to the statistics, Saxonhurst had never lost a village cricket match. They were invincible. Legend had it that, back in the 1980s, they'd played the all-conquering Somerset county side in a friendly and won. They'd bowled out Ian Botham for a duck.

Yet, as far as Adam could tell, they rarely practised and only played a few games each season. Just another piece of unquantifiable Saxonhurst luck.

On the sidelines, Adam was constantly aware of Evie, in her scarlet silk dress, cheerleading enthusiastically. Every time a Saxonhurst man was called out, she ran up to him and leapt into his embrace, snogging the face off him until Adam felt quietly sick. Since her declaration at the Bible study session, she had skirted around the subject every time they met, uncharacteristically demure and coy, not her usual brazen self at all.

And yet she would not relinquish her work at the porn set, nor was she seen any the less wrapped around hearty village lads in the beer garden of the Fleece.

'The time isn't right yet,' was all she would say.

'But surely if I have to wait, then you could at least stop all this ...'

It was no use. She wouldn't. He had to stand by and watch, it seemed. She wheedled and cajoled with soft words and apologies, but the upshot was the same. He had to suck it up.

Finally, Hamframpton gave up the ghost, having no chance of catching up with the mighty Saxonhurst total of runs – 506 for 3 at tea time.

They all trooped into the pavilion for sandwiches and cake. Adam sipped tea in a corner, watching Evie sit across two giant laps, being fed cucumber slices and strawberries. Julia, in charge of the tea urn, followed the direction of his sour looks.

The sons of Hamframpton despatched to their minibus, only Saxonhurst team members remained, with Evie. Julia and the other villagers had decamped with the empty plates and cups, and suddenly the atmosphere of affable gentility had gone with them, replaced by a kind of avid anticipation that owed everything to testosterone.

'Team talk,' said the skipper gruffly to Adam. 'Not for a vicar's ears.'

'What about Evie?'

'She's part of the team.'

'I fail to see how ...'

'You don't need to know. Thanks for your services, vicar, much appreciated. Good evening to you.'

He thought about arguing, but each of the Saxonhurst cricketers was built like a Greek god and furnished with shin pads and bats.

'Evie,' he said, his final gambit, but she smiled, a little sadly, and shook her head.

He tore off the ill-fitting coat and stormed out, leaning up against the side of the pavilion, flattening his spine against its pebbledashed wall. His arms spread, his let his fingers press into the little sharp stones, relishing the mild pain, anything to get the image of Evie with all the cricketers out of his head.

Because that, beyond doubt, was what would be happening in there.

Another sick Saxonhurst ritual involving the use to exhaustion of Evie's genitalia.

He took a few lungfuls of sweet summer air. How uselessly the sun shone a benevolent golden light over the pitch, how pointlessly the bees buzzed and flowers vented perfume and the cries of children playing with hosepipes drifted on the air.

It was all ugly, all without purpose, while Evie rutted like a mindless beast.

He crept, crablike, around the side of the building, finding the store cupboard unlocked and concealing himself in there, amidst the nets and racquets and balls and other paraphernalia of rural sporting life.

The smell of stale sweat and old rubber was none too pleasant, but he couldn't seem to tear himself away from the pursuit of knowledge that would do nothing but hurt him. He needed to know how bad it was, how very low his love could stoop.

The cupboard walls were thin and beyond them lay the changing rooms. He heard the hot splash of the showers, and shouts loud enough for the words to be made out.

'Hand 'er over, Jase. I think you missed a bit.'

Evie's shriek and a chorus of ribald male laughter. More splashing, louder, and some screaming.

'Fuck me, that's cold! Turn the dial back, you bastard!'

Slaps on wet skin, female giggling, male shouts and whistles.

'She likes it. Seen the state of her nipples?'

'Oi!' Evie's voice. 'Two against one ain't fair! No!' Rising to a shriek again. 'He's got me! Charlie, get him off me!'

But Charlie didn't seem inclined, judging by the fulsome applause and shouts of approval coming from the other side of the wall.

'Hold her down, Gav. Ready with the wet towels?'

Evie, half-laughing, half-screaming, '*No!*'

The sound of the towels flicking on to Evie's presumably bare, wet bottom was indescribably sharp and cruel, making Adam flinch and swallow and claw at the plaster.

Evie sobbed through it, yet it was clear those sobs weren't indicators of distress. Throughout, she kept up a defiant commentary.

'Just wait till I get hold of you, Ben Summers. You've got it coming to you. Ow! You ain't seen me with a whip, have you? I'm good. Shit, that hurts! Stop it!' She broke into wailing as the vicious swish-flick-swish-flick kept up its wince-making rhythm.

'Still got 'er, Gav? Watch her, she's got sharp nails.'

'Look at that arse. Bright red.'

'She loves it.'

'I know she does. Gave her 20 with my belt last week, she came before I'd finished with her.'

'Kinky little bitch, ain't you?'

'Yes, yes, I fucking well am,' she panted. 'Want to make something of it? Ow, ow, ow.'

The towel-lashing came to an end.

'Learnt your lesson, have you? Gonna be a good girl?'

'Yes, sir.'

General laughter.

'That'll be the day.'

'My bum's killing me now.'

'It'll be worse soon, once Charlie's cock's been up it.'

'I want one in my cunt, now. I'm horny as fuck. Please, Ben.'

There were cheers and a shout of 'Ride him, cowgirl!'

'Ah, oh, that's good, you've got such a good one, fills me

right up, mmm.'

Adam screwed shut his eyes and uttered a voiceless howl.

As the grunts and moans grew louder and wilder, he took a tennis ball and threw it against the wall, letting the thump of it drown out some of the sounds of Evie's pleasure.

But not all of it could be disguised. The men's voices rang out as clear as anything.

'That's it, my son, give her one.'

'Got one waiting for you when you finish with him, love.'

'She'll be 11 not out before the game's finished.'

'Bet that vicar wishes he could be in on this. Pervy sod, I reckon he is. What do you say, Evie?'

But Evie could contribute no more than inarticulate ohs and ahs to the conversation.

'Does he spank your bum when you go to Bible study? Does he get you on your knees and give you a mouthful?'

'Oh God, shut up, don't talk about him,' said Evie, finding her voice in extremis. 'You'll spoil my orgasm, you cunt.'

Adam sank to the floor and hid his head in his arms, hot tears springing into his eyes.

It was all so wrong. It could never, ever be right.

He kicked aside a net bag of footballs and slammed out of the cupboard, then he ran across the cricket pitch, faster than he had ever run in his life, all the way to Julia Shields' flat.

She let him in without a word, turning to a cupboard and taking out a bottle of cognac and two glasses.

'No, no,' he said, putting up a hand, then using it to dash the remnants of tears from his eyes. 'Not for me.'

'Drink isn't a demon all the time. Like most demons, actually. A lot of them look pretty attractive and act like good people for a large percentage of the time.'

She poured the brandy and handed a glass to Adam. It

was clear from her face that she wasn't going to brook any refusal, so he took it anyway and twisted the stem in his fingers, avoiding putting the rim to his lips.

'That makes sense,' he muttered.

'Woman troubles?' she asked, sitting on the sofa and patting the cushion beside her.

'Julia, what do you know about Evie? Clearly it's more than you're prepared to tell me. Why won't you tell me?'

Julia took a lugubrious sip of her brandy.

'It's not my place,' she said. 'I can warn you to keep away from her. I can't do much more than that.'

'That's not enough,' he said, bringing a fist down on the sofa arm. 'Why is she used like some kind of sexual talisman? What is it about her?'

'Oh, the cricket thing. I see.'

'What would happen if she said no?'

'The sky would fall in.'

'I'm serious.'

'So am I.'

He shut his eyes and took a breath, too close to blasphemy to trust himself to speak.

'Please, for the love of all that's holy, stop talking in riddles and help me understand.'

'Now listen.' She put her drink down on the coffee table and came to stand behind him, putting long fingers on his shoulders and rubbing them in. 'Poor darling. You're shaking.'

He tried to shrug her off but the series of tremors running down his spine blanked his resistance.

'Evie Witts,' Julia continued, 'wishes you no good. If she pays you attention, it's all part of a game. A nasty game that you can never win. I know you don't want to believe it, my love, but you must.'

'Evie is a victim in all this,' he said, his voice weakened by the increasing waves of pleasure. Julia's hands were confident, her thumbs pressing into the tense muscles at the back of his neck. He shut his eyes and focused on his breathing. 'I'm sure she is. There's somebody behind it all ... I wish I knew – who it was.'

'Put down your drink,' whispered Julia.

He obeyed without reflection. The fumes had unsettled him enough; coupled with Julia's seductive massage, he was in danger of losing his head completely.

'I'm in love with her,' he said, a desperate attempt to shake Julia off that didn't work.

'I know that, sweetheart. Everyone knows it. But she can't love you. She never will. Let it go. Come to the one who wants you.'

Her hands were in his scalp now, easing the pressure so beautifully. His skin fizzed and celebrated, his hair standing on end.

'The one who wants you,' he repeated, voice barely audible.

'Such lovely hair you have,' she told him, running her fingers through it. 'Lustrous, that's the word. And so dark. Dark enough to get lost in. I always wanted dark hair, but I'm the palest thing imaginable. I'm drawn to the dark, though. Perhaps because of my own pallor. Who knows?'

Adam's breathing lost its hard-won regularity as she began to twist coils of hair around her fingers, then she lowered her lips to his ear and spoke directly into it.

'God made you desirable, Adam Flint. Why would he do that if he didn't mean for you to be desired?'

'Temptation,' he murmured. 'To show strength of purpose.'

'What purpose?' She kissed the tip of his ear.

'Purity.'

'This world is impure. You belong in this world. Purity is so terribly overrated.'

She licked a little trail downwards to beneath his earlobe, the tip of her tongue pointed and probing. His breath hitched.

153

'Besides, you're anything but chaste, Mr Flint. Virginity doesn't equal chastity. Everyone knows you like to watch.'

He panicked at that and tried to rear up, but Julia pressed her hands hard on his shoulders and pinched, her nails digging into the black cloth of his shirt.

'Shh, don't, darling. Don't resist it, don't deny it.'

'What do you want from me? Why are you doing this?'

'I'm giving you what you need, for the pleasure of it. Because I want you, Adam. Very badly indeed.'

'Nobody ever wants me.'

'You try to repel them, with all your gloom and your talk of sin and your whiff of sulphur. Not literally, I mean. You smell rather nice. But you know what I mean. If you'd let that go, you'd be fending them off.'

She kissed the spot that her tongue-tip had recently bathed, then moved her lips down his neck. Tiny frissons unknotted his stomach and hardened his cock. Evie and the sports cupboard seemed very far away.

'You think I'm attractive.'

'Aw, bless you, fishing for compliments. You *are* attractive. Those lovely scared eyes, that flawless skin. Long limbs like a colt. Do you work out?'

'No. I walk a lot.'

'And you abstain from all pleasure. I suppose it keeps you fit and toned, if nothing else.'

'All flesh is grass.'

She laughed and gave his neck a playful lick.

'Negative,' she said. 'I don't like the taste of grass.'

Events were a long way out of his control. How had he lost his grasp on his morality, his certainties, his entire philosophy of life so easily? Was it the pervasive taint of Saxonhurst, or was he simply weak? He had worked so hard, all his life, at avoiding weakness, all for this – his toil and labour washed away by the easy blandishments of these Saxonhurst women.

'So you aren't going to tell me about Evie?'

154

'I'm not in the mood for telling. I'm in the mood for showing. Let it all out. Let all the bad feelings go, my love, so I can fill you up with the good ones. Let me help you.'

Her kisses on his neck grew more forceful, the vibrations they sent through him full-blooded, irresistible. His code of ethics was a balloon, floating up through the top of his head and up and away, far away, out of reach.

'Come to bed.'

'Julia, please, no.' He tried to stand but his legs didn't want to support his weight.

She gave his shoulders a final squeeze and hurried around to face him, pushing herself between his clenched legs and kneeling on the edge of the sofa there. Hooking one arm around the back of his neck, she yanked him into a kiss even fiercer than the one at the seaside, accepting nothing but full surrender until he fought back even harder, using his tongue, using his hands to envelop her, bringing her close until her trimly-skirted pubis ground against the bulge in his trousers.

She forced him to accept that he wanted and needed this contact, this connection, this liberation. Kissing as if it would save his life, he pressed his palm against her silk shirt, feeling the outline of a nipple poking through from inside its lace confines. She was excited, she desired him. The roar of power this knowledge sent straight to his head drove him to further exploration. He tugged her shirt from the waistband of her skirt and pushed his hand up inside, over her flat stomach and her protuberant ribs, up to her bra cups. The lace crackled and grazed against his skin. He closed his fingers over the little mounds, testing them for resistance, shape, texture. They felt every bit as satisfying as he'd imagined they would, in his off-guard moments.

She purred into his mouth, rotating her hips against his pelvis.

He delved inside a bra cup and rolled the gorgeously firm, round nipple he found there between his fingers, gently at first, then harder as her moans seemed to request.

'Oh God,' she gasped, breaking off from the scouring excavations of their tongues, 'you've got the touch.'

'Really?' He was more flattered than he could say.

'Really. But this isn't about me.'

She set herself to loosening his clerical collar and reaching behind him to undo his buttons. He sat almost immobile, watching her at work, fascinated by the twin flushes in her usually pale cheeks, the sheen of her brow, the unaccustomed sparkle in her eyes. She looked astonishingly pretty and, oh God, why had the word *fuckable* popped into his head? Was it even a word?

She is so fuckable like this, with her just-kissed lips and her lust glaze and the way her chest rises and falls and her throat is bare and asking for my teeth to …

He was painfully hard. He had to stop thinking these thoughts. There was no way he could stop thinking these thoughts.

Indeed, he was still struggling with his resolve when Julia lifted his shirt off him. He raised his arms, helping her, absent-mindedly obedient to her will.

'Oh, you're lovely, such a lovely thing,' she said, then she was rubbing her head between his pectoral muscles and then, oh, what was this? She flicked her tongue swiftly and skilfully over one of his nipples and he nearly bent double with the pang of pure lust she aroused in him.

He moaned and put his hands in her hair, throwing his own head back against the sofa top. It was useless now, he was defeated. Until his cock found relief, he would not be able to stop her.

She spent a long time lavishing his nipples with her attention and kisses and licks and nips and sucks. He twisted and squirmed underneath her, moving one hand to his crotch in a sly attempt to get himself off before anything more inflammatory happened.

But she thwarted his plan, grasping at his wrist and

playfully biting the nipple she had been feasting on.

'No, no,' she rebuked. 'Not yet. I want you to come in my mouth.'

He cried out at that, fatally unmanned. Why had the Lord made this such a delirious pleasure if it was sinful? How could this ever be fair? Man couldn't win against such odds.

Julia unbuckled his belt and made swift work of releasing his cock from its restraints. He couldn't look, but he could feel her breath wafting its gentle warmth around his shaft. Her hands parted his thighs a little more, then he felt her bury her face between them, licking and kissing at the soft inner flesh, the top of her head bumping exquisitely against his heavy balls so that they were caressed by her hair.

He covered his face with his hands, as if this might absolve him in some way from any responsibility, and let her do what she wanted.

He let her whisper sweet breaths over his sac and up his shaft, then paint his cock with the teasing tip of her tongue. He let her investigate his foreskin, pulling it back with eager fingers so she could bathe his uncovered end, wrapping her lips around it and subjecting it to a thorough tongue bath.

By the time she came to take him, inch by inch, into her mouth, he was so close to orgasm he despaired of lasting longer than a minute or so. He wanted it to last longer, to luxuriate in his sin now that it was inevitable, to gather all that pleasure inside him and store it for the long, lonely nights.

She cupped his balls and lowered her lips still further, sucking at him with a force he was surprised she possessed, being such a wisp of a thing herself.

She drew sensation from the crown of his head, the tips of his toes, all the extremities of his body, and made it rush pell-mell to his velvet-sheathed cock. He felt like the national grid, lit up, alive with electricity. The power surged through him, leaving him weak and tremulous, then he cried out as he filled Julia's mouth. Oh, if he could capture this feeling, remember it in its exquisite entirety, he would have riches for ever.

She looked up at him, her spark of triumph catching him like a barb. Unease possessed him; a sense that she now had a hold over him he might find difficult to escape. And yet ... She was attractive, and she liked him and ...

Evie's face transferred itself to his consciousness and he let his head fall back again, groaning. Julia swallowed loudly and released his cock, inch by inch, with teasing slowness.

'Such a privilege,' she said in a low purr. 'The first taste.' She kissed his now-flaccid prick, then sat back on her heels. 'Oh good Lord. You look as if you might burst into tears. Do cheer up.'

'I've crossed the line,' he said, to himself. 'I've crossed it. I'm damned.'

'*I'm* damned. What a lot of nonsense, Adam. Good God. Men have blowjobs every day – some of them are clergymen. Why ever do you think it would damn them?'

Adam tried to think. He didn't even know any more. Where had his sexual mores come from? Did he have sexual mores? Had all these Saxonhurst sex fiends been right all along?

'Julia,' he said, looking at the ceiling, trying to focus on a lightshade. He repeated her name, singing it this time, Beatles-style.

'Oh dear,' she said, less robustly. She came to sit beside him, rubbing his hand with sympathetic gentleness. 'This must be rather epoch-making for you. I don't mean to be a bitch.'

'You aren't,' he said, turning his eyes to her. 'You give me attention I don't deserve. I wish I knew why.'

'I've told you why,' she said patiently. 'Because I like you. I fancy you. I want to take you to bed. In fact, I want to keep you there. Wouldn't you rather be in my bed than that cold old church?'

He shut his eyes and nodded.

'Come on, then. I've got so much I want to show you.'

Julia's bed was clean and white, in a clean, white room that smelled of lilies. She led him to its foot by her hand and then stood in front of him, smiling warmly.

'I want you to undress me, Adam,' she said. 'Will you do that for me?'

He was already naked, having left his trousers on the living room floor and his shirt and collar on the sofa. He'd had to remove his boots and socks before entering the bedroom too.

His reply was to reach out his fingers to Julia's shirt buttons and undo them, neither slowly nor quickly, but in a kind of dislocated trance. It was already out of the skirt waistband following his earlier explorations, so it slipped easily down her arms, revealing to his sight her pale pink lacy bra. Such a trim little stomach, such an elegant neck and fragile collarbone, he thought. She was nothing like Evie, with her spillage of flesh, her indecent profusion of breast. But Julia's slightness hid a strength he could almost feel in his bones. She was more than a match for him, more than a match for Evie too. Why had he underestimated her?

He reached around her waist for her skirt zip, then helped the garment over Julia's hips.

'That's the boy,' she said, letting it fall to the floor and stepping out. Her knickers were also pale pink and lacy. Behind the oyster scalloping, he could see tendrils of darker hair. Unlike Evie, who was shaven. He shut his eyes, remembering the image of her at the maypole.

Julia, in her underwear, coltish of limb, bold of gaze. She was an invitation to sin. He was going to take it.

Obligingly, she turned around to grant access to her bra hooks. He was grateful at not having to reach behind, sure he would have fumbled and taken too long. Instead, he slid them from their eyes and pushed the straps down.

'Touch them,' whispered Julia.

159

He held the little mounds in his hands, enjoying the friction of palm and nipple. A woman's body was pleasant to the touch. This was how men fell ... But it was good to have the knowledge. Forewarned was forearmed.

I am better equipping myself to fight the devil.

He put his lips to Julia's neck and kissed it, unprompted. She sighed and leant into him.

'Oh, fast learner. Keep doing that to my nipples and I'll come here and now, oh sweet God, you're a natural.'

No, I'm an unnatural. Always have been, always will be.

'You like it?'

'Damn right. You?'

'Yes.'

'Good. Knickers.'

Still behind her, he pushed his fingers into the knicker elastic and lowered them. She bent slightly as they fell down her thighs, and her bottom brushed against his cock. He felt that low-down spark in the pit of his stomach, the first sign of approaching erection.

Her buttocks were trim, pert and toned – by no means as lusciously spankable as Evie's, but all the same, here was a woman's arse, and it was in his reach, and he could have it if he wanted. He cupped it in his hands, unable to resist taking a handful of it.

'You're an arse man, are you, Adam?'

'Stop it. Stop being so coarse.'

'You are, though. I know it.'

He didn't reply, busy assessing the qualities of Julia's bottom. It looked as if a few medium-strength swats might break it. He needed a robust pair of cheeks, like Evie's. There was an arse that could take a real thrashing. His cock swelled again at the thought. The way it had looked when he rubbed in that lotion ...

Julia wriggled her hips and tipped her neck back to look up at him.

'I want some attention elsewhere, love. Let me lie down

and I'll show you where and what to do.'

She took her stealthy, feline little body to the bed and settled herself on her back. Adam watched as she scissored her legs apart and drew them up at the knees, giving him a full view of her parted lips and the lush pink-and-redness within.

'Come and touch me.' She patted her pubis, with its down of dark blonde hair. 'Right here. Come and take a look. Find your way around.'

He stood like a startled rabbit for a moment, then the mysterious territory of ridges and whorls, underhung by the soft half-moons of her bottom cheeks, drew him forwards and he knelt on the bed.

'Do you need my help?' Julia whispered, holding out a hand.

Adam shook his head hurriedly. He knew what was what and where was where. As an adolescent, he had spent a very long time studying his human biology textbook, the closest he'd ever got to pornography. He knew all about the female reproductive organs, though he'd given up hope of ever seeing them in flesh.

Prematurely, it seemed, because now here was a splendid example, open and ready to receive his attentions. He bent lower, inspecting the split lips and the complex of folds inside them. Dismal jokes about how men could never locate the clitoris came into his mind, but he was not one of those men. He could see it right there, ripe and deep pink. It looked too tender to touch, though, as if it were raw or something. Would it hurt Julia if he just ...

'Touch it. Touch me.'

His hand strayed closer. The promised land, he thought irrelevantly, irritating himself. Was he able to forget the Bible for one moment? Now he felt her heat radiating outwards to his fingers. She would be wet and slippery and have that strong, alluring scent. He could smell it now. He wanted to plunge himself into it, take it, take her. The tip of

161

one finger touched the outer part of her lips, stroking the wiry hairs.

He felt her twitch beneath him. She wanted more.

He turned his hand sideways and slipped all four fingertips between the inner lips. Such warmth, such soft, giving flesh, smooth and glistening. He stroked up and down, small movements, circling her bud, watching it grow and push itself forward more prominently than before. This was a feature of female desire, he had read, all those years ago. The clitoris, emerging from its hood, engorged with blood. He felt a little detached, as if he was watching a nature documentary, but Julia said, 'Please, Adam, use your fingers, touch it,' and he got to work.

It was incredible to see the effect his manipulation of that little knot of flesh had on Julia. She began to moan and pant and wriggle fit to twist the sheets and pull them out of their tucks. The power she had exerted over him when she had him in her mouth had been reversed. Now he wielded it. He could give her pleasure or he could withhold it. The choice was intoxicatingly his.

Rubbing away, he watched the colour bloom in her cheeks, and a sheen appear on her forehead. She looked at him with imploring eyes, as if amazed that he could do this to her.

He smiled.

This was what he was good at. At last he had found it.

'Stick your fingers inside me,' she panted. 'Fuck me with them. Please.'

Oh, he could do that. Keeping his thumb engaged with her clit, he fed first his forefinger, then his index and ring fingers up inside the hot, tight, yielding little passage underneath. She sucked him in, her walls contracting around his digits, as if she meant to imprison them there. But he had the upper hand and he withdrew them a little way before pushing them back.

'Oh God, you're good, you can't say you haven't done

this before … Oh yes.'

He kept his rhythm slow and precise, yet at the same time his thumb on her clit was merciless, driving her towards that precipice he had seen Evie on, so often. Too often.

Then something else occurred to him, and he pivoted down at the hips until he loomed over Julia. Her nipples, right there, just where he could get at them. Taking one in his mouth, he rolled the other in his free hand, still working the wrist of his other furiously. Now fully occupied with the occupation of Julia, he licked and twiddled and frigged like a man possessed until he felt the sweet surrender shudder through her. Her orgasmic cries were celestial music to him, something he was given freely, something he took as his right.

It felt like so many things – freedom, victory, generosity, connection, happiness. What it didn't feel like was sin.

He waited for her vibrations to slow, for her movements to still, then he kissed her lips.

'Oh my boy,' she slurred. There were tears in her eyes, and he kissed those too. 'I won't let them have you.'

He lay down beside her. His cock was hard, but he wasn't hell-bent on dealing with it, as he had been earlier. He had given to her, and that seemed by far the higher priority. His own relief could wait until he was in the shower.

He raised his fingers to his nose and gave them a curious sniff. Julia, at his fingertips. He had given her pleasure. He felt like a king.

Vanity of vanities. All is vanity.

'Was that – all right?' he asked.

Her low chuckle satisfied his pride.

'All right, darling? It was absolutely all right. You are tuned in. You know the frequency, you uncanny little whore.'

He widened his eyes. She called him a whore!

'That was uncalled for,' he said sniffily.

163

'Darling, I meant it as a compliment. You should do it professionally. You're that good.'

Adam's head hurt with all the reversals of his concepts of good and bad. He was good at a bad thing. Did that make him intrinsically bad?

'I understand the lure of sin now,' he said.

'Oh God, don't start with all that again. Sin hurts people. Sex doesn't. Well, unless you like a bit of SM, of course. Does that float your boat, vicar?'

He sat up in bed. The world swam before his eyes. He couldn't pin down an emotion or a sentiment that would describe the way he felt. Looking at Julia, it wasn't clear whether he saw a lover or a demon, sent to corrupt him.

'You've gone terribly pale,' she said, raising a solicitous hand to his brow. 'As if all that good sexing has drained the life from you.'

'I'm sorry, I have to … Do you mind if I use your shower?'

'Not at all. It's through that door.'

He sat in the cubicle and let scalding hot water stream on to him until his skin was lobster red. The heat only seemed to harden his cock even more, though, and he saw no alternative than to kill it with masturbation. His seed splashed on to the ceramic tray, mingling with the steam and water, disappearing down the plughole.

He crouched on the floor and wept.

When the time came to switch off, he found he couldn't stand. He felt sick and his vision grew darker and darker until all was black.

When he came to, he was still in the shower, though Julia had switched off the water and stood over him in a bathrobe, her face tight with concern.

'Why on earth did you have it so hot?' she scolded. 'I'm surprised you didn't blister your skin. You silly, silly boy. Come on. Can you stand up now?'

She helped him to his feet and back to the bed, on which

he collapsed.

She brought him a glass of water and some biscuits.

'Get your strength back. I'm not surprised you were feeling a bit – sapped.'

'What am I going to do?'

He sipped at the water, turning tragic eyes to Julia.

She kissed his cheek.

'Do what you want to do, Adam. Have you ever done that?'

He shook his head. 'I mean, about Evie. I'm sorry, Julia. I like you very much, so very much, but I can't bear to see Evie with all those other men any more ... I just can't. I worry I'm going to lose control and kill them.'

Julia sighed and fidgeted with the belt of her robe.

'You know, my advice would be to stay away from her. But I don't suppose for one moment you'll be able to do that. Perhaps if I spoke to her ...'

'She doesn't listen to anyone.'

'Yes, she does. I know she does. Listen, Adam, leave it with me. Give yourself a break and try not to see her for a few days. You need some time to wind down, I think, or you're going to give yourself a stroke. And not the right kind of stroke either.'

She winked at him, but he was too doleful to brighten up.

He knew he was on the edge now, close to being consumed by his obsessions. Somebody had to save him and, for the first time he could remember, he didn't think he could put that faith in God.

Chapter Thirteen

Evie's feet were bare and her hair streamed out behind her as she ran along the path to Palmers Barn. Sultry June had turned to scorching July and the grass verges were slowly changing from lush green to yellowish and tickly.

When John emerged from the well at her summoning, he was on magnificent form, looking hale and hearty as a spirit could.

'You performed the sporting rite?' he said. 'I know you must have done. I am closer than ever to my flesh.'

'Yes, I did it. All was well. But, John, I still fear for the vicar.'

'Why?'

'It's happening too fast, too soon. And the Shields woman has warned me.'

'Warned you of what?'

'That he can't wait another two months. He won't wait. He is too close to self-destruction. He's even talked about killing my other lovers.'

'Well, I know how he must feel. If they didn't keep me alive, I would contemplate their murder myself. It is a paradoxical position for a man to find himself in. Come here, my Evangeline. Embrace me.'

In his arms, she continued to speak, her voice low and anxious.

'Shields thinks I should leave the village for a while, and I can see her point. Absence makes the heart grow fonder. If I write to him, I can keep him on the string without him going over the top, d'you know what I mean? And I've got a chance to go and do a film shoot in the south of France. Seb and Kasia want to do a beach orgy movie. So that might work really well for me. What do you think?'

'The Shields woman – I wonder at her motives. None of her kind has ever been on our side.'

'I know. She wants him for herself. But I don't think he wants her. He's dying for me, John, I'm sure of it. He wouldn't go after Julia Shields, no matter how much she flaunted herself in front of him. He's a vicar, ain't he? He'll be faithful and chaste and all that kind of thing.'

'No man can be chaste when he sees you in his visions. You have already driven him into a fever of lust. I see the quandary, however. A fever of lust is a dangerous thing and cannot be kept at a simmer until the harvest. Perhaps it's as well if you do go away. Perhaps it will give him time to let his emotions steep. When you return, he will be at your mercy.'

'So I'll tell Seb and Kasia yes, then?'

'Perhaps you should. And now, put the preacher from your mind and unbutton my breeches.'

When Evie told him she was going away, Adam tried to change her mind.

She was sitting on his desk, swinging her long brown legs, eating an ice pop. The ice pop was purple and it stained her lips, making him picture himself smearing blackberries over them.

'Where are you going?'

'France. Nice, I think. Nice in Nice, ennit?' She grinned at her own wit.

'Who are you going with?'

'Seb and Kasia.'

He felt his facial muscles tense into a ferocious scowl.

'Oh.'

'It's a work thing. Got to earn the crust, ain't I?'

'When you come to me, you'll have to give all that up.'

'What, my job? What if I don't want to?'

'I'm a vicar. I can't be married to a porn actress.'

Evie stared.

'Married? You're a bit previous, ain't you?'

'I'm not going to live in sin with you.'

'Hark at him! Living in sin. So, come on, then. Where's my proposal?'

Adam, caught out and forced into action, looked around the room as if for an escape route before taking the ice pop from Evie's hand and pulling her to her feet.

'Evie Witts,' he said, dropping to one knee. 'Will you marry me?'

He felt ridiculous, a character in a play. This couldn't be reality, proposing to the beautiful woman who had slept with every man in Saxonhurst except for him.

She giggled. 'I really think you're serious.'

'Yes,' he said, a mite crossly. 'Yes, of course I am.'

'Of course you are. You always are. You're very sweet, Adam, but can I think about it? I've never really thought about marriage.'

'Marry me and I'll get you away from all this.'

'All what?'

'All this sordid reality. Having to do these things for Saxonhurst. Who chose you for this? Who is making you do it?'

She tried to tug her hands out of Adam's grip, her face suddenly scared.

'Nobody. Let go of me. Nobody pulls my strings. I do what I want.'

Her voice was defiant, but Adam saw the unease in her expression and knew he was close to the truth.

'You could just tell me and it would all be over. We could leave this place together, go and live somewhere far away. You could be yourself and I could love you.'

'You already do,' she said tauntingly. 'Or else why are

you proposing to me?'

'Say yes,' he urged. 'We could leave today. I'll take you to France.'

'I can't,' she said. 'Don't ask me to. Let me go and I promise I'll think about it. Please?'

Reluctantly, Adam loosened his grip on her and rose to his full height again, feeling foolish, wishing he could take back the past few minutes, or weeks, or months. In fact, if he could just avoid ever coming to Saxonhurst, that would be perfect.

'I'll write to you,' she said softly. 'Or something. Have you got Skype?'

'No.'

She tutted. 'Luddite. You've got email, though?'

'Yes.'

'I'll email you then. I should go. Got to pack.'

'Evie,' he put out a hand, preventing her attempt at a flit away. 'How long will you be gone for?'

'About six weeks, Kasia said.'

'I'll miss you.'

'Aww. I'll miss you too, love. I won't be gone long.'

He couldn't remove his hand from her shoulder. Surely now, surely she must kiss him?

'Evie.' He bent his head towards her, his heart beating faster with each inch of distance covered. 'Let me kiss you.'

'I can't. I can't. If I do, it'll all be too soon.'

She snatched up the melting ice pop and shoved it into her mouth, twisting and turning under his hand until the only way he could keep her still was under duress.

He took his hand away.

'Why?' he asked. 'Why will it be too soon?'

'I'm only asking you to wait.' Her voice was high and a little panicked now.

Adam watched her make her escape. Once she was at the door, she softened.

'Please,' she said. 'Wait for me. I'm on my way to you. I

just need a little time.'

She left and he turned to the desk, where a puddle of purple juice dripped on to the carpet.

That night, the dream returned.

Tribulation Smith stood outside his bedroom door, turning a key in a lock. Inside the room, he heard the weeping of Evangeline.

'You cannot keep me prisoner here. Let me go.'

'You are my wife. You cannot leave me.'

'I bear you no love. There is nothing I can give you.'

'You will give me yourself.'

A pause.

'Is there nothing I can do or say to sway you?'

Tribulation shook his head, although she couldn't see him.

'You are mine, and will ever be.'

'Then I cannot fight the will of God. Come in. Come to bed.'

Was it then so easy to gain her capitulation? Surely she sought to sweeten him for some further assault. Yet her voice, so seductive and low, beguiled him beyond reason.

He opened the door.

Evangeline sat on the bed in her nightgown, holding the taper that had lit her way to the chamber. As soon as she saw him, she smiled and dropped the lit candle on to the bed, where it quickly set fire to the cover.

'Evangeline!' He dashed forward in alarm, taking the pitcher from the bedside and emptying it on to the smouldering linens. In the time it took him to do this, Evangeline had gone.

Out of the house he ran, seeking her shadow, listening for the tread of her foot. Where had she run to?

Not to the old crooked house she had shared with her kinswomen, nor to the church, nor to any of the darkened, shuttered cottages huddled around the village green. She must have taken one of the footpaths though the fields.

He bellowed her name, hearing it echo around the timber frames of the village. From behind a cloud, the moon appeared and with it a flood of silver light. In that light, he caught sight of something, no more than a movement, but he followed it, along the footpath that led from the northern end of the village.

It was a lonely, little frequented path, for the southern road led to many more destinations. The grass grew high, almost obscuring the little dirt track. His legs swished through the vegetation, gaining on the figure ahead.

Past an old well, she ran to a shack, a tumbledown, hastily constructed affair that could not have been there long. He watched her enter and slowed his pace. She had not realised he followed her. He would retrieve her with ease. But was she alone, or did this shack house someone? The lover who had taken his bride's maidenhead?

He stole up, as quietly as he could, keeping low out of the moonlight.

Soon he heard voices, Evangeline's shrill and weepy, blending with a male voice that rose in anger.

By the time he reached the shack, the voices had stilled. The place had no windows to peer into; all he could do was creep around to the entrance and try to fit his eye to the many gaps.

Inside, there was low light from a candle. A bed of rags in the corner was occupied by Evangeline, who lay in the arms of a man.

'We shall leave for Taunton as soon as you are ready,' he said. 'Now that you have come to me, nothing holds me in Saxonhurst. Besides, the witchfinder will be back, and this time he will take you too.'

'What of my husband?'

'Call him not your husband.' The man spat on the floor. 'The preacher, you mean? What can he do? He is already a laughing stock for marrying a witch. He will be too proud to

171

pursue you.'

'I do not know that you are right. He is close to madness, John.'

'You are enough to drive any man to it.'

He kissed her. Smith's fists clenched.

'He will seek us out. I shall never feel safe.'

Smith carried a blade in his belt, the legacy of the civil war when no man was safe from sudden assault. He took it now and unsheathed it, holding it up to the moonlight. This, beyond doubt, was the man who had deflowered his Evangeline. This was John Calderwood, coven master and fugitive.

Before he had considered the consequences, Smith forced open the door. Evangeline screamed and hid behind Calderwood, who rose to his feet.

'Speak of the devil,' he sneered.

'It is you! You who are the devil,' blustered Smith, beside himself. 'You are the evil influence on this village and you must be flushed out.'

Calderwood swaggered up to him until their faces almost touched.

'Say you? Evil? It was not I who caused innocent women to swing. It was not I who forced a maid to wed against her wishes.'

'It was not against her wishes. She consented.'

'In fear of her life, yes.'

'She is my wife.'

'No, Preacher, she is mine. We are wed, perhaps not in a ceremony you would recognise, but a true knot was sealed, some months ago.'

'You have not wed her, you have simply violated her. That is not a marriage in the eyes of God.'

'You have no claim on her.'

'She is mine.'

'Shall we let her choose? Shall we make that Evangeline's decision?'

'It is God's will that she be mine.'

'Who do you choose, Evangeline?' Calderwood tossed the question over his shoulder. 'Only you can end this quarrel.'

'You know I choose you. I choose John Calderwood.'

Smith made an incoherent sound of mingled rage and pain. The blade he clutched recalled itself to him and he drew back his hand.

Calderwood saw it too late.

'Now this is not –' he said, but he never finished the sentence. For the blade plunged deep into his heart, putting an end to all words.

It seemed to Smith that he took a long time to die. Evangeline rushed to him, screaming and sobbing, putting her hand over the wound, trying to stop the blood that pumped everywhere, including all over Smith.

All he could do was watch. The world had slowed down. Perhaps it might even stop and there would be Calderwood, suspended between life and death for ever while he, Tribulation Smith, experienced an eternity of the knowledge of his mortal sin.

After an age of mourning and wailing and blood, Calderwood hit the dirt floor, all the light out of his eyes, the shell of the man who had stood there seconds before.

I have killed a man.

Evangeline looked up at him once and he shrank from the anguish and hatred in her eyes.

'You have killed the father of my child,' she said.

Smith, unable to bear the implications of her words, took flight.

His hands stained with blood, his limbs moving only mechanically, as if beyond his own agency, he threw a rope over the strongest limb of the yew tree …

Adam woke up, shouting words he didn't understand.

The dream was more horrible than he could process at first. He needed to get out of bed, to pace up and down, to go to the kitchen and make tea, before he could settle his thoughts.

The clock read 3.47. He couldn't go back to sleep. He was afraid to go back to sleep.

Instead, he dressed and walked into the churchyard, shivering with horror as he passed the yew tree.

At Julia's flat, all the lights were off, unsurprisingly, but he rang the doorbell all the same.

There was no reply, so he rang again. Still nothing.

Perhaps she was afraid to answer her door at this time of night. He took out his phone and rang her, standing on the doorstep with the mobile to his ear, marvelling at how profoundly dark the village was at night.

The call went to voicemail. He shrugged, sighed, and made his way down the path, back towards the village green. Perhaps a walk ... But nowhere near Palmers Barn, which appeared to occupy the very site of that shack in his dream.

It was as if the whole village had switched itself off. Not even a cat prowled, or a fox menaced a chicken coop. The night was so still he thought he could hear the snores of the sleeping villagers behind the curtained windows. All dreaming, all except for him.

Memories of his nightmare occluded his thoughts, turning the tranquillity of the village into something more sinister. His skin prickled and every corner seemed to turn to John Calderwood's shack.

He stopped at the manor house gates and looked bleakly through them, thinking of the earlier building and what had taken place there. Witch trials, abductions, torture. He shuddered and turned away, but his attention was caught for a moment by light in one of the upstairs windows.

He looked harder and detected a shadow of somebody in the room.

But they had all gone to France, hadn't they? Taking Evie with them.

Maybe a housesitter, he thought. But he was uneasy. He

174

had spoken to Sebastian before they left, just a light conversational exchange outside the shop, and he had mentioned that the house would be empty.

Here was something to chase the dream away. An investigation. Taking a deep breath, he walked on to the spot where the wall curved round into the woodland and followed it round, knowing where to find the little broken-down section that could be climbed. The thicket was intensely dark and eerily quiet. Adam felt something ancient and primitive in the air, something he would almost describe as evil. It was if unseen eyes watched him. Once or twice, he almost called out in bravado, but he persuaded himself that the dream had put him in a strange frame of mind and he should ignore his errant thoughts.

He blundered his way through, snapping twigs and tripping on roots, until he found that part of the wall he had climbed over before. He was quick, weaving through the trees until he arrived at the moonlit back lawn. The pool was empty, its cover spread over it, and the tennis court had no net. The gardens were still fragrant, though, and the swinging chairs lazed on the veranda, waiting to be occupied by lascivious bodies.

All the curtains were drawn across the French doors, so he couldn't see inside, but he walked slowly around the perimeter of the house, trying to find a window he might peer into.

It appeared to be a fruitless task. Even at the front, great wooden shutters were drawn against the outside world.

He looked up again at that lit window. The light was still on. Had he imagined the figure? Perhaps it was just for security.

He marched up to the front door and rang the bell. If it was thieves, he could disturb them, at least. He imagined them haring over the back lawn, arms full of computers and film equipment.

The lit window opened but by the time he'd looked up,

the face had gone and the window was shut again.

His heart thundered. He was close to solving a mystery. He hoped the solution would be a benign one. He stood on the step, looking out into the night, until he heard footsteps behind the door and he turned back. The noise of locks carried on for some time, but eventually the door swung open.

'Julia!'

She smiled delightedly. 'Adam, it *is* you. Do come in.'

'But what are you doing here?'

'At four o'clock in the morning, I could ask you the same question.'

She stood, grinning from ear to ear, in a silk bathrobe and satin slippers.

He looked around to make sure nobody was watching, and followed Julia into the entrance hall.

'Couldn't you sleep either?' she asked in a conversational tone. 'I meant to go to bed, but I found all this *stuff* in one of the spare rooms and I couldn't resist a look. I'm afraid I've been in there all night.'

'Stuff?' said Adam vaguely, walking into the main reception room after her.

'You know. Sex toys and equipment and all sorts. Fascinating. I'll show you.'

'Oh, you needn't bother,' he said, suddenly aware of how tired he was. 'Look, what are you doing here? Did Seb and Kasia invite you to housesit?'

'God, no. They wouldn't be so stupid. They know that they'd never get me out, once I was in.'

'Julia, please tell me you didn't break and enter.'

'Of course I didn't. I kept back a set of keys.'

'That doesn't make it legal.'

'It's not right that this house is theirs,' she said, eyes narrowing as she sat down on a cream leather sofa, beside Adam. 'It's not right that they've filled it with all this awful furniture. It looks like some stupid soap opera set now. I want all my dark wood back, my antiques, my beautiful ormolu clock and my Victorian escritoire.'

'Julia,' he said gently, 'you don't own this house any more.'

'Morally I do.'

'No,' he said, more firmly. 'Morally you don't.'

'I'm not leaving,' she said. 'Never. This is the seat of the Shields. They'll have to kill me and carry my body out in a coffin.'

'Julia, for heaven's sake!'

'I mean it. Don't try and talk me out of it. I won't listen. Anyway,' she said, turning to him, 'why are you here?'

'I saw the light.'

'Marvellous! But I thought you vicars all saw the light long ago. Sorry. I shouldn't tease you, even if you are so beautifully teasable. So you were out for a walk in the dead of night, were you?'

'Actually,' he confessed, 'I was looking for you.'

The way her face brightened at his words was both wonderful and mystifying to Adam.

'You were? Darling, I know you've been confused but now, with Evie gone –'

'I had a dream. I think you can explain it to me.'

'Oh. I see.'

'Tribulation Smith killed John Calderwood and then committed suicide. Am I right?'

Julia nodded.

'Just my luck,' she drawled. 'Dream lover comes to me in the middle of the night and wants to talk about 17th century history.'

'Yes. It's history,' he said fiercely. 'But why am I dreaming about it? Why is it happening to *me*? And so vividly. Every detail ... And the girl is Evie. And Smith – well, Smith is apparently me. Why is it happening, Julia?'

'How should I know? That book of Lydford's. Vivid imagination.' She shrugged, but her eyes were guarded.

'Where is the book of Lydford's? I want to read it to the end.'

'You can't. He never finished it.'

'I still want to read it.'

'I don't have it. Look,' she said, speaking over Adam's increasingly frustrated expostulations. 'I can tell you all about it. Are you sitting comfortably?'

He grimaced, but leant back in the sofa as if ready for story time.

'Then I'll begin. Saxonhurst has always had its rituals. The one you saw, for Robin Goodfellow, is one of the earliest. Nobody knows how far it goes back, but it certainly pre-dates the Civil War. For centuries, people left Saxonhursters alone to our funny little ways. There was, I believe, always an "Evie" – a village girl at the heart of the rituals.'

'Why did it all start?'

'I've told you. Nobody knows. Presumably it used to be more widespread, but gradually died out everywhere else. Now it's only us carrying it on. I don't know if it's behind our amazing harvests, but I don't think anyone wants to test it.'

'It's ludicrous.' Adam shook his head but Julia shushed him.

'So it seems, to a modern mind set. But we're not big on modernity here in Saxonhurst. And neither are you, are you, darling? But your archaic attitudes are different to ours – that's all.'

'Mine are from God.'

'You keep on telling yourself that. Anyway, this was Saxonhurst, carrying on in its merry little way until the Civil War happened and we had Puritans and witchfinders crawling everywhere. You know how that affected us. Saxonhurst was deemed a village of witches and heathens. Tribulation Smith was sent to clean it up, but he couldn't do it alone and the witchfinder was called in.'

'Who was John Calderwood?'

'An ancestor of mine.'

'Of yours?'

'Yes. He should have been lord of the manor, but his father disinherited him after some scandal or disgrace. He set himself up as a coven master and tried to start a cult of some sort. Obviously the Cromwellians took a dim view.'

'He said he was married to Evie.'

'I suppose they did some daft binding ritual or other. She was pregnant by him, though, and eight months after all the business with Tribulation Smith, she gave birth to a daughter.'

'And was she all right? Was her life – all right?'

'I don't really know. I suppose the village rallied round. They look after their own, in Saxonhurst.'

'I see. She looked exactly like Evie.'

'That whole clan does – the women, anyway. Have you met her grandmother?'

'Yes.'

'Exquisitely beautiful woman. She did all the ritual stuff before Evie.'

'So she's doomed, by her blood, to be this village – sex toy.'

'Ah, you're going to start all that salvation stuff again, aren't you? Hasn't your dream taught you anything?'

'What do you mean?'

'You can't save Evie. She doesn't want to be saved. She has a Calderwood of her own, and you're their pawn.'

'I don't understand you. What Calderwood of her own? Who?'

Julia rubbed tired eyes with her fingertips.

'Listen, darling. Bad things happen to vicars who get involved with Evie and her forebears. Take it from me. You don't want to follow in their footsteps.'

'What bad things?'

'J.E. Lydford. He went mad. Ask Evie's grandmother all

179

about it. She knows.'

Adam could only stare.

'That Victorian missionary. It was him who was killed at Palmers Barn. Another Evangeline was right there at the scene.'

'I had a dream about him too,' muttered Adam. 'Earlier. He was teaching her about the Bible ...'

'Just like you and Evie, eh?'

'So, look, what you seem to be saying is that if I continue to pursue Evie, I will die. Is that what you're saying?'

'I'm afraid it is. And I really shouldn't be saying it. But I want to warn you, even if it makes me seem insane and simply sends you running far away from me. At least I'll know I tried.'

'Why shouldn't you be saying it?'

Julia sucked at her bottom lip as if unsure whether to say anything more.

'Let's say I might be in for some unpleasant dreams of my own. My ancestors won't be happy with me.'

'They haunt you?'

'Yes. They do. They're very good at it too. They certainly worked their magic on my parents. And my husband.'

'What?'

'The really clever thing is they used me as their vessel. When I was a child. They made me drive my own parents mad with fear. Isn't that cunning of them?'

'Julia ...'

'You don't believe me.'

'Have you ever had proper grief counselling?'

She laughed, a high-pitched shriek that did nothing to reassure Adam's doubts about her sanity.

'Oh dear.' She dabbed her eyes. 'Grief counselling. That's a good one. You're so sweet. So innocent. Despite my best efforts to corrupt you.'

'Ghosts, though. There's no such thing.'

'Oh yes there is. It's why I daren't go to sleep while I'm here.'

'Nightmares.'

'Will you stay with me? They might not come if you're here.'

'I can't control your dreams.'

'You can keep the ghosts away. They won't want you to believe in them. If you believe in them, they lose.'

'I don't begin to understand this, Julia. But you're really afraid, aren't you?'

'I've upset them enough already. Losing the house – marrying who I did … And now I'm telling you, when I shouldn't be. I don't know what they might do.'

Adam considered this for a moment.

'Perhaps if you came back to the vicarage with me.'

And tomorrow I'll make you a doctor's appointment.

'No, I have to stay here. I have to do that much for them. Now that the pornographers are gone, I stand a chance.'

'But they haven't gone for good. They'll be back.'

'They'll have to get the police to evict me. I'm not moving.'

'Julia, this won't work …'

'I don't care.' Her agitation was physical now, her hands trembling.

Adam took one of them in his, wanting very much to drive the demons out of her. He felt a tenderness for her that threw him, since it wasn't part of his plan. This woman was the spanner in his works, but a rather nice spanner all the same. If it wasn't for his all-consuming passion for Evie …

'All right,' he said. 'I'll stay with you. Look, it's half-past four. If we're going to get any sleep at all …'

'The birds have already started. The sun will be up in an hour or so. Come up.'

The bed was a huge wrought iron number with fur-lined manacles attached to the headboard.

'Not mine,' said Julia shortly. 'I suppose they film in

181

here.'

He noted also the mirror on the ceiling and the intense faux-Victorian décor.

'It's a right tart's boudoir,' she said, putting his politer thoughts into words.

She turned to him, smiling through her fatigue.

'Are you going to get undressed?'

She untied her robe and let it drop to the floor, revealing instant nudity.

Adam, taken by surprise, coughed and tried to look away.

'Oh, don't,' she said. 'You've seen it before. Look, see these nipples? They're hard. That's because you're here.'

'Julia – get into bed.'

He took off his jacket and draped it over a chair.

'If I'd known you were coming I'd have given myself a trim.' She ran her fingers over the fuzz at her pubic triangle.

While Adam unbuttoned his shirt, she dared to move closer, reaching out for him. He took her wrist in one hand and held it firmly, keeping her at arm's length.

'I have not come here to fornicate with you,' he said with purpose.

'I know. But now you're here ...' She put one hand beneath her right breast and squeezed it, lifting it to better show off the rosy little nipple.

'Get into bed.' He tried to push her away, but as soon as she was free she leant on the bed post and dipped a finger, infinitely casually, between her thighs.

'Have you ever wanted to taste?' she asked, licking it. 'Mmm. Try it.'

She stepped up to him again, proffering the finger.

He took her by the elbow, smacked her bottom and pushed her on the bed.

'I won't tell you again,' he growled.

Julia, thrilled, slipped under the sheets and pulled them up to her chin.

'Oh my goodness, slap and tickle!' she exclaimed. 'You

are kinky. I thought you might be. Just wait till you see what they've got in the store room. You'll love it. Whips and paddles galore. The things you could do to me ...'

'I shall leave,' he said, swallowing. 'I shall walk through that door and go straight home, if you don't shut your eyes and go to sleep *now*.'

She lay down and screwed her eyes shut.

'Gosh, you're so masterful. At the most inconvenient times.'

'Good night, Julia.'

Down to his underpants, he laid himself down at the extreme edge of the bed.

'Good night, Adam. Sweet dreams.'

The dreams were not sweet, nor were they disturbing, for none came. Adam was enveloped in a pure blankness that carried him pleasurably through to the moment he was awoken by ...

Was that a hand on his cock?

His eyes flew open, to find Julia smiling lazily into his face, her warm, naked body pressed up against his, her hand, yes, on his cock. His erect cock.

'What are you doing?' he gasped, the words not coming out quite right in his haste.

'What's the story, morning glory?' she drawled. 'Thought you might like a hand with it.'

'You're a – a sex pest,' he accused, but the touch of her fingers sent a message of fatal weakness all the way up his nervous system to his brain.

She took them off and rolled over, presenting her back to him.

'Oh dear. Wouldn't like to be a sex pest. Certainly not.'

She pushed her bottom against his groin. Somehow his hand landed on her hip and held it there while his cock pushed against the yielding flesh.

'Mmm, that's nice,' she said. 'Now put your other hand on my breasts.' She did it for him, and he was once more powerless to resist. How did she do it?

He felt it imperative that he put his lips on her neck and kiss it, long and lasciviously, pushing the tip of his tongue into the skin, testing it for flexibility. She seemed to enjoy this, and he enjoyed the passage of her moans through her throat, feeling them vibrate beneath his lips.

'Careful, you'll give me a love bite,' she warned, but she continued to encourage him in all his works, rubbing herself joyfully against him.

Slowly and inexorably the hand he'd placed on her hip began to creep round in front, heading for the heated core between her legs. He needed to feel that warmth and wetness on his fingers, he needed to know how plump and full her clit was for him. And he needed to know, ultimately, how ready she was to accept him inside her.

His body knew what it wanted. His body had the upper hand over him this morning.

'Oh yes, touch me right there,' said Julia, grinding against his fingers. People gave the impression that the clitoris was hard to locate, but they were wrong, badly wrong. It bloomed under his touch, an obtrusive, fat thing, slippery with juices. If he rubbed it a bit harder, Julia seemed to melt against him.

If sex was sin, why did it bring such pleasure for both parties? Why did women have a clitoris, such a superfluous little thing if one considered the purpose of copulation to be procreation? Adam thought about this as he continued to stimulate Julia until she panted. Why would you give someone the means to masturbate, if you considered masturbation to be wrong?

He took his fingers away, much to Julia's chagrin.

'Don't stop.'

'No, I just want you to lie on your back. I want to see what I'm doing.'

She obliged him, spreading her thighs so he could make closer inspection.

What he saw between them was both the same as that oft-scanned biology textbook and different. The patterns were familiar, but the glistening, vivid colour and the intoxicating scent were not. He needed to breathe the scent in, to receive its full impact. He bent his face towards the spread folds and inhaled. It was like a drug, a perfumed steam that entered his senses and bewitched them.

Now that he could see her clit, peeking from the centre of the complex of whorls and swirls, he saw the best thing to do with it. Much better than touching, surely. He bent his head closer and put out his tongue.

'Oh God, you're a marvel.'

His instincts had been correct. He licked on, following every little pathway around that central focus, lapping and tickling while Julia grabbed his hair in great handfuls. How would he describe the taste? He pondered this, while his tongue investigated. It was a delicate flavour, almost overwhelmed by the strength of its scent. And the feel of those soft undulations beneath his questing tongue certainly added to the piquancy.

While he thought about this, he decided to push his fingers inside Julia, the way he had done the last time. She had enjoyed it then and she seemed to enjoy it now, for she was easily accessible. His fingers slipped in without encountering resistance. She felt tight and hot and gloriously wet.

His cock throbbed. He wanted to put it where his fingers were. He wanted that very badly indeed.

'Oh Adam,' gasped Julia, pushing her cunt into his face. 'Oh yes. Fuck me. Please fuck me.'

How could any man be expected to resist such a plea?

He gave her clit one last salutary lick, then he rose up on his knees, looking down at Julia's ravenous face.

'You're going to, aren't you?' she asked.

He nodded.

'Right, you'll need one of these.'

She reached for the bedside drawer and scrabbled blindly inside it, never taking her eyes off Adam, until she retrieved a box of condoms.

'I bet you've never put one of these on before,' she said, removing a foil package and tearing at it with her teeth.

He shook his head. He remembered some of the boys at school filling them with water and throwing them down the stairwell in the science block. Detentions had resulted.

'I'll give you a hand,' she said, sitting up, brandishing the circle of latex. 'Gosh, good thing I bought the large size, isn't it? That's quite a boner you've got going on there. Making up for lost time, eh?'

Adam frowned at her, feeling himself the butt of her sly humour.

'Do you want it or not?' he asked gruffly.

'Oh. You *are* a fast learner. Talking the talk now.' She popped the ring over the tip of his cock then skinned it on with a certain degree of difficulty. 'Sorry,' she said, grimacing. 'I haven't done much of this.'

'Haven't you?' Her touch felt exquisite, even with the sheath of rubber separating her fingers from his cock.

'Not since – you know. There hasn't been anyone else.'

Adam almost wanted to ask questions. Almost. But his overriding desire to sink his cock inside Julia's tight and willing cunt soon made its presence felt and the questions fled his mind.

'Do you know what to do?' Julia whispered, lying back down.

'I ... In principle. I think so.'

'Don't worry. I'll help you.'

He took his cock in his hand and bent over, guiding it towards the place his fingers had prepared. Julia lay with her legs bent and her bottom slightly raised, making his target easier to penetrate.

He let the tip nestle in the shallow basin, preparing for a move forward that he could only assume would hurt Julia.

He seemed too thick, too wide, for that tiny little entrance. He knew there was yield inside, but was there that much?

'You're big, but you'll fit,' she said reassuringly. 'You won't hurt me. I can't wait to feel you inside me. I think you're going to fill me up so beautifully.'

He had to stop and hold himself still, her words arrowing with deadly accuracy down his hard shaft to his straining balls. Just the thought of it was almost enough to bring him to orgasm. He was so close to that moment, that sweet, mad moment when he would be inside her flesh.

Julia's flesh.

Suddenly, the image of Evie, brown-skinned and wanton and laughing, flashed into his head. It should be her flesh, on their wedding night. This was wrong. It was not meant to happen this way.

But it was too late now. It was going to happen this way. He couldn't turn back.

He braced himself over Julia on one arm, the other hand still holding his cock at the root and made that first tentative nudge forward.

How easily she widened and gave way, as if welcoming him in. It couldn't be this simple, could it?

He edged in slowly, wanting to feel every tingle, every iota of friction, every second of warm, velvety cling as he glided up the passage. It was so good, better than he even imagined it could be. So good that he worried he would not be able to hold himself back for long.

'How does it feel?' asked Julia, her voice far away and contented. 'Your first time?'

'Heaven,' he whispered. 'Oh, heaven. Please. Don't move. I must keep still for a moment.'

She chuckled and ruffled his hair.

'You sweet thing. I understand. You feel divine, you know. You're a perfect size and length. I could keep you in here for ever.'

'Oh.' He shut his eyes and tried to control the blood that

pumped so wildly through him. He was connected, physically, to another individual, a woman.

He was no longer a virgin. He was her lover. Her sinful, fornicating lover.

And he didn't care.

Once he was sure he had a grip on himself, he drew back and then thrust forward. How many times could he repeat that motion without climaxing? This was the question of the moment.

He kept up a languid pace, keen not to disappoint Julia, though she seemed anything but disappointed. She had put her fingers on her clit and was stroking it. The sight of her, abandoned to her pleasure, did nothing to hold back his threatened orgasm.

He couldn't help himself. He began to speed up. His brain was beginning to blur, his self-control flying beyond reach. Julia put her other hand on one of her breasts and pinched a nipple. He bent down and kissed it, and she moaned, loudly and ecstatically. Was she finished?

'Adam,' she said, stretching out the final "m" for miles. He felt a spasm, a convulsion around his cock. Yes, that had to be it. She had come.

Now he didn't have to wait … But if he came, then it would be over, and he didn't want it to be over … But his cock would have its way and it plunged him into the darkness, followed by the starburst sky of orgasm. Lights flashed behind his eyes and the force of it was like being flung from some precipice. He poured himself out, all his lusts, all his repressions, all his fears, into Julia. She took them all.

He collapsed on top of her.

'My little virgin,' she crooned, stroking him. 'All grown up now.'

'I'm sorry,' he whispered. 'Sorry, sorry, sorry.'

'God, why? You've nothing to be sorry for. Come on, love. Look at me. Lay yourself down and catch a breath.'

He pulled out and climbed off her, flopping down on the bed on his back.

'Come on, what's this nonsense? Sorry? What for?'

'I've ... I shouldn't have.'

'Yes,' she said, irritation in her voice. 'You should have. You've given me the most wonderful time. You're a terrific lover, a natural. You should be sorry you didn't fuck me before. Very sorry.'

'I've opened Pandora's box,' he said to himself.

'My name isn't Pandora. It's Julia. Stop being so daft.' She kissed his forehead.

'How will I be able to stop, now I've started?' he asked, feeling a sense of panic. He was going to become one of those sex addicts. He could see it in his future.

'I hope you won't,' she said robustly. 'My doors are always open to you, sweetheart. You know that. You can stay here and shag me until the cows come home.'

'Or the legal owners.'

'Don't start that again. Honestly, Adam, if sex is going to make you tetchy and navel-gazing, perhaps we should see about getting your dick removed.'

'Perhaps you should,' he said bleakly.

Julia sat up, shaking her head.

'I should have known there'd be remorse. I wasn't expecting it to kick in so quickly, though. What's good for sexual remorse? Tea?'

Adam could barely see through the fog of exhaustion swirling behind his eyes.

'Sleep,' he suggested. And that was the last word of the conversation.

Somehow, Adam couldn't leave the house. He thought about staying away, about giving Julia a wide berth, but every night of that sultry July, he ended up back at the manor, in her bed.

What was it he felt for her? He couldn't put his finger on

it. He didn't think it was love, because when they were apart, he barely thought of her at all. Indeed, at his desk in the vicarage, all his thoughts were of Evie, of what she might be doing in France, of how they would be together when she returned.

She sent him emails every day and he treasured them, although they were no more than little notes, full of trivial detail about her days. She never referred to her promise that they would be lovers. Perhaps she had forgotten she ever made it.

He would read and write sermons and visit the sick and tend to his other parishes and eat the tea Mrs Witts had cooked for him. Then, as soon as the sun began to sink in the sky, something would draw him out towards the manor house and Julia.

Nobody seemed to realise she was squatting, for she lived there completely undisturbed. He spent every night in her bed; she taught him every position imaginable and some that weren't. He was an eager learner, somehow able to sublimate the guilt for as long as he was with her, though it always hit him with ugly force as soon as he was outside the manor house gates.

His skills were considerable now, in the last week of July, days before Evie's return. He knew where Julia's G-spot was and how to stimulate it. He knew the best positions for deep penetration. He had explored endless variations on where to put his hands and his mouth while his cock was sunk deep inside her cunt. He could identify the first stirrings of her orgasm, and he could facilitate it or frustrate it at will.

Her initial control of the situation was waning. He knew how to give to her, and he knew how to take away. She, it seemed, was quite under his spell and he enjoyed the power of it.

Climbing over the broken section of wall for the last night before its rightful owners' return, he pondered the possibilities. They had ransacked the toy room and tried out the vibrators, massagers, probes, plugs, paddles, shackles in various combinations over the last fortnight. Adam had gone from a man who didn't know what clover clamps were to a man who knew exactly how to apply pressure to the most exquisitely tormenting effect during the course of their use. He pictured them on Evie's fat brown nipples while she stood on tiptoe, suspended by fine chains from a ceiling hook. He would have a riding crop and smack it down on her bum while she twisted and moaned. Then perhaps he would fuck her with it until she came, multiple times in succession. Her eyes would roll like Julia's did and he would kiss her body all over and take her down and carry her to the bed, setting her down tenderly before rubbing in more of that cream.

He was hard before he reached the door.

He pushed it open, finding it on the latch, and peered around the hallway.

'Julia.'

He took a few steps inside, then suddenly a figure leapt on to his back from behind and slipped a blindfold over his eyes.

'What on Earth … Julia …'

'Yes, lover.'

'What are you doing?'

'Surprising you.'

'Consider me surprised. Can I take this off now?'

'No, keep it on. It's the last night before those impostors come home and I want to make the most of it. I want to feast on you. Take me upstairs.'

'I can't see,' he objected. 'You'll have to get down.'

'Oh.' She climbed off his back and took him by the hand, leading him away. 'I've got so many treats lined up for you tonight.'

'Are you really going to leave tomorrow?' he said hopefully, dreading a huge scene between Julia and the pornographers.

'No, I'm not. But I suppose you will. I'll miss you.'

Adam was silent as they walked along the landing towards the room Julia had reclaimed as her own. Things were going to change. This peculiar idyll was drawing to its close.

He heard her shut the door behind them, then she pressed herself against him and fed him with her kisses, which he devoured without second thought. Her hand reached for his dog collar, ripping it off, exposing his throat. He let her undress him, still joined at the lips, and made no demur when she laid him backwards on the bed.

She warmed him up with a thousand little tricks of fingers and mouth on his straining cock, until he bucked upwards into her face, begging to fuck her.

'I want to tie you up first,' she said.

'You? Tie me?'

It had been done the other way around, but Julia had never tried to restrain Adam, being too keen on the unrestricted movements of his hands upon her.

'Yes. For a change. I'll drive you wild with desire and you won't be able to do anything about it.'

'I'm not sure …'

'Please, Adam. Just this once. Then you can do it to me. Is that a deal?'

'All right. You won't hurt me, though? I don't like pain.'

'I won't. I promise.'

He held his arms still while she wrapped black silk ties round and round his wrists, then attached them to the bed posts. He had never felt such on such high alert, everything much keener and sharper than he usually felt it. Her fingers on him made him shiver now, with a kind of apprehension, for he would not be able to stop whatever she decided to do.

She repeated the process with his ankles until he lay spread-eagled and helpless, unable to see, but certainly able to feel how straight and tall his cock stood in the middle of it all. And now she would tease him again, kissing the shaft, flicking her tongue over the tip, squeezing his sac and stroking his perineum, even poking a finger against his tight-shut anus.

'Julia, have mercy,' he pleaded.

'Poor baby,' she crooned, but to his immense relief, she began to wrap the condom over his cock, then she straddled him. He felt her lower herself slowly, a gorgeous gush of warmth over his rubber-clad length, moving downwards, silky smooth and tight. He tried to thrust, but his capacity was limited and she held all the cards. She established a slow rhythm, grinding hard then pulling back, while her fingernails grazed his nipples.

'We'll do this my way,' she gloated, almost removing her cunt entirely from his cock. 'You're my boy tonight and I'm not letting you get away.'

Adam's heart thudded. What did that mean?

He decided she was talking only about the sex. That was all. She meant to take her pleasure from him one last time before they had to part company.

'Ride me,' he said faintly.

'Oh, I'll ride you all right. Let's go.'

She set a merciless pace then, as if she intended to wear his cock out, gripping his shoulders tight, digging her fingernails into his firm flesh. The friction built rapidly and he knew he wouldn't last long.

When she bent right down and sucked his earlobe, he lost control and let her milk his orgasm out of him, enjoying for that delirious moment the additional element that his bound helplessness brought to it.

'Oh, I knew you'd like it, deep down,' she taunted, popping a finger into his mouth. 'I knew your rampant cock would like to get used while you were tied up. Well, perhaps we can try that again sometime.'

'Again?' He shook his head. This was the end for them. Tomorrow Evie would be back.

'In the meantime,' she continued breezily, ignoring his confusion, 'I need a little help. You were a bit ahead of me there.'

She climbed off him, letting his softened cock lie.

The next thing he knew, a waft of her heat and scent hit his nose. She was going to sit on his face.

'Come on, sweetheart,' she wheedled, squatting over him. 'Use that lovely tongue of yours.'

He never missed an opportunity to taste those secret, hidden parts and he satisfied her whim with a will, licking her clit and sucking at it, pushing his tongue up inside her just-fucked cunt, until she could take no more and her thighs quivered at the sides of his face.

'Oh, that was nice.' She bent her head to his and kissed him, tasting herself. 'Now you could do with a little rest, I expect. I'll leave you to it.'

'What?'

He tried to sit up, but of course, he couldn't.

'Where are you going? Julia!'

But she had shut the door.

Chapter Fourteen

When Julia arrived at the wishing well, she performed the same ritual Evie used to call up the spirit of John Calderwood.

He was not best pleased to be aroused, and especially not by Julia.

'What are you doing here, woman? I must conserve my energies. And you do not have the authority to summon me.'

'I have come with a plea.'

'A plea from a Shields? How are the mighty fallen.'

'Yes, we are. And much is changing in Saxonhurst. I don't have the manor any more. And it's time you released Evie.'

'You are talking nonsense. Release her? She is bound to me, by love as well as duty.'

'Unbind her, then. Set her free. If you love her as you claim ...'

'If I set her free, then I die for all time. We will never be together. That is not what either of us desires.'

'It would be best for the village.'

Calderwood roared with anger.

'You dare tell me what is best for my village? You, you miserable little jumped-up heir of sycophants.'

'All right. Keep your hold on Evie, if you must. But leave him alone.'

'The preacher?'

'Of course.'

'You love him?'

'It doesn't matter what I think about him. He does not deserve what you have planned for him. Let him go. Find some other way to be with Evie.'

'There is no other way.'

'If you will not leave him alone, then I will take him away from you. I will protect him. I don't care what I have to do.'

'He has to die. His predecessor –'

'He is not Tribulation Smith! None of those others were either. He is a peaceable man, a little out of his depth, just beginning to know himself. He is an innocent.'

'He wants his hands on Evie. He is not so innocent when it comes to her.'

'I can keep him away from Evie. I can stop the repetition of history.'

'You can't.'

'I will do everything it takes.'

'Do what you will. He will die. And Evangeline and I shall live.'

It was a warm night, and Julia's activities had certainly added to the heat, but after 20 minutes or so, Adam was starting to feel decidedly chilly. Stretched on the bed, without any covers, and with no means of getting them, he felt the cold keenly on his nipples, which throbbed in their suffering. He tried twisting his hands and feet, to keep the circulation going, then he worked at every strategy he could to wriggle out of the tightly tied ribbon, but nothing had any effect. Julia had trussed him up in fine style.

The cold intensified, beyond what he expected of an English summer night. Suddenly he was shivering, teeth chattering. It felt as if the seasons had done a dramatic and unannounced swap.

'Lord, have mercy on me, a sinner,' he muttered between his teeth. Perhaps here at last was God's vengeance on him for all this fornication. He would have to bow to it, accept it

196

as best he could. He had no defence prepared.

In the corner of the room, he heard a crash, as if something had fallen from the chest of drawers. A vase, perhaps. He tried to sit bolt upright, wrenching his arms in the process.

'Who is there?'

But no reply came.

An icy wind blew over his body now. He heard footsteps, small ones, pattering about the room.

'Julia? This isn't funny, you know.'

All those stupid, mad stories she had told him about the ghosts of her ancestors crowded into his mind. Her husband and his sudden heart attack – was he now in line for one of those? His toes and fingers curled while he tried whatever he could to seek warmth.

Somewhere close to his ear, a chain rattled, then there was whispering, as if from multiple mouths, very faint, but finally crystallising into recognisable words.

'Your time is short,' it whispered over and over again. 'Your time is short.'

'Who are you?' he begged. 'Lord, have mercy on my soul. May the power of Christ smite those who deny Him. I invoke the name of the Lord.'

But the whispering continued, and so did the cold. He heard rattling, as if an earthquake or a heavy thunderstorm struck the room, making every loose item vibrate.

'Get thee behind me, Satan,' roared Adam, trying to make himself heard over the growing din. He began to sing *Rock of Ages*, concentrating hard on the words in order to keep his mind, which threatened to slip away into a black maw of terror.

Something else crashed to the ground. Then he felt a pain, like the blade of a knife, dragging up his thigh.

'Get away!' he shrieked. 'Go away!'

At that moment, a light snapped on and he heard Julia's voice.

'Oh, for pity's sake. Leave him alone. Go after me if you must, but he's done nothing to offend you. Good God, it seems every ghost in Saxonhurst is after you.'

The noise ceased and the air in the room gradually reheated.

Adam tried to talk to Julia, but his mouth failed to co-operate and all he could do was twist his wrists and ankles in a mute appeal for freedom.

'Oh dear,' she said, sitting down on the edge of the bed. 'They are awful. They're in a terrible mood at the moment, but I wasn't expecting them to take it out on anyone except me.'

Adam found his voice and croaked out a few words.

'Either I'm mad – or you're sane ... I don't know which ...'

She stroked his cheek.

'It's all real enough.'

'Untie me.'

'You know, I'm not sure I should.'

'Julia!'

'You aren't safe and I want to keep you out of harm's way. What would be easier than keeping you up here, locked away from the world, until the danger has passed?'

'You can't kidnap me. For pity's sake, set me free.'

With a sigh, she set to unravelling the tightly wound ribbons, first at his ankles, then at his wrists, until he was able to sit up, stretching his arms and legs to dispel the pins and needles brought on by the bondage. He took off the blindfold and stared at Julia's despondent face.

'What was that? The noises, the – feelings?'

'My ancestors. Poltergeists. I didn't think they'd bother you, but they're having an angry phase, so ...'

Adam shook his head. 'And I was going to insist you saw a doctor, once you were out of here.'

She smiled. 'I'm not mad. But perhaps you'll believe me now. There is danger, and Evie is the one charged with leading you right into it.'

'These ghosts ... Don't they haunt Seb and Kasia?'

'They've never mentioned it. They wouldn't haunt Evie's friends, though. Evie has special protection.'

Julia's voice was bitter.

'Special protection?'

'As the village mascot. The one who performs all the rituals.'

'I *am* going mad,' muttered Adam. 'Dear Lord and Father of mankind, have mercy on me. My indulgence of the flesh has poisoned my brain and I suffer delusions ...'

'Stop it, Adam. They are not delusions.'

He stood up and started collecting his clothes from the bedroom floor.

'They drove my parents mad, by inhabiting my body when I was a small child. The things they made me do ... You've seen the film *Poltergeist*?'

'Never.' He paused in the midst of putting on his trousers to frown at the concept of horror movies, of which he strongly disapproved.

'Oh, never mind. And my husband's heart attack – that was their doing. Not that I entirely blamed them for that one ...'

'Julia!'

'You mustn't go. Please stay.'

'I can't stay. You are in league with Satan. I have to go.'

'I just want to save you ...'

'You are damning me. You and your – perverse lusts.'

'Hey – they're your perverse lusts too. Don't put this on me. You're every bit as sex-mad as anyone in this village. You just can't handle it, that's all.'

'I was pure. I lived a chaste life, until I came here. I have to leave. I have to get away. This is what they call a breakdown, is it?'

He laughed wildly.

'Don't go.'

She lunged for him, but he had put on his boots and he sidestepped her, hurrying through the upper corridors to the main staircase, looking left and right for signs of the presence that had so terrified him, but it was gone and he left the house unhindered.

He ran across the moonlit lawn and vaulted the broken wall. He did not break his pace until he was back at the vicarage.

He went straight to the study and booted his computer, then fired off an email to the Archdeacon.

'I have been feeling unwell both in body and spirit since coming to Saxonhurst and I would be very grateful if you would agree to giving me some time off for a retreat. There is a place on the Welsh borders I have visited before. I suspect some weeks spent in solitary contemplation will revive my wearied mind and re-invigorate my faith. Please indicate as quickly as you can whether this will be possible.'

He sat awake, staring at his inbox for hour after hour, not that he expected a reply at least until morning.

'Please respond,' he whispered.

Evie was due back today. He had been unfaithful to her. He couldn't face her. And besides, he was going mad. The faith that had been so strong was unravelling, falling away, breaking into chaos. He sat back in the chair and shut his eyes, but then he opened them again, afraid of what he might dream.

The Archdeacon's reply, a terse nod coupled with some griping about how hard it would be to find a stand-in at such short notice, came just after Mrs Witts had arrived to prepare the breakfast.

With ineffable gratitude in his soul, he trudged upstairs to pack a bag.

Aquinas House stood in a shallow valley hidden deep in the Forest of Dean.

Adam had spent the month of August in prayer and

anguished efforts at atonement. If he'd known how to make a hair shirt, he would have done so. Instead, he spent three hours at a stretch on his knees on the cold stone floor of the chapel. He fasted for three days out of every seven. He went on long forest walks, letting the brambles scratch him and the nettles sting, never stopping until he was physically incapable of moving any further. Then he would lie where he was and sleep until he was able to walk back.

He struggled daily with the knowledge of what he had done. He had gone to Julia, night after night, and given in to the lusts of the flesh. Yet when he tried to think back to how it had happened, what had been the moment of fatal weakness, he could never put his finger on it. How had he fallen, so far and so fast? It was witchcraft. There could be no other explanation.

'Lord, deliver me from this evil woman,' he prayed. 'Turn her away from her sin and direct her to the path of righteousness. I failed to do so. I was weak and I became her vessel. Oh, how shall I ever atone?'

Kneeling, naked from the waist up, he reached beneath the bed that took up most of his Spartan cell and found the instrument he had made from a handful of birch rods, bound together with twine. He whipped it over his shoulder, letting the branches swoop down on his back, establishing a dull, painful rhythm, carrying on past the point where he thought he could bear it, until he broke down in tears and fell on his face on the floor.

After perhaps an hour, he stood up shakily, put on his shirt and jacket and went out into the forest.

He hadn't walked far when he became aware of sounds behind him – twigs snapping on the forest floor, a cough. He was being followed.

He turned around and groaned with dismay.

'Evie. What are you doing here?'

'Why did you leave us? I've had to call in a few favours to find out where you were.'

'I needed some time. Saxonhurst ... Well, it's not a healthy place for me to be.'

'It's healthier than that holy prison up the road.'

'I fell into an abyss. I'm trying to find my way out.'

'That's very poetic, Adam.' She stepped closer.

Dear Lord, she was even more beautiful than before. Autumn was in the air, and she wore tight jeans and a figure-hugging long-sleeved T-shirt, a headscarf making a nominal effort to tame her mass of dark curls. A jewel flashed on the right side of her nose and her lips were plumper, her eyes brighter, her skin more touchable than ever.

He sat down on a felled tree trunk, winded.

'Why have you come?'

'I missed you. Came back from France, couldn't wait to see you. Ran all the way to the vicarage, but you weren't there. Aunty said you'd gone on retreat. Retreat from what? From me?'

She sat down beside him.

If she touches me, I am lost.

'From Saxonhurst,' he said. 'The most godless village in England. They weren't wrong.'

'We have our gods. Our own ones.'

'I can't work with that, Evie. Polytheists. Witches. Heathens. That's all Saxonhurst is made of. It's no place for a man of God.'

'You're saying you want to leave?'

'I think that's the decision I've been building up to, these last weeks. God has shown me that I don't have the strength to prevail in that place. He has showed me my weakness ... I pray every hour of the day for His forgiveness, that I might be made worthy. But I will have to prove myself in some other arena. Saxonhurst has defeated me.'

Evie, who had been smiling and shaking her head, suddenly looked anxious, pale beneath her tan.

'No, Adam, you ain't defeated. You needed a rest, that's

clear. But you'll come back stronger and you'll build up that congregation. I'll round up some of the locals, get them down the church next Sunday.'

'Church attendance is immaterial. They have to have true faith, or it's meaningless.'

'They just need time, that's all. They'll come round. Get a choir together, some good rousing hymns. They love a bit of singing. Have a jumble sale.'

Adam put his head in his hands.

'A jumble sale,' he said, laughing unsteadily. 'I can't go back. I can't ever go back.'

'But Adam.' She put her hand on his thigh. 'What about us?'

I am lost.

'You don't mean it,' he said. 'You're toying with me.'

'Toying with you? D'you call this toying?'

She pulled his hands away from his face and knelt up on the branch. She clasped her hands around his neck and moved slowly forward, gauging his response, which was to remain stock-still and petrified.

When their lips met, he felt the penances of the past weeks come undone. As quickly as the washing of a wave, he was a man of flesh and blood again, drowning in his desires.

She was his nemesis and he would never be able to resist her.

Her soft mouth on his, she nipped at his lower lip, catching it delicately between her white little teeth, pulling at it. He plunged his tongue into her dark recesses, gathering her up, possessing her with a force that frightened him. She squirmed and gasped on his lap, her bottom grinding lusciously on his erect cock.

They kissed ravenously and without stopping for breath until a dog rushed by, hotly pursued by its owner, causing them to break apart with blushes on his part, though not on hers.

'Come back to Saxonhurst, Adam.'

'I want you. But I don't want Saxonhurst.'

'You can only be with me there. It's my home.'

'I hate it.'

'Look,' she said. 'Why don't you apply to the diocese for a transfer? We can sort something out, I'm sure. Maybe a nice little suburban church in Parham? All yummy mummies and bake sales.'

'But you would be in Saxonhurst.'

'As long as you weren't too far away, it'd be all right, wouldn't it?'

'Evie, I want to marry you. If I marry you, we live together. I'm not leaving you in Saxonhurst.'

'Well, we can cross that bridge when we come to it. But you can't stay here for ever. And the Archdeacon'll want you back. Don't trash your career for the sake of some stroppy villagers. If it's that Julia Shields you're worried about –'

'What's she said to you?'

Evie smiled slyly. 'Nothing. I know what she's like, that's all.'

'She's a witch.'

'Just come back for a little while, darling. Just until the Harvest Festival. You've got to do the Harvest Festival. It's the one church thing everyone goes to. Put on a slap-up supper and a barn dance. The place'll be heaving at the rafters.'

'I can't …'

She kissed him again, gently as air.

'You can, lover. You can.'

'Where the hell did you disappear to?'

Adam had not bargained on bumping into Julia. He finished pinning up the notice on the board and turned to her, his face set in unwelcoming blankness.

'I needed to get away. To think. I've thought. Now I'm

back.'

'I see. Care to share any of these thoughts?'

'Yes, actually.' He dropped his voice, looking over her head for any passing villagers, but the lane outside the church was quiet. 'What happened between us was wrong and it's over. I wasn't myself. It won't happen again.'

'You weren't yourself? It's the one time you've ever been entirely yourself, Adam, you silly, silly man. It's the one time you've dropped those ridiculous inhibitions and scruples and been the natural Adam Flint. I know it and, deep down, so do you. But you'll keep lying to yourself because it suits you.'

'We'll have to agree to disagree,' he said. 'Are you still at the manor house?'

'No. Got turfed out with a police escort. Made it into the local paper, actually. You'd have seen it if you'd been here. I needed you, Adam. You left me when I needed you most.'

'What you need,' he said, 'is a doctor. A psychiatrist.'

'Oh, how dare you! You're going to deny everything that happened, aren't you? God, you're an idiot.'

She seemed about to flounce off, but the poster caught her eye and she stopped to read it.

'And so it begins,' she said, in a tone that made Adam's hackles rise.

'What do you mean? The Harvest Festival? It's pretty usual to have one at this time of year.'

'Her idea, was it?'

'Actually, it was both of our ideas.'

'At least you'll get a full house for that one. Adam.' She put out a hand suddenly, touching his forearm. He snatched it away. 'I wish you'd listen to me. You mustn't go to that festival.'

'It's a church event, Julia. How can I not go?'

'You won't come out of it.'

He shook his head with exasperation.

'Look, all that village history stuff – Tribulation Smith,

the Lydford book, the generations of Evangelines – I'm going to put it behind me. I got too involved in it and it affected my thinking. From now on, I look to the future. My future and that of Saxonhurst as a Christian village.'

'And the future of Evie.'

He glared.

'Yes. Yes, why not? The future of Evie.'

Julia turned away from him.

'You're next, then,' she muttered, before stalking off towards the post office.

Adam shook his head and re-entered the churchyard through the lych gate. It was a gloriously mellow late-summer day, the air ripe with the smell of fallen apples.

When he walked into the vicarage, Mrs Witts called out from the kitchen, 'Evie's come to see you. She's in the garden.'

Adam's heart glowed and he walked out into the neatly tended back garden, finding her sitting at the far end of the lawn in her scarlet dress.

She waved at him. As he drew nearer, he saw that her mouth was stained a delicate purple.

'You've got a ton of blackberries, vicar,' she said, pulling a few more off the hedge and cramming them into her mouth.

'So I see.'

'Aunty's making a crumble with 'em, but there's loads left. Come and have some.'

He sat down beside her and took off his hat.

'How many have you had?' he asked laughingly.

'Loads. I love 'em. Don't you?'

She put one to his lips and he accepted it, biting down so that the slightly sharp, mildly flavoured juice burst on to his tongue.

'Very nice,' he said, swallowing it down.

'Have another,' she said.

She popped one in her mouth, then she lifted her face to

Adam's, putting her hands around his neck and pulling him into a kiss. Once she had prised open his lips with her tongue, she pushed the blackberry into his mouth. Their tongues competed to burst it first, Evie winning the race.

'Mmm. Let's do that again.'

They consumed a lot of blackberries in this manner, the juice running down their chins, their lips and teeth bumping together, their tongues stained purple.

Adam grasped Evie around her waist and pulled her down so they lay, entwined and panting and surrounded by smashed blackberries, in the shadow of the hedgerow. Now the kissing continued without the fruit, sensual yet solemn, while the sun looked down upon them.

The lushness of her body beneath his hand made him moan with desire. The way she filled her dress, curving and spilling over, was too perfect to bear. He ran a hand up her thigh until he was inside her silky skirt, close to her silky briefs.

Evie broke off the kiss. ''Ere, vicar. You're coming on a bit strong, aren't you? Didn't think you knew how to feel a girl up. I see I've got a lot to learn about you.'

'You are going to marry me, Evie, aren't you? Say yes.'

She sat up, dried grass stalks in her hair, blackberry juice on her breasts. God, she was obscenely gorgeous.

She put a finger on his lips, smiling fondly.

'You're covered in juice stains,' she said. 'What a funny bloke you are, Adam. You're serious, aren't you?'

'You know I am. I love you so much it chokes me. I love you so much my vision goes black around the edges when I see you. I love you so much it's driving me slowly insane. Well, not that slowly, actually.' He laughed mirthlessly and grabbed her hand. 'You have to say yes.'

'All right then,' she said. 'After the Harvest Festival. OK.'

'Really? You will?'

'Yeah, why not? You're fit as fuck and you'll do for me.'

She giggled. 'Imagine Evie Witts as the vicar's wife. I'll never hear the end of it.'

'Oh Evie. Oh, you've saved my life.'

He threw his arms around her and locked her in a passionate kiss that threatened to drown the pair of them.

'Steady,' she laughed, emerging in even more of a mess than she had been before. 'Where's my ring then?'

'Ring? Oh! Of course. Well, are you busy? Shall we go to Parham and look in the jewellers?'

'I'm never too busy for new diamonds, lover. Not that I've got any old ones, mind.'

Mrs Witts, who had been watching from the back porch, mixing bowl under her arm, congratulated them as they passed by. The look exchanged between aunt and niece was a little strange, loaded with something. But Adam was too immersed in his private rapture to think about that too much.

'You'll have to give up that porn film work. If you can call it work.'

They lazed in the shade of a spreading oak tree by the river in Parham. Evie's ring finger sparkled. She held it up to the sun, admiring it from every angle.

'Why? I'm a modern woman, Adam.' She laughed at his face. 'I'm only joking. I know it'd get you in trouble with the bishop. Dunno why, though. It's just sex.'

'Evie! You can't have sex with anyone else but me. We'll be married. "Forsaking all others", remember.'

'Oh, you religious types,' she sighed, stretching out on the grass. 'Funny lot you all are.'

'You're going to have a lot of adjustments to make,' said Adam anxiously. 'Perhaps I should help you understand what Christian marriage is. Perhaps we should focus on that in our study sessions.'

Evie laughed, a trill that sent the ducks quacking over to the other bank of the river.

'You want to teach me how to be a wife? You're classic,

Adam, you know that?' She rolled over to face him, smiling up at him. 'But I do like you.'

'More than like, I hope.'

'Yeah.' She reached up to stroke his cheek. 'More'n like.'

'Our love must be faithful and exclusive,' he said earnestly. 'Nobody else can have you now.'

'We ain't married yet.'

'Evie!'

'Tell you what. Let's go back to yours and – get a bit of practice in. For the wedding night, like.'

'No. No sex before marriage.' A flashback to all those nights with Julia, so vivid his stomach ached, burst into his brain. 'We should wait.'

'Who'd care? Your God? He don't care. He knows I've been around the block, I should think, what with being omniscient and all.'

'Evie. I want to do this properly.'

'Can you do it properly, though? That's my question. When it comes down to brass tacks – have you had a woman?'

Adam swallowed and looked out over the river.

'Adam. I asked you a question. Are you a virgin?'

He shook his head.

'Really? I thought you were, for some reason. Bad boy, were you, back before you took up wearing that dog collar?' She curled her fingers inside it, poking his neck. 'Love it. Such a sexy look. My man in his dog collar. Not like the ones we put on the subs at work. They really are dog collars, leashes and all.'

'Yes, well, the less said about that the better.' Adam's tone was stiff. 'And you're going to have to learn to stop saying everything that comes into your head. I can't have you talking about – *subs* – at the Bishop's palace garden party.'

Evie pouted. 'Why not? What am I supposed to talk

about?'

'The weather. A good book you read recently. A charity you support.'

'I support the Saxonhurst cricket team. Will that do?'

Adam clenched his fist, remembering that awful afternoon in the sports pavilion.

'I have a lot of work to do on you,' he said under his breath. 'But I'll get there.'

'That sounds ominous.' A cloud covered the sun and she sat up and hugged herself. 'We going home for that shag then, or what?'

'No, we are not. But I do need to book the service and call around for a clergyman to officiate. I take it you want to use St Jude's?'

'Register office'd do me fine,' she said sulkily.

'Don't be silly. Come on. Let's get home. We can call at your parents' on the way back – tell them the good news.'

If they thought the news good, Evie's parents didn't do much to show it. Her father, out in his combine harvester, wasn't available, and her mother stood at the counter in the farm shop, counting out eggs into boxes without even looking up.

'Yeah? Right. What you wearing, Eves?'

'Dunno. White dress. How funny!' She burst into peals of laughter. Adam tightened his grip on her arm.

Evie's mother looked up briefly, her eyes flickering between the pair of them.

'Make an odd couple, you do,' she said. 'Can't believe she caught you.'

'Caught me?'

'You being a vicar and her – not.'

'We are in love, Mrs Witts. You can count on my being the best husband to her you could ever wish for.'

'Can I now? You'll need a bloody tight rein, vicar, if you don't mind my saying.'

The blood rushed to his groin. A tight rein on Evie. Her

luscious body, wound around with thin leather straps, her breasts round and prominent, her bottom framed by the shiny bonds. He, with his hand on the leash, leading her across the lawn. *I have to keep you like this, my love, so that your wicked impulses cannot be indulged. I have to hold you in check.* Why had she had to say that?

'Oi, ma,' objected Evie. 'I'll be a brilliant vicar's wife. Do all that baking and flower-arranging and visiting the sick and whatnot. Just watch me.'

Her mother turned back to the eggs.

'Yeah,' she said listlessly. 'When's the big day then?'

'After the Harvest Festival,' said Adam. 'The weekend after.'

'Course it is, love,' she said. 'Course it is.'

'Your mother is a strange woman,' commented Adam, entering the wedding date into the church ledger.

'Funny, coming from you,' snorted Evie. She twirled around the altar steps, her heels tip-tapping on the old, cold stone. 'They don't come a lot stranger than the Reverend Adam Flint. Should I call you Reverend? What does it mean? Am I meant to revere you?'

He looked over at her.

'Don't do that.' She had her palms down on the altar cloth, as if she were contemplating climbing aboard.

'Why not?'

He took her by the arm and marched her swiftly into the nave.

'Do we really need to have a chat about respecting the sacred character of the church?' he asked, shaking his head. 'My church?'

'Your church? Ain't it God's?'

'Evie, this will never work if you can't learn to control your impulses. You don't have to voice every single thing that comes into your head, and neither do you have to do everything your body tells you to.'

She put her head to one side, coquettish, irresistible.

'Aw, where's the fun in that?' she said. She put out a finger and prodded at his chest, moving it down towards his stomach. 'I thought you liked my impulses. Like, right now, I've got this really strong impulse to touch you.'

'This is the house of God,' he whispered.

'He ain't in. Nobody can see us.'

She put her hand on his waist and stood on tiptoe, brushing her nose against his.

'Give us a kiss.'

The scent of her, its warmth and spice, was a drug, confounding his senses. You could kiss a woman in church, couldn't you? *You may now kiss the bride.* It didn't break any rules.

He cupped her face and darted forward, meeting her challenge, pressing his lips to hers. She moaned with pleasure and held on to the back of his neck, massaging it with her fingertips while the kiss deepened in intensity.

It was like scratching the worst and most persistent itch, Adam thought. She was a mosquito who had been biting him over and over and over all summer and now he finally had the antidote. If she bit him again, he could bite her back. The relief sank into him like balm, while his tongue sank inside her mouth, embedded in her warmth and wetness.

He was a drowning man, but he wanted to drown.

When his eyes half-opened, the first thing they saw from their blurred corners was the crucifix that hung over the altar. The nailed Christ looked down upon them, sorrowful and crowned with thorns.

Adam broke away and wiped his mouth.

'Not in here,' he said apologetically.

'I want to do it on the altar,' said Evie, trying to lure him into another kiss, but he shook her off.

'Don't be so blasphemous,' he growled, trapped in the agony of an erection that couldn't be used. 'I'm serious, Evie. You need to learn to control yourself. What will it take?'

'Perhaps you should spank me,' she suggested, hitching up her red silk skirt until it sat just above her thighs. She bent over teasingly, presenting her bottom through the tight scarlet cladding.

Adam put his hands over his face.

'Go on, Adam. Teach me a lesson. Make me a good girl for you.'

With an incoherent cry, he turned on his heel and strode up the nave, taking deep breaths as he walked towards the light from the open door.

'Oh, don't be like that,' she called, running after him and taking his arm. 'Don't go all uptight on me again. I just can't help myself around you. You're so much fun to tease.'

'You can't marry a man just because you like teasing him,' he muttered, entering the churchyard.

'It's more than that. Hey. Don't give me daggers. I love you, vicar. Honest, I do. I love you so much I want you to take me to bed right now and give me the seeing-to of my life.'

'We have to wait,' said Adam, although it was closer to a shout.

'Why? You didn't wait for that other girl, the one that popped your cherry. Why should I have to? Ain't I as good as her?'

'That's not ... That was meaningless. I didn't ever want to marry her. I want to marry you. I want our wedding night to be special.'

'That's so sweet. But it'll be special whether you fuck me now or not. It'll be special 'cos it's our wedding night and we'll be together.'

'I want to do everything the right way. For you, Evie. I want to treat you the way you should be treated. Not the way you're used to. The way you deserve.'

She was quiet for a minute, the usual breezy repartee knocked from her by Adam's words.

'The way I deserve?' she said, and Adam saw a shimmering in her eyes. 'What's that then?'

'Like the precious, amazing soul that you are, that you're capable of being. I don't think anyone's ever really cared for you, Evie. It's always been about what they could take from you. I want to care for you. So much. I want to show you what you're worth.'

She inhaled a ragged breath. 'Fancy words,' she said, but her voice was uneven.

'Words from the heart,' he said firmly. 'Words that are meant.'

'I suppose you'd think the same of me if I looked like an old sock, would you?'

'Evie, don't. Nothing you can do or say will ever change the way I feel about you. I love you absolutely. I always will.'

She smiled, but she still looked as if she might burst into tears at any moment.

'So you're saying a quick knee-trembler's out of the question, are you?'

He shook his head with fond exasperation then bent to kiss her gently on the lips.

'Until we're married,' he said. 'Then you can have as many as you like.'

'Right. You'd better take me down the pub, then. Let's have an engagement party.'

Adam felt like the man who broke the bank at Monte Carlo as he entered the bar of the Fleece with Evie on his arm.

All eyes swivelled over to him and he held Evie's hand up deliberately high, drawing attention to the sparkling diamond on her ring finger.

'Evening, vicar, Evie,' said the landlord, looking up from his pump. 'What'll it be?'

Evie got in first.

'Drinks all round,' she announced, turning to the room.

214

'To celebrate my engagement to our lovely vicar here. Go and tell them outside.'

There was an immediate scrum for the bar. Adam was buffeted this way and that by passing backslappers while the women all crowded around Evie to coo at the ring. A few villagers muttered congratulations to him, but nobody seemed to want to catch his eye.

Indeed, it was Evie who got all the attention while Adam stood on the sidelines, sipping at his mineral water. They moved outside into the beer garden, making the most of the mellow evening sunshine.

At a table by the swings, they spotted Sebastian, Kasia and some of their entourage. Evie ran over to them while Adam followed at a slower pace, rehearsing some lines that he imagined would be immeasurably satisfying to deliver.

'You're marrying the *vicar*?' Kasia's tone suggested that Evie had announced her engagement to a toad.

'Yes, she is,' he confirmed, pulling up alongside Evie and taking her hand. 'So I hope you'll have her P45 ready on Monday morning.'

Sebastian stared. 'We're starting filming on a new feature tomorrow. Evie's the star. After all the press coverage we got, she's our biggest asset.'

'Not any more. She's *my* biggest asset now.'

'Can you see the headlines?' said Kasia slyly. 'Vicar weds porn star.'

'I'll stand by her. I don't care what anyone says. People can change. And Christianity, after all, is about forgiveness and finding redemption.'

'I don't think she's done anything that needs to be forgiven,' said Sebastian. 'And if you do, then you're not right for her. Evie, have you thought this through? Is it really what you want?'

'You'll have to postpone filming *Lesbian Discipline*,' said Evie.

'I can't. Everything's set for tomorrow.'

'Tomorrow'll be too soon,' she said stonily.

Adam glanced at her. Too soon? What did she mean by that?

He didn't have time to think about it, though, because he was sharply tugged away by a hand on his forearm.

'Julia.'

'You're engaged to her?'

'Yes.'

They walked to the barn where functions were sometimes held and stood by the door, leaving Evie with her erstwhile work colleagues.

'The wedding'll never happen,' said Julia bluntly.

'I've booked it. It's in the church planner. I just need to hire the hall and do something about a reception.'

'When's it booked for?'

'End of the month. The weekend after harvest festival.'

'Weekend after? Well, if you want to marry her that much, go ahead. But if I were you, I'd get a special license. Marry her before harvest festival.'

'Why?'

'Because you'll still be alive then.'

'What the ...?'

'Suggest it to her. Go on. See what she says.'

Adam emptied the bitter dregs of his over-lemony water on to the grass.

'You aren't jealous, are you?'

'As a matter of fact, I am. Why wouldn't I be, Adam? I love you, after all. But you don't love me, so there's an end to it.'

She turned and walked away. Adam looked after her. Something urged him to follow her, to apologise, or plead, or ... That curious pull she had. He fought it until she was out of the beer garden and out of sight.

He looked back at Sebastian and Kasia's table. Evie was no longer there. He scanned the garden, searching for her among the knots of drinkers and laughers, smokers and jokers. She was nowhere to be seen.

He strode over to Sebastian.

'Where did Evie go?'

Sebastian shrugged.

'You'll need to keep tabs on her better than that,' he said maliciously. 'She's gone with the wind, that one.'

The words were an echo of her mother's warning. Warnings everywhere today. Should he heed them? He was past that now.

He went inside, ducking under the lintel of the low door, pushing through the crush of drinkers, careless of their pints spilling over the rims of the glasses as he shoved. In the lounge bar, no sign of her either. At the foot of the stairs, he was assaulted with a horrible memory of the time she'd been up there with Trevelyan.

No, she wouldn't be up there now. She wouldn't. She knew she belonged to him.

Perhaps she had gone back to the vicarage. He crossed the lane hurriedly and ran through the lych gate, calling her name. Then he stopped. He could hear something. It was coming from the church porch.

Heavy breathing, panting, grunting. Someone was having sex right in the doorway of the church.

Recoiling in disgust, but filled with righteous anger, Adam marched up the path towards St Jude's. The first thing he saw was a hairy male backside, flexing as it thrust, jeans around ankles. A pair of shapely brown legs was wrapped around the man's waist. The shoes. Those shoes. Those scarlet high heels.

'No,' he shouted, lurching forwards. 'No, you can't.'

He saw dark curls spilling back, crimson nails clinging to the man's shoulders.

'Get off her!' he screamed, but the man paid no attention at all, intent on his fucking.

Adam felt as if he were in one of those nightmares where your voice won't come out, however hard you try to yell. It

217

seemed that neither of them could or would hear him.

He tried one last time.

'Evie!'

She began to gasp and keen.

'Oh fuck, yes,' she wailed, hanging on to the man for dear life. 'Fuck yes, I'm coming, lover. Give it to me.'

The man pistoned hard and then roared.

Adam grabbed him around the neck, yanking him back, before punching him hard in the face.

'Adam!'

Evie looked down at the man's inert form.

'You'll get yourself arrested.'

'You … You …' Adam was having no more luck with coherent speech. He stared at Evie, who stared back.

'I'm sorry,' she said at last.

The felled man managed to push himself into a sitting position.

'Sorry, vicar,' he said. 'I suppose I asked for that.'

'You ain't going to tell, are you, Dan?'

'No. I'll get off now, then.'

'Go and bathe that cut lip, lover.'

'Yeah.'

Adam simply watched the man shamble off. His eyes wouldn't seem to stop popping and he felt trapped in something; a thick, oppressive air that stopped up his breath and roared in his ears.

Evie touched his arm. The action brought him back to life and he fended her off before turning to the church wall and resting his head against the cool, rough stone, letting his legs bend until he had slid down to a crouching position, in which he rocked and moaned.

'Why? Why? Why me, O Lord? Why?'

'Adam,' said Evie nervously from somewhere behind him. 'I don't expect you to understand. I don't think anyone not from here would. But there was a reason why I had to do that. I didn't want to. I'd rather wait for you. But

218

something – something means I can't do that. Oh God, if you can't forgive me, we're all lost ...'

He turned, sitting with his back to the wall, staring up at her with tear-leaking eyes.

'What do you mean? What is making you do this? Evie, once and for all, just tell me the truth.'

'You won't believe me.'

'Try me.'

'I can't tell you.'

'Evie!'

'But I can show you. At the Harvest Festival. I'll show you what makes me this – sex machine.' She laughed miserably. 'And once we're married ...'

'Married?' Adam screwed his eyes shut in a futile effort of resistance against the tears. 'I'm a laughing stock. *You* have made me a laughing stock.'

'If you don't want me, I can't make you,' she whispered. 'But that's up to you. I'm leaving it all up to you. Goodnight, lover.'

Through blurred and squinting eyes, Adam watched her back as she swayed up the path to the lych gate.

Everything he wanted in life was contained in those curves, but she had corrupted herself beyond his endurance now. She had been unfaithful to him, and would probably continue to be so. He should never have come back.

Chapter Fifteen

Mrs Witts had excelled herself, and so had her gang of village cronies. The trestle tables in the church hall were thick with produce, the snowy cloths barely visible underneath it all. Huge baskets of fruit and vegetables, tureens of soup, plaited loaves, giant cakes, gargantuan pies – plenty as far as the eye could see.

'It's almost indecent,' said Adam, walking between the aisles. 'That one village should produce this bounty while elsewhere in the world people starve.'

'Well, the leftovers'm going to the old people's home, ain't they?' said Mrs Witts. 'That's charity.'

'It seems wrong, somehow, to feast like this.'

'It's tradition. A harvest supper. A celebration of how good – God has been to us.'

'You believe, Mrs Witts?'

Adam stopped pacing and smiled at his housekeeper. She set down the pie she was carrying, took off her oven gloves and passed a hand over her reddened brow.

'Well, y'know. I can't say one way or another. I'm on the fence, let's say.'

'I hope I can bring you over to my side. Won't you come to Sunday service tomorrow, at least? Make up your mind one way or the other?'

'I dunno about that, vicar.' She went to look through the window, across to the village green which lay beyond the tree-lined walls of the church grounds. 'They'll be setting up out there.'

'Setting up what?'

Adam joined her, seeing heads bobbing up and down, some kind of structure being erected.

'The after-party. After the feast.'

'What are they making?'

'Corn dollies. Giant-sized, like.'

'Oh. And is this a typical Saxonhurst party?'

He asked, not wanting to hear the answer, not wanting to know that his devout gathering would turn into a bacchanalian orgy, like everything in this village did.

'I don't think this one will be,' said Mrs Witts after a pause. 'This'll be different.' She turned to him and looked behind her to make sure nobody was listening in. 'Our Evie misses you,' she said.

'Don't. It's over. I've applied for my transfer. By the end of this month, I'll be gone.' As long as I don't see her again. As long as she doesn't look at me. As long as she doesn't touch me, I can tell myself I don't want her.

'It's a shame. She just needs someone steady.'

'She had someone steady.' Adam tried not to shout.

'Won't you at least talk to her? She wants to apologise. Talk to her tonight. She'll be here.'

'I've nothing to say.'

Mrs Witts clicked her tongue and went back to arrange a wheatsheaf.

Adam watched her, his heart pounding, his brow slick.

Two more weeks and then this is over.

The door opened and Julia walked in. She looked good, in knee-length boots and a short burgundy tweed skirt, pearls looped and dangling to her waist.

'Adam,' she said, with an air of getting directly to the point. 'I need your help with something.'

'I'm a little busy at the moment, Julia. We start in half an hour. I still need to organise the sound system for the folk group.'

'It's a spiritual matter,' she said.

'Can't it wait?'

'No. It's old Mrs Randall at the forge. She's dying. She wants Extreme Unction.'

'That's a Catholic sacrament –'

'Oh, whatever. Whatever it is you do. She needs it.'

'I see. I'll need to get my bag from the vicarage. Let me speak to Mrs Witts.'

'No, no time. You'll be back for the feast, I daresay.'

They left the hall and hastened up to the vicarage. Adam hurried into his study, packing his prayer book and Bible. He was scrabbling in his desk for a pack of communion wafers in case she felt up to taking it, when he was suddenly and instantly aware of a fierce burst of pain at the back of his neck.

He heard Julia say, 'Sorry, Adam,' a millisecond before everything went black.

There was pain, redness behind the eyes, and a fuzz in his head when consciousness began seeping slowly back to him. He could open his eyes, but it was dark and he was somewhere very uncomfortable, wedged in between wooden walls, brushed by hanging fabrics. A wardrobe. He put his hands out and felt the clerical robes. His wardrobe. He pushed at the door. It was locked.

He blinked over and over again, and some of the pain receded. It was an ache now, and a dryness of the throat, but that was more to do with the dust in there than anything else.

Julia, he remembered. She must have hit him. Knocked him out.

He kicked at the wardrobe door, but it was sturdy Victorian oak and the lock was a good one. With a rush, he realised that he was missing his own Harvest Supper. This was ridiculous. Everything about his ministry here had been ridiculous and now it was ending on an appropriately bizarre note.

He tried to stand, but couldn't do more than hunch over. He reached up for a wire coat hanger and worked in the dark at picking the lock with it, not that he had much aptitude for that kind of thing. He should have paid more attention at that James Bond spy club he'd joined at junior school. He was sure there'd been something about picking locks ... What did that boy say? Oh, it was no use. He couldn't remember.

He scratched away, kicking at the door intermittently in the hope of weakening the clasp, but at heart he was resigned to being stuck there until Julia deigned to release him. If she ever did.

He must have been working on it for over an hour by the time he heard the bedroom door open.

'Let me out!' he bellowed. 'Julia!'

He heard footsteps and saw the handle turn, but whoever was there could only wrench at it. They didn't have the key. It wasn't Julia.

'Hold on!'

It was Evie's voice. Even her voice made him flare up with love, even now.

'I'll get help, lover.'

He heard her run out again. Ten minutes later, someone was picking at the lock, rattling the handle like fury.

The catches lifted and the doors were flung open. Evie held out a hand to him. She was more maddeningly beautiful than ever, in a flowing full-length dress, her hair pinned up with a rose. Staggering out of the dark, he perceived an aura of shimmering light around her. She was his saviour.

'This'll be the work of that Shields,' she said.

Adam nodded.

'Well, screw her. Let's go to the feast.'

'Is it still going on?'

'Nearly done, but there's the party on the green. Come on.'

The locksmith walked through the door in front of them.

'First,' said Adam, holding her back.

'What?'

'This.' He held her face and kissed her, all the pain

223

forgotten, all the indignity and heartache melted away by the sight of her.

'Are we back on then?' she asked softly, touching his cheek.

'Do you want us to be?'

She nodded. They held each other in silence until the locksmith called gruffly from the foot of the stairs, reminding them that the night was young.

'Sorry, emergency, got called away,' he explained, striding up the aisles, past tables that looked like disaster areas, piled up with meat bones, crumby plates, wine spillages and half-eaten bread rolls. The villagers were merry enough, singing along to *Kumbaya* while the folk band strummed away.

'You and Evie back together?' somebody called out.

Evie turned to whoever it was and nodded gleefully, at which a barrage of banging knives and forks broke out, together with cheers.

Adam looked around for Julia, meaning to tell her that he was going to have her charged with assault, but she wasn't there. Presumably she thought her work for the night was done.

He waited for the folk band to finish their set, then rose to give a speech of thanks and a final prayer. The villagers rose as one and streamed out of the hall, towards the green.

'You coming, vicar?' Evie pulled him up by the hand.

'There's a lot of clearing up to do,' he said, waving at the scene of devastation.

'Oh, nonsense. You go. You've worked so hard getting this organised,' said Mrs Witts. 'Go and dance with Evie. We'll sort out this mess.'

'Ta, aunty,' said Evie, beaming as she ran with Adam towards the open doors. 'Come and see what they've done to the green. There's a band and dancing and all, and a big bonfire.'

'A bonfire? Is that allowed?'

'Course it is.'

Outside, the air was heavy with shouts and laughter. An accordion started up, then a fiddle joined in. As they wended up the path, Adam saw the golden flicker of the bonfire, sending orange sparks high into the darkness. It illuminated strange and unsettling shapes, a row of them, ranged behind the bonfire.

'Are those the corn dollies?' he asked, stopping at the lych gate to observe the scene.

'Yeah. Dead clever, ain't they? Take ages to make.'

'They look – obscene.'

Each shape unmistakably depicted people in the act of intercourse.

'They're a bit primitive,' admitted Evie. 'But that's tradition.'

'What kind of tradition demands you make a corn dolly of ... Of ...' He broke off, glaring at the stylised figures of two people engaged in fellatio.

'It's Saxonhurst,' said Evie with a shrug. 'Don't let it get your knickers in a twist, lover. Come and dance with me.'

Looking around him at the towering tableaux of coitus, Adam allowed himself to be led by the hand into the heart of the action, joining the villagers in a rousing country dance. Joyful faces glowed in the firelight, heads thrown back, teeth revealed, eyes bright and wild. Swiftly a ring formed around Adam and Evie, who danced more slowly, swaying in each other's arms.

'They're pleased for us,' she whispered. 'They want to celebrate. This is a big night for us.'

'Harvest Festival?'

Evie smiled and nodded, but something in her eyes suggested that he had misunderstood her. The fire grew, sending out powerful waves of heat. Adam feared an errant spark might catch on a corn dolly and set light to it, but Evie forced his attention away from the looming statues, cupping his face in her hands so he could look only at her.

'Are you happy, lover?'

Adam looked into her endless dark eyes, let the music coil around him, the fire burn his face, the scent of wood smoke creep into his soul.

'I've never been happier.'

'Hold on to this moment. Keep it. You've known happiness in life. No one can ask for more than that, can they?'

The villagers' dance had turned primitive now. People flung themselves around, falling on the ground, flailing arms, grabbing each other, kissing, wrestling.

Evie's lips touched Adam's, and a hysterical cheer broke out. Immediately, the people swarmed forward, pushing and jostling against them. Adam struggled to end the kiss, aiming to try and direct them backwards, but Evie clung to him, biting down, pushing her tongue in his mouth.

Arms braced around them, hands grabbed hold of him and he felt his feet leave the ground. Evie still held on to him, the pair of them joined in an embrace while the village men bore them aloft, laying them down across dozens of forearms. Adam, alarmed now, broke free of Evie, but a pair of men walking alongside yanked his hair and forced his face back into hers.

'Kiss her,' they demanded. 'Keep close to her.'

Somebody else was winding something around the pair of them, binding them together. It was some kind of twine, a flexible tree branch, perhaps willow.

'What are you doing?' he yelled, escaping Evie's lips again, kicking and thrashing, but powerless against the combined strength of the Saxonhurst men.

'Relax, lover,' cooed Evie. 'It's just a silly tradition. Don't worry.'

'I know your traditions. What are you doing?'

'We have to join together. Make the fertility of the summer last another year.'

'*What?*'

'There's no point fighting it now, Adam. The time's here. You might as well just …'

'You mean …?'

Adam and Evie were set upright and then more twine was wrapped around them, securing them to the largest and most obscene of the corn dollies, a vivid representation of a woman being taken fore and aft by two lovers, one on either side of her.

'You can't mean this,' yelled Adam, to the villagers as well as to Evie. 'You can't say all the other vicars have done this. Or is this some kind of joke? A sick Saxonhurst joke for a sick place.'

'Kiss me.'

'Evie, this is wrong. I love you, but this – this is wickedness.'

'I'm sorry. I can't go against the tradition.'

'I love you so much. All I ever wanted to do was love you.'

She looked away for a moment, into the leaping flames. The villagers thronged around, some writhing on the grass, some lighting brands from the fire.

One man took a knife and cut a line down Adam's clothes, pulling them off through the twine. It was a long and painstaking process and Adam had to hold completely still if he didn't want an injudicious cut. The same was repeated with Evie's dress until the pair of them stood, bound and naked, on display to the village.

'There's nothing for it,' said Evie softly.

Adam shut his eyes and groaned, feeling her breasts squashed against his chest, his cock pressed to her hip. Despite everything, he felt it twitch, eager to harden.

'You want me, don't you, lover?'

She caught his mouth in another kiss. The cheer was loud and shrill, rising above the crackling roar of the fire.

He knew there was nothing else to be done. All was finished. He would leave Saxonhurst, never to return. But this once, he could have Evie. Evie could be his. Perhaps she would even leave with him.

He let his reservations fly and threw himself into the kiss. If he was to corrupt his soul, at least he could do it wholeheartedly. He ravished her mouth, fidgeting with the twine as his tongue lunged. But it was tied so fast and so tight, there was no way of releasing them.

Evie's skin undulated, warm and yielding, against his. She ground her hips, inviting him to feel the wetness between her legs. He felt it, felt it stronger than the sting of smoke in his eyes or the pressure of the bonds or the humiliation of being exhibited this way. Its rapacious allure shot through him, into his bloodstream, straight to his cock.

Oh, at last, at last he could have her. At last he could plunge inside that luscious, dangerous cunt of hers and take it, take it, take it. He could know earthly pleasure, never mind damnation. It didn't matter any more. And besides, he had no choice.

'She's wet!' shouted a female voice. Adam opened one eye to see a woman crouching by their legs, inspecting them. 'And he's getting hard.'

More cheers, then a chant opened, ragged at first but growing swiftly in volume.

'Fuck her, fuck her, fuck her.'

'Hold on,' said the woman. 'I'll need to put him in.'

Adam felt eager hands grasp his shaft. Shockingly, this turned him on all the more, especially when they began to pump him, working him to full erection. Then she manipulated him into position, seating his tip just at the velvet opening of Evie's pussy.

'Get inside me,' gasped Evie, breaking out of the kiss. 'Fuck me, lover.'

The woman pushed Evie's bottom forward so that he advanced, slowly, exquisitely, up her tight channel. The crowd screamed approval until he was all the way in, balls deep. He felt her tighten her muscles around him, holding him in. Tears leaked from his eyes.

'Oh God,' he whispered. 'Evie. My love.'

Then something happened to the fire and it shot higher, causing the crowd's screams to heighten, in terror rather than excitement, and many of them to jump back.

Adam stared transfixed as the flames contorted into strange shapes, like arms reaching up, then a head appeared, then a torso, and the flaming head developed features, male features. The fire had become a man.

No. This was a hallucination. It was one of his dreams. He looked around desperately, trying to flex his muscles, to bring himself back to consciousness, but he was still there, still with his cock in Evie's cunt, still looking at a man made of fire.

'Saxonhurst.' The voice came from the flames, low and echoey.

The villagers were making a horrible keening noise now, their arms held aloft.

'The time has come.'

'What's he talking about? Who is he?' Adam asked Evie, his voice coming out in a panicked trickle.

'My beloved,' she said. 'John Calderwood.' She was staring just as hard as anyone, and she looked afraid.

'Raise them.'

A group of village men gathered in a tight formation about the corn dolly and began to lift it from the ground.

'What is this?' Adam flustered, gripped with terror.

'It's time,' said Evie faintly. 'Time for us to burn. And then Calderwood and I can live freely again.'

'I don't ...'

'You have to burn. You have to die for us to live.'

'Evie, this is ...Stop! This is murder!'

The villagers carried the corn dolly closer to the fire.

'Tribulation Smith. Your time of tribulation has come.' Calderwood smiled.

'You give your life for a greater good. Take comfort.'

'This is murder!' he reiterated. They were so close to the fire that he could feel it singe his hair and begin to strip his skin.

'My Evangeline,' said Calderwood softly. 'You have brought him to me. And now we can be together. Say the words.'

Evie simply stared all the more.

'Say the words,' Calderwood prompted her. 'The spell we devised together, before Smith murdered me. Say it.'

The blank, glazed expression on Evie's face snapped into life. She lifted her chin.

'John, this ain't right,' she said.

'Say it,' he hissed. 'Tribulation Smith must die.'

'This isn't Tribulation Smith. This is Adam Flint. He's done me no wrong, nor you.'

'He wants only to possess you, like his forerunners. Evangeline! You know it.'

'No, I don't. He ain't quite the same. I don't think he wants to do those things. I think he just wants to love, and he don't know how.'

'He comes to Saxonhurst in a direct line from Tribulation Smith. He is the same man in a different time. He must be sacrificed. Evangeline, if you don't say the words, I am doomed to another hundred years …'

'What will you do if you gain your life?'

'I will love you. I will be lord of Saxonhurst. We will rule together. Say the words.'

The villagers lurched forward, as if they meant to pitch the corn dolly on the fire regardless.

'That won't work!' Evie shouted. 'If we burn without me saying the words, it all goes bad anyway. It's my choice. I have to want to.' She looked Calderwood directly in the eye and spoke softly. 'And I don't want to. I don't think you've earned my conscience.'

The roar of rage from the fiery Calderwood was enough to deafen all who heard it. The flames reached to the stars, while the villagers howled around them.

Adam thought he might faint, overwhelmed with smoke and heat and terror, but he held on, trembling in Evie's bounden arms, teeth chattering.

'Begone,' yelled Evie at the full force of her lungs. 'Begone, Calderwood. I compel thee.'

The fire turned black and then it was no more than smoke and ashes, thick and choking, turning the villagers' cries to coughs with instant effect.

'Shit.' Evie hacked along with the rest of them. 'He's a cantankerous old sod. He did that on purpose.'

Adam couldn't reply. He felt as if his entire body and soul had been filled up with awe and dread, so much so that it was pouring out of him. Awe of Evie, dread of everything else.

'You OK, vicar?' she croaked. 'Sorry. Bit intense, yeah?' She raised her voice. 'Will someone untie these fucking ropes?'

'What you playing at, Evie?' asked the woman who had coupled them sourly. 'That wasn't meant to happen.'

'I'm through with that bloke,' she said. 'He's all talk. He won't do nothing for the village. He'll just try and take everything over and be Lord Ego. Do we need that?'

'He's supposed to get his vengeance.'

'I'm bored of vengeance. He's been avenging himself for centuries. He needs to start thinking about forgiveness instead. Ain't that right, vicar? Forgiveness.'

'It's – a virtue,' said Adam weakly.

The bonds began to loosen and he tottered, Evie holding him upright, her head on his shoulder.

'He loves you, though, Eve,' said the woman, finally releasing Adam and Evie from the corn dolly before setting to work on releasing them from each other. 'Such a romantic story.'

'He don't know about love,' she said wistfully. 'Not really. And I don't call it romantic. Getting me into

231

witchcraft, knocking me up, letting another man marry me while he runs off and hides from the witchfinder. It's not romantic, really.'

'You aren't – the same person – surely,' said Adam, the words coming sporadically from a still-slack mouth.

'Well, no, not literally. But her DNA is in me, you know, and so is her soul. Calderwood made it happen, not sure how. She's travelled down the line for generations. I'm just the latest poor sap to get lumbered with her.'

The final bond was loosened and the pair of them fell to the ground, still entangled. Adam's legs were weak as he scrabbled about, trying to get up before the ugly-looking crowd closed in on them.

'What did you do that for?' demanded one man of Evie, brandishing a flaming torch. 'What happens to us now?'

'We live our lives,' said Evie, defiant and unafraid.

'But what will Saxonhurst be? You'll keep the traditions going, won't you?'

'I haven't decided yet. Leave us alone. I'm taking Adam here home.'

They bunched together, menacingly tight, but Evie shouted at them to get back.

'You can't do nothing to me,' she shouted. 'I'm your goose that lays the golden eggs. If you hurt me, the village can't prosper.'

They loosened their formation, muttering.

'What about him?' One of them jabbed a thumb in Adam's direction. 'We don't owe him anything.'

'Let him alone. He's in shock. Here.' She helped him to his feet and began to stagger away from the green. 'Best not go back to the vicarage tonight,' she muttered as they limped onwards. 'Wouldn't put it past that lot to torch it.'

'Christ,' said Adam, still far from recovered. His thoughts flew about, untrammelled by reason, refusing to settle.

'We'll go to the manor. Seb and Kasia'll look after us.'

*   *   *

Kasia answered the door, pale as milk.

'Come in,' she said, hugging Evie to her. 'Jesus. What was that?'

In the living room, Sebastian poured them all substantial brandies.

'I knew this village had its quirks,' he said. 'All the sexy stuff – we loved that. We felt we fitted right in. But what happened out there …'

He shook his head.

'They would really have burned both of you alive?' asked Kasia.

'Yeah,' said Evie, sipping her drink. 'For God's sake, Adam, get it down your neck. It's not poison.'

Adam gave in and let the fiery liquid burn a trail down his throat.

'I don't like it,' said Seb. 'It's … I'm calling the estate agent tomorrow. You agree, Kas?'

'Yes. I can't stay in this place. They are murderers.'

'Well, to be fair, nobody got murdered in the end,' Evie pointed out.

'All the same … I'll go and make up a couple of guest rooms.'

Kasia drifted out and Seb left the room to take a call on his mobile phone.

Adam turned to Evie, alone with her at last.

'You saved me,' he said, grimacing as another mouthful of brandy set light to his chest.

'Don't mention it,' she said dryly, then she gave him a guilty look. 'I got you into it in the first place. You shouldn't be thanking me. You should hate me for the way I've treated you.'

'I couldn't hate you.'

'I used you.'

'That man – Calderwood. He used you. He had a hold over you, didn't he?'

'He must have done. When I look back, he ain't even all that good-looking.' She shrugged. 'I think by turning him down I've broken some sort of spell.'

'You only needed your own strength. Magic couldn't beat that.'

She smiled. 'Yeah. Reckon you're right.'

She wandered over to the drinks cabinet and poured herself another brandy.

'You'd best get away from here, vicar,' she said, her back to him.

He watched her silently, afraid to ask the question.

He downed the rest of the drink and gathered his courage.

'Are you coming with me?'

'Oh Adam.' She came to sit beside him. 'I'm sorry. I never loved you. I can't marry you or any of that stuff.'

He looked away.

'Oh, I see.'

She put her hand on his.

'But I do care about you. I care a lot. I must do, mustn't I? Or things would've been very different out there.'

'I love you, Evie.'

'Mate, you don't love me. You're obsessed with me. That ain't the same thing. You'll get that, one day.'

'Everything's lost,' he said blankly. 'Everything's changed. I've lost you and as for my faith ... I just don't know any more. All this magic and witchcraft ...'

'You just need a bit of time to work it all out. Go back to that freaky monastery place in the forest. Sort your head out. You'll be fine.'

She stood up, yawning.

'Now, if you don't mind, I'm going to bed. I'm cream crackered. Sweet dreams.'

She bent to kiss his forehead, then skipped out of the room, as lightly as if she'd done nothing more arduous with her day than eat strawberries under the shade of a blossoming tree.

Adam put his head between his knees and let the blood rush forward.

He was alive. He could have been dead, but he was alive.

Was it the will of God? Or was it the will of Evie?

He no longer knew which of the two was more powerful.

But he was leaving Saxonhurst. Leaving tomorrow. Nothing and nobody could make him stay.

He looked up, sensing another presence, though the room was empty. Over by the French doors, something moved beyond them, a flicker of pale light, some colour. He heard a tapping and his throat closed up, fearing pitchfork-wielding villagers or Calderwood in a towering rage.

Shakily he rose to his feet and went to the window. The lawns were just as always, stretching onward to the swimming pool and tennis court. But the harvest moon illuminated the trees further on. Somebody leant against a trunk, wearing a burgundy skirt.

'Julia,' he murmured. His hand went instinctively to the back of his head, where she had hit him so hard earlier on. 'I want a word with you.'

He opened the French doors and strode out, breathing in huge lungfuls of good, sweet, clean air. But then the tang of wood smoke interfered with it, bringing a bitterness that made him want to retch. All the same, he continued towards her, face set in a frown.

'You knocked me out,' he accused, once she was within hearing range.

'Of course I did. They were going to kill you.'

'You knew?'

He stopped short, then gasped as she launched herself at him, throwing her arms around his neck and bursting into tears on his chest.

'Hey, hey,' he soothed, slowly bringing his arms around her. Even to his racked, sore body, she felt good. He wanted to keep her there, hold her, breathe her in. 'It should be me falling to pieces. I'm the one who nearly ended up on the

235

fire.'

'I thought you were dead. I thought they'd done it.'

'Evie refused.'

'Oh God, I think I love her. I'm going to have to love her now, aren't I? What a pain.' She laughed amidst the tears. 'And I suppose you love her more than ever now. Even though she was stringing you along.'

Adam squeezed Julia tight, light-headed with the closeness of her.

'She won't ever want me,' he said.

'But I do,' said Julia, looking up at him. 'That's the pathetic thing. I've let myself fall so much in love with you I feel I might die of it. I'm such a fool. I could kick myself.'

'I can't imagine why you'd fall for me,' said Adam, looking at her, drinking her in.

'No, neither can I, but the fact is, I have. And now I don't know what's to be done.'

'Perhaps you'd let me love you back.'

She stiffened, held herself perfectly still for a moment.

'You don't love me, Adam.'

'Don't I?'

'You've no idea how you feel.'

'Oh really? And yet I do have an idea what I want.'

She rested her forehead against his chest, looking down. Adam had seen the traces of a smile twitch at the corner of her lips before she ducked.

She looked back up, clearly suppressing an urge to grin.

'And what is it that you want, Reverend Flint?'

'I want to kiss you,' he whispered.

'Well, a kiss can't hurt ...'

There might have been more to that statement, but she wasn't given the chance to add anything because Adam's lips pressed against hers, silencing her.

He needed comfort, solace, communion with another soul and hers had touched him, reaching out with infinite tenderness and affection. She was, he realised as their kiss deepened, everything he needed in his life, his mirror image, his soul mate. He gave himself to her, poured his hopes and dreams into their passionate embrace, trusted her to keep them safe.

'Adam,' she panted, breaking off. 'Are you sure about this? Don't break my heart.'

'I want you,' he said.

'You can have me.'

She lifted her skirts and Adam saw that she was naked underneath. No restraining force of guilt or shame held him back this time. He unbuckled his belt, needing to get to her, having no other thought on his mind than being one flesh with her. He let his trousers and underpants fall to his ankles and lifted her thighs, pushing her back against the tree trunk.

Within seconds he was inside her, right up to the hilt, her legs wrapped around his hips. Her sheath was tight, holding his cock in its close embrace. They fitted so well together. He had known it, all those times in the manor house, and yet he had not allowed himself to accept it. How stupid he had been.

Now he would prove it to her. He showed her his dedication to her happiness with strong, sure thrusts, keeping her pinned to the tree while he seated his cock over and over. She grunted each time he drove forward, her lips fastened to his neck. She trembled all over and he felt the wild fluttering of her heart, felt it join in with his own ragged beat.

He reached down for her clit, rubbing it as he fucked harder and faster. She began to moan and kick her feet behind him.

'Yes, come,' he breathed, then he held her fast, crushing her into the bark for as long as it took for his own orgasm to grip and then release him.

They stayed in that position until Adam's legs could no longer support them, then they slid slowly to the ground, rumpled and sweaty and full of love.

'I can't stay here,' he said, looking up at the moon. 'You know that, don't you?'

'I know. I don't want to live here any more. I've come to hate this place.'

'Really? I thought you'd never leave. You're so attached to this house.'

'It's a pile of bloody stones. That's all it is.'

He hugged her tight, smiling into her defiant eyes.

'And Seb and Kasia are about to put it back on the market too.'

'Are they?' She shrugged. 'Good luck to whoever forks out for it. I'm done with Saxonhurst. I don't have a single good memory of the place. Well ...' She corrected herself, smiling slyly up at Adam. 'I do have a *few*. But if I want more, I need to go with you.'

'I don't know where I'm going yet,' he admitted. 'I'm still getting used to being alive. And loved. I am loved.'

He shook his head as if this was the greatest mystery ever encountered.

'Haven't you ever been loved before?'

'Not really. No.' His face crumpled as he realised the truth of this.

'That's why you're so bad at life, darling. You don't know what love is, so you made up this strange version of it and you clung to this unloving vengeful God of your imagination. I don't know if there's a God or not, but if there is, I don't think He or She is anything like the one you've been preaching about.'

'All my beliefs have collapsed. And I don't feel bad. I feel good.'

'You *are* good. You will be good. We both will.'

'Is love enough?'

'It's more than enough. It's all we need.'